Also by Kristin Cast from Bloom Books

TOWERFALL

The Empress

The Lovers

SWORDS TAROT TOWERFALL

(novellas co-written with Gina L. Maxwell)

King

Two

FORTUNE

A Towerfall Novel

KRISTIN CAST

Bloom books

Cover design by Nicole Lecht/Sourcebooks
Series design by Laia Tinaut
Cover art © Maria Andreea Cruceru - thesleepingfoxy
Chapter opener image © Elena Konchukova/Getty Images

Published by Bloom Books, an imprint of Sourcebooks
1935 Brookdale RD, Naperville, IL 60563-2773
(630) 961-3900
sourcebooks.com

Cataloging-in-Publication data is on file with the Library of Congress.

Printed and bound in United States of America.
LSC 10 9 8 7 6 5 4 3 2 1

To Gina, you fucking troublemaker.

TOWERFALL TAROT
THE WHEEL SPREAD

TOWERFALL TAROT

The Wheel Spread

This spread is designed as a way to witness the forces that guide you from one phase of your life into the next. Each of the eight outer cards represents a spoke on the Wheel of Fortune. They'll help you to uncover what is shifting within you, what patterns keep repeating, and what you're ready to claim next. The center card is the anchor, the still point in your life around which everything turns.

This is a deeply personal pull. Approach it with curiosity. Let the Wheel show you the parts of your journey you've already survived and the momentum that's building as you continue forward.

USE THIS SPREAD WHEN:

Use this spread when you're moving through a moment of change and need help understanding the cycle you're in, the lessons rising to the surface, and the truth that nothing stays the same for long.

TIPS & TRICKS:

As you pull your cards, remember that every card (or aspect of your journey) has its season, and each season touches the next.

Everything in the circle relates back to the center. Return to it often as you need, the way a compass will always pull you back to true north.

Watch for circular imagery as you lay out your tarot cards. Wheels, moons, rings, spirals, etc.—these symbols deepen the reading by reminding you of the cycles of time.

Ask yourself: What cycle am I completing? What cycle am I stepping into? What does this pull say about where I've been and where I'm going?

THE CARDS:

CARD 1: Your Center

This is your still point. It's the truth that remains constant while everything else shifts. This card holds the piece that anchors you through each season, each ending, each beginning. It reveals the part of you that guides every turn of the Wheel.

CARD 2: What Is Beginning

Energy that's rising, opportunities forming, or truths gaining strength. This card speaks of what's ready to enter your life.

CARD 3: Forces Outside Your Control

This card shows you the elements of fate that are bigger than you, and what you're meant to surrender to rather than shape.

CARD 4: The Turning Point

This card reveals the shift you're approaching or already experiencing while on your journey.

CARD 5: Forces Within Your Control

The choices you can make right now that influence how the Wheel turns. This card highlights your power in the midst of change.

CARD 6: What Is Fading

A force, belief, or chapter that's losing power, even if you're continuing to hold onto it. This card reveals the ending already in motion.

CARD 7: The Supporting Current

This card highlights what uplifts you, steadies you, or carries you forward as fate takes hold and your journey continues to shift.

CARD 8: The Pattern

Habits, fears, buried feelings, or desires. This card highlights what continues to come up for you and will continue to until it's acknowledged.

CARD 9: What Awaits

While it might not be a fixed destiny, this is the direction fate will continue to take you. But remember, the Wheel of Fortune—your life—is always changing.

ONE

DECLAN: If I were there right now, I'd start with your thighs. Spread them wide. Pin your knees. My mouth full of you.

ME: Mmm, big promises for a man who's never actually seen what he's working with.

DECLAN: I've seen enough.

DECLAN: Especially after the photos you sent last night.

ME: Speaking of pictures…

DECLAN: You want more?

ME: Maybe

DECLAN: All you have to do is ask.

ME: Will you send more pictures?

DECLAN: Nicer

ME: Please

DECLAN: Almost…

ME: Can I have more please, Mr. Thorne?

DECLAN: I can't wait to hear you beg for more when I'm finally touching you.

ME: Bold of you to assume I'll be the one begging.

ME: Maybe you like being told what to do.

DECLAN: You'll find out soon enough.

ME: In person? And ruin the fantasy by making this real?

ME: Sounds dangerous… But maybe worth it.

The cab lurches over a pothole, jostling me sideways against the cracked vinyl seat. Outside, Manhattan blurs past in jerky bursts—corner bodegas, scaffolding, a guy in a Cookie Monster suit lighting a cigarette. Horns blare. Someone shouts.

In real life, I do not feel like a sexy, snarky, choose-your-own-adventure heroine. But I want to. I want to be the version of myself I've carefully curated for Declan Thorne over the past three months—witty, witchy, confident. The woman who sends artfully posed nudes and talks about tantric sex practices like she doesn't routinely cry in the parking lot of Trader Joe's.

DECLAN: Maybe?

DECLAN: I'll fuck that maybe right out of your mouth.

I chew the inside of my cheek and drum the fingers of my free hand on my knee. There's no real harm in being a little more myself. It's not like we're actually getting together in person. I'm safe from that as long as Declan is off living his jet-set businessman life, collecting stamps in his passport, and, I'm assuming, women in every time zone. He has no time for anything real.

Neither do I.

So I type it out. A little truth slipped inside the game.

ME: If you keep talking like that, I'm not sure I'll want whatever's happening between us to just be a fantasy.

DELIVERED.

SEEN.

I stare down at Flutter, the dating app open on my phone with the soft pink logo and the borderline-insulting algorithm that seems convinced my soulmate is either a man-bun-sporting yogi who calls his mom "goddess," or a crypto bro in Austin who owns a neon sign that says HODL.

I hold my breath as Declan types out a reply. We're not exactly in the habit of baring our souls. If what I said can count as vulnerability. It does to me. Then again, I'm not sure I've been vulnerable enough with anyone to really know.

The three dots disappear. No message arrives.

DECLAN THORNE: OFFLINE

"Oh." I swallow through the dryness that coats my tongue like sand.

That's fine. Totally fine. I'm cool. Very chill. A glacier sliding around in the back of a sticky cab. I exude *can't be bothered*, and nonchalance basically drips out of my pores.

But what I sent plays on a loop in my head. A cringy, borderline desperate loop I wish I could unsend.

My phone buzzes in my hand, and I fumble it, swiping too fast, heart kicking in my chest. The logo for my work email flashes across my screen, and I grimace. Six new messages from my boss. On a Saturday.

When I started working in publishing, I wanted it to be my calling. I thought I'd be championing the voices of fierce, fearless women, shaping the culture of the literary world one award-winning manuscript at a time while simultaneously ushering in a new era of inclusive storytelling. Instead, it's been ten years, and I'm still an editorial assistant who proofs jacket copy, tracks deadlines I have no power to enforce, and spends most of the day pinging people on Teams.

So, basically, *not* my calling.

But that's okay, because I've also started an online brand. It's like if Goop and a witchy Pinterest board procreated. Only instead of moonstone vibrators and $100 collagen gummies, I recommend grocery store incense and DIY lavender bath soaks people can actually afford. The vibe is accessible mysticism with a hit of meme energy.

Maybe my calling is helping other women to have the same thing my brand of spiritualism has given me—protection. A little padding between me and the rest of the world. A pocket ritual to pull out in a bathroom stall when a first date tanks. A sentence to fall back on when thoughts run dry. A metaphorical or literal candle to light when the darkness starts to press in.

I post daily rituals, handpicked playlists, lunar cycle alignment affirmations, and the occasional Reel where I soft cry/launch a new income stream. But the brand isn't exactly making me money or even reaching the people I want to help.

It could have something to do with the fact that I change up my online persona more than I change my sheets, which means my audience (all 749 of them) is never quite sure who I am. That's the thing, though. Even in my thirties, *I'm* not really sure who I am. I just keep hoping that one of these days I'll post the right message and channel the right energy and everything will fall into place. I'll go viral, my savings account will contain more than twenty dollars, and I'll finally know: *that's my calling*. That's the rest of my life, ready and waiting for me. I just have to keep throwing different personality traits at the universe's proverbial wall to see what sticks.

All while being quietly terrified that nothing ever will.

Right now, I'm in my "*positive thinking,*" "*manifest your life,*" and "*totally unbothered*" era. Or at least, I'm trying to be. On the outside, anyway. Inside, none of it's really clicking. Although, I could be onto something. Maybe attempting to be this kind of woman long enough will help me become her. Or maybe it'll just be another version of me that doesn't stick. I guess we'll see.

But, hey, at least Dating App Amanda is thriving. She's glossy and mysterious and knows her angles. Real-Life Amanda is…between therapists and a bit of a mess.

Regardless, I'm doing the work to find myself. I'm gearing up with rituals to make my day predictable when my emotions aren't. I have the vision boards. The affirmations. The moon rituals and manifestation sound baths. I'm drinking green things and speaking kind words to my full-moon-charged water bottle. I even did a spell to cleanse my inbox last week. Not that it helped, considering the six weekend emails.

The point is—the universe eventually has to listen.

Right?

I step out of the cab with my purse, my phone, and a green juice in a compostable bottle that's approximately two seconds away from melting in my palm. The paper straw has already given up on life. It's bending in on itself like it, too, has a mound of student loans and a podcast idea it never launched.

Skin shimmering with highlighter, Hepburn-style corset dress flowing like I just drifted out of a LaceMade ad, I am the picture of calm. That Goop-meets-witchy-woman Pinterest board come to life. Inside, though, I'm running on three hours of sleep, two oat milk lattes, and one deeply personal vendetta against the upstairs neighbor who decided 3:12 a.m. was the perfect time to lift weights while blasting Skrillex.

Look, I'm not saying the universe hates me. I'm just saying, if Mercury's only in retrograde a few times a year, then I must be making up the rest. Maybe I'm the problem.

It doesn't help that my best friend, Gemma, just returned from a two-week wedding/impromptu sabbatical in South Carolina looking like the after photo in a skincare ad. Her hair is shinier, her aura is brighter, her skin is the kind of dewy that twenty-year-old influencers talk about. And, oh yeah, her drop-dead-gorgeous boyfriend is a billionaire.

"Speak of the devil," I mutter under my breath as I glide past a gaggle of said influencers snapping photos and staging slow-motion twirls outside the venue.

Gemma's billionaire boyfriend is loitering just inside the brightly lit, wide-open entrance to the stone-front

Midtown high-rise, checking his watch like he's waiting for someone. He sees me the moment I see him. His face lights up, smile wide and lopsided as he bounds toward me like a golden retriever.

"Amanda!" Alder wraps me in a hug like we're old friends. I stiffen on instinct, the soles of my strappy high heels hovering above the red-carpeted sidewalk as he literally lifts me off my feet. "Gemma has said so much about you. I feel as though we've already met. In another world, perhaps."

"Alder." I grind out his name like it tastes bad and bare my teeth instead of smile. Luckily, or maybe unluckily, he'll never know since my face is smashed against the shoulder of his tailored suit.

As much as I want our first in-person meeting to be all unicorns and rainbows, I can't ignore how much of an ass he's been to Gemma. She's my best friend. Has been since the publishing company's corporate retreat a decade ago when we both got lost during a team-building hike and trauma-bonded over blisters, granola bars, and a shared hatred of the friends-to-lovers trope. She's basically family. And family means I smile through gritted teeth and swallow my objections to their on-again-off-again soap-opera-drama of a relationship. For now.

He sets me down gently, hands steadying me like I might float away. Then, as if it's the most natural thing in the world, he reaches into the inside pocket of his blazer and pulls out a small, delicately wrapped bundle—brown parchment paper tied with a silk ribbon the color of French marigolds.

"I saw this at the market this morning," he says, offering it to me. "Gemma mentioned you like crystals."

A palm-size cluster of green fluorite. Its facets jut from the stone like ice. Light glides across the translucent edges, catching in pale sea-glass depths that shift between sage green and teal. Along its base, tiny crystals glitter like frost. It feels both fragile and indestructible, a secret the earth revealed in slow angles.

"It's raw. Not heat-treated," I say, smoothing my thumb over the uneven facets. "That makes it way better for enhancing mental clarity and focus…activating the third eye. Basically all the things that help open the mind."

"You know your crystals." His wide mouth tips in a smile.

I shrug, but of course I know my stuff. Wouldn't a knight thoroughly check their armor before going into battle?

"And I know," he continues, "that most things are more powerful when they haven't been altered."

I thought Alder would be more sinister, a stick-up-his-ass domineering overlord with a chiseled jaw and a god complex. Instead, he's charming and thoughtful and disarmingly sweet. For a second, I forget that I hate him.

Then I remember the last time Gemma called me snot crying because he'd tried to convince her that therapy was "self-indulgent" and that she should try being grateful instead of feeling sorry for herself. And *bam*, my clarity returns.

Still, I tuck the gift into my purse. I'm not a monster.

"Yes, well," I begin, clearing my throat. "It's nice to finally see…how tall you are in person."

Totally normal thing to say. I want to throw myself directly in front of the nearest cab.

Instead, I move to down another sip of my tragically lukewarm green juice when Alder smoothly links his arm through mine.

"Shall we?" he says, and before I can reply, he sweeps me past security and inside the old Midtown hotel.

We follow a steady stream of black-tie guests through the marble foyer, past a gleaming concierge desk, and straight through a pair of doors into the ballroom. The ceiling sparkles with faux constellations—tiny LED stars pulsing in time with the ambient music, casting soft glimmers over the crowd. Silk drapes cascade down the walls in long, shimmery waves, pooling on the marble floors like spilled moonlight. Laughter and soft chatter sweep through the space as cater waiters in cream tuxedo jackets float by with trays of apps.

Everywhere I look, it's silk, silver, and crystal. The kind of space designed to make people feel important and vaguely immortal. I, on the other hand, feel like I wandered in from a different timeline. One where I still use coupons and haven't ever figured out if I'm filing my taxes correctly.

I'm scanning the room for Gemma when I realize Alder has been talking.

"There are many aspects of my past I need to explain," he says, his voice low and serious.

My fingers stick to my green juice bottle, whiffs of wheatgrass rising from the sloshing liquid.

"I was—"

"An insufferable twat."

He snorts.

Shit. Said that very inside thought out loud. Well, it's not the first time, and it definitely won't be the last.

"Precisely." He flashes a grin so devastatingly charming that, despite myself, I smile back. Damn him.

The crowd shifts, and I finally spot Gemma in a backless emerald-green gown, her honey-blond hair swept to one side and held in place with a glimmering silver and sapphire clip.

She looks *happy*. Radiant in a way that can't be faked. At least, not without a bank account with more commas than mine.

She holds up her hands and lifts onto her toes as we get closer. "Amanda! I am so happy you're here!"

I smile, because that's what you do when your best friend says they're happy you've arrived. But in the back of my mind, Declan's "OFFLINE" is blinking like a low-battery warning. I wonder if I'd look as happy as she does if I had someone I wasn't terrified of scaring off.

My phone stays heavy in my hand, screen dark, no new messages.

But that's fine.

I'm fine.

I have more important things to do than angst about whether or not a man I've never met in person is second-guessing our dynamic.

Alder slows beside her and deposits me at her side with a slight bow. "I'm sure you two have much to catch up on and would prefer to do so without me present."

He turns to Gemma, brushes an errant curl from her cheek, and murmurs something in her ear that makes her blush like a summer sunset. Then he kisses her hand, gives her a wink, and vanishes into the crush of the crowd like a very well-dressed mirage.

"Umm, excuse me," I say, mouth open as I recover

from mild whiplash. "When did Mr. Emotionally Stunted turn into Prince Freaking Charming?"

Gemma's blush deepens. "I have *a lot* to tell you. But first—" She wraps me in a hug that squeezes the sarcasm right out of me.

I return it with gusto, a soft little exhale escaping my chest.

"I missed you," she says as we pull apart.

"I missed you too." My smile wobbles as I motion around us, a sweeping gesture that translates roughly to *what the actual hell, Gemma?!* "I mean, we usually talk at least once a day. And then I don't hear from you for two weeks, and when I do—"

"I know. I know." She grabs two glasses of champagne from a passing waiter and offers me one.

I shake my head. This green juice bottle is practically glued to my palm by a thin film of sweat. "You're okay, right, Gem?"

Gemma sets both flutes on the closest cocktail table and turns back to me with a soft smile. "Yeah." Her eyes gloss over with tears, a full-to-the-brim joy I haven't seen on her face in a long time. "I am *unbelievably* okay."

"And everything with Alder…?" I ask carefully, watching her expression for the smallest twitch, flinch, or cringe—any sign that I should throw a drink in his face and then run him over with one of the valeted sports cars.

She takes a deep breath and brushes an escaped tear from her cheek. "Is perfect," she says. "*He's* perfect."

"Good."

And I mean it. I do. Well, I want to mean it. But

it's hard not to feel like the only person still stuck in the opening act of her rom-com while everyone else is already well into their glow-up montage.

But tonight, I'm pulling it together. Gemma's back. I'm off my couch, wearing real clothes and a full face of makeup. All I need is one good night. One little spark. A reminder that my story is still unfolding.

And something to help me forget that, against my better judgment, I inched closer to being a very tiny bit emotionally naked with Declan. A man I've never actually met and now probably never will.

I set my phone face down on the table and dip a hand into my purse until my fingers brush the familiar edge of rose quartz. A talisman against heartbreak. A way to hold myself together when I start to come apart.

However, there's still hope for me yet. I mean, maybe my own two-week glow-up starts right now.

"You know..." Gemma says, sipping her champagne, a secretive little grin creeping across her face.

"You didn't go drunk shopping and order a bunch of those creepy, toothed monster key chains again, did you?" I tease, because I've seen that smile many times. Usually right before we're reading a website's fine print about returns.

"God no. I am never getting online after two drinks again."

We both laugh, the sound slipping easily into the familiar groove of ten years' worth of inside jokes.

"No," she says, still smiling. "You were right when you called him Prince Charming."

I follow her gaze across the room to Alder, who towers above the crowd with his blue eyes, golden hair, and devastating cheekbones. He looks like the live-action reboot of every animated prince who ever twirled a princess in a castle ballroom.

"He's definitely got the whole original-Disney-hero thing going for him."

And, okay, I *know* I don't need a man to save me. I light a candle every morning before work to fortify myself against emails and capitalism and to remind myself that I'm a feminist with a full-time job and a high-yield savings account I opened during a full moon. The black tourmaline on my coffee table tells me that I know how to rescue myself. But being whisked off my feet by a handsome billionaire wouldn't be the worst thing in the world.

Not that it's an option. In order to be saved by Prince Charming, I'd have to make myself completely emotionally available. Possibly even open to true love.

No thank you.

I've got enough to juggle just keeping up with the rituals that numb the panic long enough for me to move one foot in front of the other.

Declan leaving me on read is for the best.

I take a drink of green juice, and Gemma cringes.

"It's healthy," I explain, swallowing a mouthful that tastes like wet grass.

She gestures toward one of the servers weaving past us, silver tray stacked with decadent bites. "You know this event is fully catered with food that's chewable and seasoned."

I eye a platter of grilled shrimp skewered between blistered cherry tomatoes and creamy balls of mozzarella.

"I'm recalibrating my gut biome," I say primly.

"You're recalibrating your taste buds into an early grave."

I snort and crack a smile. I missed her so much.

"Laugh all you want," I say, lifting the compostable bottle and sipping again, grimacing only a little. "But this chlorophyll elixir is going to keep me radiant well into my third divorce."

Gemma shakes her head. "There's no way you'll end up married three times."

"I could get married if I wanted." The words tumble out faster than I mean them to, and my cheeks flush hot. "It's not like there aren't guys who want to marry me."

I'm not destined to be alone. I'm just wary of putting myself out there. A lot of people would say my pessimism is healthy realism. And it's not like I'm the only one hiding behind a carefully crafted dating persona and reinventing myself biweekly.

My dating technique is…protective. Whatever. I don't have to justify my decisions. Point is, I'm not in a healthy, stable romantic relationship because *I* don't *want* to be in one. So…there.

"If I wanted to be with someone." I continue my justification aloud even though I definitely do not feel any type of way about it. "I could be. I *would* be. Men would be lined up around the block to—"

"Okay," Gemma cuts in gently before I'm forced to find an end to that thought. "I'm not saying you couldn't get married three times. You're fucking amazing, Amanda. What I'm saying is that once you find your person, you're going to be with him forever."

A lump rises in my throat. It's sudden and uninvited and so full of hope I don't know what to do with it.

"And I can't picture you having an actual wedding," she adds, swirling her champagne. "Not in a traditional sense anyway. You'd shout your vows over an exploding volcano or… I don't know." She tilts her chin, thoughtful, a teasing glint in her eye. "WWAD?"

I shake my head. "I don't—"

"What would Amanda do?"

What *would* Amanda do?

Hopefully Gemma has the answer, because I have no fucking clue.

My phone trills, breaking us both out of our trances.

My heart rate ticks up as I flip my phone over and swipe eagerly, checking the notification from Flutter.

"App update," I groan. "Who needs a notification about that?"

Gemma shakes her head and laughs into her champagne flute.

I chew my cheek, pretending that she doesn't see what I'm trying to hide. But she does. We've been too close too long for her not to.

"Gimme." She holds out her hand, and I know exactly what she wants without having to ask.

I sigh and pull up his profile before handing her the phone. "His name's Declan Thorne."

Her mouth drops the same way mine did when his picture first came across my screen.

"*Okay*," she says slowly. "Second hottest man I've ever seen."

"Right?!" Excitement lifts me onto my tiptoes as she swipes through the photos I've drooled over at least one hundred times. "He looks like one of the guys from the Mafia books that always land in my inbox—tall, dark, handsome, and riddled with enough emotional damage to make a therapist salivate."

Gemma rolls her eyes.

"You know I have a type." I shrug, trying to keep it light. Trying not to sound like I'm already invested in a man who only exists on my phone.

"Yes," she says, handing the phone back. "I know your type. We used to have the same type, remember?"

"And you kissed that tall, blond toad and turned him into a tall, blond hero. I can do the same. Just not with a blond guy. Obviously. Yuck."

I wait for her to laugh again, to roll her eyes and tell me I'm ridiculous even though I really want to hear that it's possible—that I can find a man who looks like trouble but is soft and kind and doesn't go offline when I attempt to be myself...all from the comfort and safety of my own home—not that my romantic ideals are completely unrealistic or unhealthy.

But Gemma stays quiet, gaze soft and far away.

So I push forward, babbling like I'm trying to outrun the vulnerability painting my cheeks red. If I stuff the silence with enough words, maybe I won't have to sit in it.

I reach back into my purse and fully palm the rose quartz.

"The best part about dating apps is the total control. No food in my teeth, no uncomfortable outfits, no shaving my entire body for the mere possibility of being seen naked. Just posed photos that won't reveal my identity if they're ever put online, thought-out texts, and minimal opportunity for embarrassment."

And sexting. Though I'm probably not going to

mention the sexting until we crack open that bottle of wine. Plus, I'll need a few glasses to go over my *I'm not sure I'll want whatever's happening between us to just be a fantasy* text. Ugh.

I pause. Then add with a shrug, like it's no big deal, like it isn't my entire coping strategy dressed up in a punchline, "It's kind of perfect, when you think about it."

Gemma doesn't say anything right away, but I feel her watching me. Present in that gentle, steady, nonjudgmental way only someone who's become your chosen family can be.

I hate it.

"It's like one of those story apps," I blurt, vaguely aware that I'm strangling my juice bottle, filmy green liquid sloshing dangerously close to the compostable rim. "Choose Your Billionaire or whatever, where you get to text flirt with a morally gray CEO who wants to ruin you in a sexy way while also, like, supporting your small business. I get all the drama with none of the consequences."

Gemma's brow creases, her chin jutting slightly as she tilts her head. "You're comparing your potential future partner to a choose-your-own-adventure smut app?"

"No," I scoff, because I am very clearly doing just that.

Her gaze stays on me, and there's a sinking sensation in my stomach like I missed a stair in the dark.

"So..." she starts gently. "You haven't actually met him?"

"What do you mean by 'met'?" I force a laugh, light and breezy, as if my cheeks aren't on fire and I'm not scraping my nails against a crystal for any ounce of stability.

Meeting him isn't the point. What we have now is *working*. If he'd just reply to my last message, everything would be great.

"Babe..." Her voice is quiet, warm. Kind in a way that makes it harder to ignore. "How do you know for sure Declan Thorne is who he says he is?"

Her concern wraps around my chest and squeezes.

I didn't ask for rational. I didn't ask for gentle. I didn't ask for this version of Gemma—the evolved one, the responsible one, the glowing-goddess-with-clear-boundaries-and-a-billionaire-boyfriend one. Right now I want the Gemma from ten years ago. The one who would've said *fuck it, have fun*.

Who cares if ten years ago neither of our brains were fully developed and that we consistently put ourselves in ridiculous situations?

"He sends real photos," I say quickly, yanking my hand from my purse to point at my phone like it's evidence in a trial. "And his grammar is flawless."

I glance up, practically begging for the eye roll, the smirk, the head shake that will let me stay in the delusion a little longer.

Instead, Gemma tilts her chin and narrows her eyes. "Wait a second." She leans in. "You *like* him."

"Well, yeah." I bark out a laugh that's way too loud. "You saw the pictures."

"No." She shakes her head slowly, her champagne flute seemingly forgotten in her hand. "You have real feelings for him. You might be able to lie to yourself, but you cannot lie to me."

Sweat beads along my hairline. "Okay, maybe a little. But not *real* feelings. Just…" I shrug and try to sound breezy. "I like talking to him. I like the version of me I am when I talk to him."

Gemma doesn't say anything right away, and the silence fills with the ghosts of the things I don't want to admit.

Finally, she says, "Amanda, I love you, and I can't help but worry about you. You've never been in the same room with this guy or talked to him face-to-face. What if the version of Declan Thorne you've built up in your head, the version of him you're connecting with, doesn't vibe with who he actually is?"

The words land harder than I want them to. Because if that's true—if Declan's presenting some shinier, edited version of himself—then he's just doing what I'm doing. And I really don't want to think too hard about what that means.

Gemma grips my hand in hers, smooths the soft pad of her thumb along my knuckles. "I feel like sometimes you fall for the idea of a person so quickly, you forget to ask if they're even real."

Pop.

The balloon I've been clinging to—inflated with hope and fantasy—deflates in a single breath. Now there's just the slow hiss of reality.

I try to laugh it off, but the sound gets stuck in my throat.

"Hey." Gemma squeezes my fingers. "I'm sure this guy isn't some lying loser. I'm sure he's exactly who he's presenting himself to be. I don't think terrible assholes even know how to employ proper grammar."

My laugh is paper thin. "It's fine," I say, forcing a smile that feels like it's glued on crooked. "I'm fine."

"You don't have to be." Her voice is even softer now, like she knows I'm barely holding it together. "I just want you to find something real. That's all. You deserve that."

I nod, but I can't quite speak. My throat is too dry. My rib cage feels too tight, my dress too fitted, the air too warm. Not even chugging the rest of my green juice is going to help, and I added ashwagandha to this batch specifically for calm and clarity.

My phone buzzes.

I practically leap for it, breath whooshing out of my lungs like I've been underwater.

Saved by the bell. Or the buzz. Either way, it's an excuse to look anywhere but at her.

DECLAN: Are you free tonight?

My stomach flips, equal parts anticipation and dread. The kind of drop felt at the top of a roller coaster right before the plunge.

I glance at Gemma. Then back at my phone as it vibrates again.

DECLAN: I leave for Dubai in the morning, but before I go I want to make this fantasy real.

DECLAN: Rendezvous at 9. At Ember. Dress code's: make me regret not meeting you sooner.

I read the messages once. Then again. Then five more times to be sure I'm not hallucinating.

He wants to meet me.

Tonight.

My entire body goes rigid. My soul rolls over and plays dead. A weird, nauseating cocktail of *it's finally happening* and *I might throw up* swirls in my gut.

It's not that I didn't think he'd ever ask. I just didn't think he'd ask *now*. With no warning. With less than an hour of mental preparation. I thought I'd have time to memorize new affirmations and rituals that make pretending I'm fine feel almost the same as actually being fine. Instead, I've been dropped into the deep end of a pool I built myself—tile by tile, text by text, fantasy by fantasy.

"Okay," I whisper, squeezing my phone until my knuckles go white, "what the actual fuck am I supposed to do?"

Gemma's lips form a tight O, eyebrows raised like she's been waiting for this exact moment. "The dating app god wants to meet."

"I hate how psychic you are."

She lifts one shoulder in a lazy shrug. "It's part of my charm."

I pick up my previously ignored champagne flute and down the entire thing. Bubbles burn a trail down my chest, fire with a floral finish, and I nearly cough it back up.

"Tonight," I sputter. "At a club he told me last week that he *co-owns*. Because apparently the universe didn't think this situation was destabilizing enough."

Half of me hopes he cancels.

The other half would be crushed if he did.

Gemma leans casually against the cocktail table. "So go."

"I can't just *go*," I hiss, arms flailing. "I've only seen

his face on a screen and talked to him through an app. What if none of it's real?"

Even as the words leave my mouth, I wince. The irony that I've spent the last half hour defending the very real, extremely valid, definitely-not-a-catfish existence of Declan Thorne like I was his personal publicist is not lost on me.

Gemma's smile is amused, a little smug. "Or what if he's emotionally available and no longer wants to hide in your DMs?"

Without thinking, I unglue my hand from my juice bottle reach inside my purse. "Let's see what the universe has to say, shall we?"

"You don't need to outsource your decision-making to the universe. You are capable of figuring out what to do on your own."

"I know that." But I'm already elbow deep in my purse, rifling through its contents like a witchy Mary Poppins. "I'm just looking for, you know, *clarity*—"

"Zero risk."

We both say it at the same time.

"Potato, potahto," I chirp and pull out my Break Glass in Case of Emotional Instability kit: travel-sized tarot deck, affirmation flashcards, a bottle of rosemary and lavender room cleanser, and a rose quartz stone the size of a chicken nugget are just the highlights.

Gemma eyes the cards warily. "You better be careful with those."

"This night can't get any worse."

She inhales deeply through her nose, and that feeling washes over me again. Like she knows something. Like she knows—

"Gemma!" Alder weaves through the crowd beside us, straightening his tux as he flashes a grin that could fund a small country. "So sorry to interrupt," he says smoothly. "There are a few donors I'd love for you to meet before the auction starts."

Gemma's gaze flicks from him to the cards spread on the table. "Don't even think about touching those until I'm back," she warns, giving my arm a pointed squeeze. "Promise?"

"Promise, weirdo."

She narrows her eyes, unconvinced. "I'm serious, Amanda."

"Okay, okay, I won't." I kiss her cheek. "Now go be Ms. Billionaire."

Alder takes her hand in his, and moments later they're lost inside the glittering crowd.

As soon as they disappear, I let out a slow breath and glance down at the cards. My fingers twitch toward the deck despite her warning. They're just harmless cards. More habit than actual belief. One of those little buffers I use to keep the mess hidden.

"I just need a sign," I murmur. "A tiny push in the right direction. And I am not doing this to outsource my decision-making."

A woman draped in silver satin glides past, pearls swinging at her throat, and shoots me a look like it's abnormal for well-adjusted people do tarot readings in the middle of fancy charity galas to prove they're on the right path.

I give her my brightest smile, snag another champagne flute as a waiter drifts by, and down half the glass in a single gulp before turning back to the cards.

"Okay, universe," I exhale and whisper to the cards. "Could this thing with Declan Thorne be real, or is this just another fantasy I've gotten too attached to?"

I flutter my fingers over the tarot deck, eyes half closed, waiting for the tiny tug that's supposed to mean intuition but probably just means my brain likes patterns. When it finds me, I draw.

The Wheel of Fortune.

I stare down at it, unimpressed. "Wow. Shocking." I roll my eyes. "This is the fifth time I've drawn this card this week."

Twice just this morning. Once after I lit my candle and chanted badass feminist affirmations over my first latte and again after I ugly cried into my dying fiddle-leaf fig while listening to a Divine Feminine Realness playlist. At this point, it's less of a sign and more of a stalker.

"Come on, universe," I groan. "Mix it up. Give me literally anything else. A burning bush. A pigeon with a scroll. Skywriting. Surprise me."

I frown down at it and absentmindedly twist the stem of the champagne flute. "So we meet again," I mutter. "Let's see, you're all about cycles, change, fate, divine timing. Plenty of that cosmic self-help jargon." I wave a hand in the air, shooing away the potential gravity of pulling the same card so many times in a row. "Basically, a move from one phase of life to the next. Groundbreaking."

I finish the rest of my champagne in one gulp, warmth spreading through my chest and down my legs. "A girl comes to you for answers," I say to the card, "and instead gets psycho-spiritual babble. Typical." I sigh. "Maybe this isn't working for me anymore. Maybe I should order one of those crystal pendulums I keep seeing in those targeted ads..."

A server floats past, and I snag a small silver dish of truffle-dusted popcorn, popping a few kernels into my mouth as I scan the ballroom for Gemma or Alder, but they've both vanished.

"Where are you, Gemma?" Anxiety buzzes under my skin, itchy and bright, and I worry my lower lip between my teeth.

I glance back down at the card, the golden wheel at the center glinting in the overhead lighting.

This is what I wanted, right? A message. A sign from the universe. The modern-day version of a carrier pigeon. If Gemma texted me the same thing five times in a row, I'd listen. But I know her. I trust her. She's real. These are cardboard coping mechanisms. And, yes, maybe I do use them to pass the blame if I do make a wrong move.

But real relationships come with expectations. With timelines and vulnerabilities and the terrifying possibility that someone might see the parts of me I've gotten really good at hiding. The ones I can't filter or edit or rebrand.

I could meet Declan—the dark-eyed, grammar-fluent fantasy I've carefully kept behind the safety of a screen. Or I can end it now. Pull the plug. Laugh off my last message and retreat into the comfort of sexts and emojis and low-stakes make-believe.

The Wheel of Fortune catches the light again, winking up at me.

I slide the card back into the deck and down the rest

of my ashwagandha-infused lawn sludge in one grim, defiant gulp.

"Well..." I mutter, wiping the corners of my mouth with a cocktail napkin. "Fuck it."

TWO

Ember's logo is etched in copper above a sleek, black facade—a wand engulfed in flame, twisting upward like a question mark made of fire. The wand is subtle, almost hidden unless you know what you're looking for. Which feels like a metaphor. For what, I don't know yet. But it feels important and ominous in a cursed-object kind of way.

I weave through the crowd, people pressed together in clusters, dancing, drinking. Music pulses low. The lighting is soft but strategic, red glows from the shadowed corners like flames, and a gold wash fills the space, making everyone look a little glossier, a little more like a dream.

I'm trying to hold myself together. Trying to channel Dating App Amanda—the mysterious, effortlessly flirty version of me who sends eggplant and water emojis and strategically plans double texts.

But in reality, I'm a vibrating mess in strappy stilettos and a dress that seemed like a brilliant idea when I was going to a fundraiser and not moments away from meeting the man who has an express pass to my nervous system.

Declan casually leans against the back bar—a gleaming stretch of black stone veined with copper that glints under the dim glow of low-hanging sconces. Behind him, a wall of backlit liquor bottles rises like an altar. He holds a crystal tumbler in one hand, the other tucked lazily into his pocket.

Holy shit. He's real.

I mean, I *knew* that. But seeing him in the flesh, watching his body take up space like this… I guess I didn't fully believe someone like *that* was actually DMing someone like *me*.

He doesn't move when he sees me. Doesn't wave. Doesn't smile. He just watches.

I draw in a breath. It catches halfway.

His profile said six foot three, but seeing him now, he's somehow…*bigger.* Taller than expected. Broader too. Dressed in a sleek black suit, every line tailored to make the most of his impossibly muscular build. And his stillness—that coiled, tightly reined-in quiet—is magnetic in a way that feels like a challenge. A dare cloaked in wool and shadow.

His molten gaze glides over me like he's already unwrapped me and is deciding which part he wants to taste first. He lifts the tumbler to his lips and takes a long pull, his throat working, his jaw flexing ever so slightly. Without breaking eye contact, he drags his thumb across his full bottom lip.

All I can think about is how I want that thumb dragging across me. My lips, my throat, chest, stomach, lower.

My nipples harden. My ovaries sigh. And my vagina lights up like a chakra that's just been unblocked.

This whole meeting-in-person thing is going to be a lot more complicated than I thought.

I bite the inside of my cheek. Flirting through a screen I have down. But being near this man—breathing the same air, watching his mouth move, seeing the way he looks at me like I'm the next thing on his to-do list—is something else entirely.

All at once, I'm devastatingly aware of every inch of my body. Every beat of my heart. Every shallow breath.

I take one step. Then another.

My walk is too stiff. Or maybe too bouncy. Is there such a thing as seductive but grounded? Like a ballet dancer who moonlights as a dominatrix?

I try to picture what I must look like, which of course only makes it worse.

Tucking my chin, I adjust my shoulders. Then I untuck my chin. I have no idea what my arms are doing. Why do I have so many limbs?

My ankle wobbles.

Oh no. No no no.

This isn't going to be a cute little trip. Not a flirty stumble. Not an *oopsie, tee-hee* kind of moment. This is a *flat on my face* sort of blunder. A full rom-com pratfall.

If I could just make it to the bar…touch something solid…

No such luck. My ankle gives out, and I death grip my purse as I pitch forward.

Directly into Declan Thorne's chest.

Colliding with him is like hitting a wall of heat and

muscle that somehow smells expensive—earth and spice layered over woodsmoke.

One solid arm wraps around me, catching me hard against his chest before I can slide down his torso like a cartoon character and end up on the floor.

His suit jacket is smooth velvet, but there's no missing the broad, unyielding muscle beneath. My hands press against him, fingers splaying over firm pecs that flex as he moves. My nose brushes the hollow of his throat. The scent there—skin and warmth and something that might be clove—hits so good and deep it makes me sigh.

Would it be weird to live off this smell and one green juice a day? Because honestly, I'd thrive.

A low sound rumbles in his chest as he clears his throat, and my whole body jolts like I've just remembered how to function.

Looking up takes effort. My face burns.

The soft curve of his mouth twitches. That little smile is slow, smug, and completely unfair.

"You always make an entrance like this?" he asks, voice low and bone-meltingly deep.

And holy hell.

That voice.

It's richer than I imagined. A slow scrape of gravel against my bare arms.

"Apparently only when I'm trying to seduce someone," spills out of my mouth before I can stop it.

Kill me. Kill me now.

His breath flutters my lashes as he leans in, close enough to feel the heat of it against my cheeks. "Then I'd say it's working."

Something tightens low in my belly—want or warning,

I can't tell—and for a second, the noise of the club fades to a low, echoing hum. Just me. Him. And the acute awareness that this man is not going to play fair.

I clear my throat and shuffle ungracefully backward while smoothing my dress and hooking my purse over my arm. Hopefully getting some distance will erase the fact that I just inhaled him like a human incense stick. My hand flies to my hair, fingers raking through my shoulder-length cut that I'm praying doesn't resemble a poodle caught in a windstorm.

Declan reaches out with the languid grace of a man who's never had to rush for anything and drags his fingers up my arm, leaving a trail of sparks along my bare skin. Each second stretches like taffy as he slowly hooks the strap of my dress back up over my shoulder

Breath locked in my throat, I focus on not leaning in.

But my body betrays me, shoulder shifting a fraction of an inch into his palm before I can stop it.

"There," he murmurs, voice a slow pour of honey. His gaze locks onto mine, dark and steady. "Perfect."

Perfect.

The word smolders in my chest. My skin buzzes where he touched me. My brain scrambles to reboot. And beneath the heat and the want and my resting level of anxiety, a single, unnerving truth rises like a warning bell:

I am in so much trouble.

THREE

"So," I say, voice higher than I'd like, "you do exist."

The corners of his mouth curl into a devastating smile. "Don't sound so disappointed."

"I'm not."

I *absolutely* am not.

I just wasn't prepared for him to be real in the kind of way that's ruining every coherent thought in my head.

He studies me for a beat, gaze unreadable, like he's trying to decide if I'm what he expected or maybe just how much trouble *I'll* be. Then, without a word, he tilts his head toward the roped-off hallway behind him. Tufted leather panels line the walls like the inside of a very expensive coffin.

"Come with me."

Of course he has a private room. A man like Declan Thorne—the co-owner of this club and the kind of guy who swoops in, buys majority control of a good-but-struggling business, and turns it into a money-printing machine—doesn't lounge on the main floor with the rest of us commoners sipping overpriced cocktails and pretending not to people watch. He disappears into places no one else enters without invitation. Places with locks and passwords and consequences.

I trail him, trying very hard not to stare at his ass. But holy hell, the way he moves. Fluid, composed, like the air bends around him. His shoulders shift with an easy, rolling rhythm beneath the precise lines of his tailored suit, spine a perfect arrow. Even the movements of his hands, swinging loosely at his sides, seem choreographed.

We reach a tall, black door at the end of the hall, and he opens it with the barest flick of his wrist.

I have the sinking, thrilling sensation that he's the kind of man who barely has to touch anything to make it his. A man who gets what he wants just by existing in its proximity.

I dig my teeth into my lower lip.

He hasn't looked at me in a full thirty seconds, and I already know, if he pressed me up against that door right now, I wouldn't just let him. I'd say thank you.

The door glides open, heavy and silent, and he steps across the threshold without glancing back to see if I'll follow.

I hesitate for half a second, because that's what smart people do before walking into the dragon's den wearing four-inch heels and a dress designed for breathing shallowly. But then I step in after him because I'm not always smart.

As the door eases shut behind us, the thrum of Ember's main room fades, sealed behind thick walls. The atmosphere changes. It's warmer and quieter, intimate in a way that feels both luxurious and a little treacherous.

Candlelight spills across the space in molten waves. Dark crimson walls soak in the glow while the flickering flames dance across the booth nestled in the back corner like a confessional box.

Another sleek black bar stretches along the opposite wall. Behind it, glass shelves hold bottles of amber and jewel-toned liquor lined up like artifacts. Gold accented armchairs flank a low mirrored table that throws the candlelight around the room like a moody disco ball.

The scent here is intoxicating. Cedar, cardamom, a trace of smoke and cinnamon and something spicy that clings to Declan and this space like power in pheromone form.

It's the kind of room where things begin.

And maybe end.

We close in on the leather booth, and he gestures for me to sit.

My legs ignore every rational directive and opt for immediate, unthinking surrender, and I instantly drop my purse and shimmy in.

He slides in beside me, unhurried and confident, his thigh almost brushing mine. The heat radiating from his body makes it feel like the air between us is thinner—less oxygen, more tension.

"You need a drink," he says, voice all silk and shadows.

It's not a question, and part of me likes that he didn't ask. That he just decided.

I should decline, ask for something citrusy and nonalcoholic since the champagne from earlier is fizzing in my bloodstream, trying its damnedest to suppress my better judgment. One more drink, and I'll slide right out of Dating App Amanda—polished, flirty, vaguely mysterious—and land squarely in the territory of Real-Life Amanda, who is a tangle of anxiety and overthinking and one emotional hiccup away from hiding in the bathroom.

Declan lifts a single finger like a king summoning a feast.

A bartender who must have been part of the furniture a second ago, because I did not notice him, appears without a sound. He sets down two crystal glasses before fading back into the atmosphere.

My drink is cold, pink, and perfectly poured. The sugared rim sparkles like frost under the candlelight, and a crescent of grapefruit rests on the edge like a wink.

I blink at it. Then at Declan.

"Should I be worried?" My lips twitch. "Or just impressed?"

Declan leans back slightly, his gaze steady. "Try it," he murmurs, "then let me know."

The glass is cool against my fingers, condensation kissing my skin as I lift it to my lips.

One sip and I'm hit with sharp citrus, a whisper of liquor, and a punch of botanicals. It's tart, unexpected, and strong enough to make my mouth water.

"Is this elderflower?" I ask, surprised. "And…tequila?"

His smile is sly and full of secrets. "I figured you'd want something pretty," he says, lifting his own glass filled with darker liquid, "that knows how to punch back."

My brows rise. "What made you think that?"

"I can tell you like a little beauty with your burn."

He takes a sip of the dark, heavy drink in his glass, his gaze never leaving mine.

Beauty with your burn.

The words stick to my skin. Wrap around my ribs. That's the whole illusion tonight, isn't it? All dressed up, hoping he doesn't notice the restless fire in my chest. The sharp edges I've melted down into flirtation.

We sip our drinks in silence, and I try not to obsess over how close he got with those four little words.

Every second he waits to speak is another inch of rope tightening between us. Like he's giving me enough slack to bolt only so he can enjoy it more when I don't.

The air between us crackles, thick with tension and citrus and candle smoke. My skin hums. My knees press together. My fingers toy with the stem of my glass.

"So," I say too brightly, the word bursting from my lips like it escaped. "This place is...*wow*. It's very you."

I grimace. What does that even mean?

"Like, very mysterious," I continue, because of course I do. "All dark wood and sexy lighting. It's got that whole Bond villain meets underground jazz club energy, but in a cool way. Not in a murder-y way."

"Hmm." He lifts his glass to his mouth, watching me over the rim. "You think of me as a villain, Amanda?"

A strangled sound that's halfway between laughter and choking leaves my throat. "No, of course not." I purse my lips and bite the inside of my cheek. "But...*maybe*. I mean—I work in publishing. I'm always thinking of the world like a story. And you do co-own a club with a secret back room, and you are very...large."

One brow twitches, but otherwise his expression remains neutral, giving me absolutely nothing to work with.

I press on. "I just mean you have presence. Like a tall, expensive, slightly villainous presence."

"And who do you see yourself as in this story?"

The question knocks the breath from me. I take a giant sip of my cocktail and nearly choke on the sugar.

I should be calm. I've read enough manuscripts to know exactly what role I'm playing. I know what this is.

And what it isn't.

This isn't a love story. This is attraction and desire and two people playing a game they both understand. It's sex à la carte. A fantasy with a body no matter what either of us might have said in our last round of DMs. A man who wants me in his bed, not in his life. That much is obvious, since he made the decision to meet right before he's about to leave town. And that's fine. If he wants to pretend like I never said I'd be open to catching feelings, I'm more than happy to do the same.

No messy surprises. No broken promises. No vulnerability required.

That should be comforting. Reassuring, even. A clean transaction.

Instead, it feels...unsettling. A twisting ache deep in my chest, threaded with the sharp, electric awareness that this man—this moment—could undo me if I let it.

"You seem like you're about to run."

"I'm not," I lie, laughing too loudly.

"Good." He sets his glass down slowly, carefully. "Because I don't chase."

The air between us snaps tight, and I sit up straighter. Adjust the strap of my dress even though it's already in place. Cross my legs way too fast and knock my knee into the underside of the table with a solid, echoing *thunk*.

"Ow! Shit." I hiss in pain and slap a hand over my drink just in time to keep it from toppling.

Declan shifts toward me. "You okay?"

"Fine," I blurt on a pained exhale. "Just a little blunt force trauma."

His full lips twitch in a suggestion of a smile as he leans back, stretching one long arm across the back of the booth, relaxed and unreadable. I can't tell if he's being a gentleman and giving me space or a predator who enjoys watching injured prey limp closer on its own.

Does it matter?

Either way, I'm already caught.

Whatever this is, my body said yes long before my brain could weigh in. Now I just have to survive it.

I shift in my seat, run a hand over my throbbing knee, and take another sip of the cocktail that's going straight to my head.

"You're quiet," I say, grasping for normal conversation even though nothing about any of this feels normal. "Is that part of the whole mysterious, velvet suit vibe, or are you just not an in-person conversationalist?"

He tilts his head, studying me. "Do you want me to talk more?"

"I don't *not* want that."

"What would you want me to say?" he asks, not missing a beat. "That I'm dangerous? That you should run? That this is a bad idea?"

"That feels like a lot for a first meetup."

"You're still here." He lifts his drink again and takes a slow pull.

"I'm curious."

"About me?" he asks, one brow lifting.

"About whether this..." I gesture vaguely between us. "...translates from screen to real life."

Declan watches me carefully. "So far?"

"So far what?"

"Does it translate?"

I open my mouth. Close it again. "I don't know yet. You're...different in person."

He nods once. "And you expected what, exactly?"

"Less brooding? More charming? Definitely more conversing and less intense staring."

"Would it be easier if I smiled?" he asks, tone unreadable. "You did say you'd like me to be more charming."

That pulls a startled laugh from my throat. "I *like* knowing where I stand. You're kind of the opposite of that."

Declan tilts his glass. Dark liquid sloshes from one side to the other, catching the candlelight. "Tell me something."

Jutting my chin, I tuck my hair behind my ears. "I feel like I've just told you a lot of things."

"Tell me more."

Whatever spell was taking hold loosens.

Every word he's said since I walked in has been about me. Reflections, deflections, questions lobbed back. He hasn't revealed a single thing about himself. Not one.

Sure, he's gorgeous, built like a fantasy, and smells like a luxury candle. And yes, I found this persona compelling and mysterious and sexy on the app. I also understand how Declan could expect me to purr and flirt—play my part and match the version of myself I created online. That's completely fair. I did build her and then hide behind her.

But here now, in person, with my dress stuck to my thighs and my anxiety gnawing on my brain, I'm realizing there's a part of me that might actually want something that doesn't fit the script. Not a full-blown relationship. Not forever. Just proof that I exist outside the version of myself I've been choreographed and ritualized into existence.

So him sitting there, cool and composed and unreadable, stings more than it should. Because I've made this about more than it's supposed to be.

This isn't only about the heat that's been building between us. It's about wanting to know if I can have a real connection without losing the armor that keeps me functioning. And if this *is* a real sign from the universe and not just coincidence, then maybe this time I'm supposed to stop performing long enough to actually feel something.

Fuck. I hate self-reflection.

"Okay," I say flatly, setting my glass down. "You haven't said anything meaningful since I got here. You expect me to do all the work, carry the conversation, guess what you're thinking, and somehow still look hot doing it. And I get what this was supposed to be about, but it hasn't even been an hour, and I'm already exhausted."

Before I finish the drink—or let my vagina convince me to stay—I push to my feet.

"This was fun," I say, managing a smile that feels clean and final. "But I think I need to figure some shit out. Meeting in person was a mistake."

I slide toward the edge of the booth, chin lifted, ready to sashay off with my boundaries and self-respect. Only my purse catches on something under the table.

I tug. It doesn't come unstuck.

Declan shifts, rising halfway to help.

"I got it," I say through gritted teeth, yanking harder. The strap refuses to budge.

"I really don't—*shit*—need—*ugh*—help—"

We both reach under the table at the same time, and we crash into each other, forehead to forehead, like two actors in a slapstick routine.

"Shit!"

"Damn it."

Declan gently pries the bag free with one smooth movement. "It was caught on the purse hook," he says, lifting it up triumphantly.

Rubbing the spot above my brow, I snatch it from him and straighten my spine. "Great. Thanks. Good night."

Before I can spin on my heel and storm off in a blaze of righteous dignity—

"Amanda, wait." The steel in his voice is gone, softened at the edges. "You can go. I won't stop you." He stands to his full height, hands open, expression stripped of all its glossy, closed-off coolness. "But I'd like the opportunity to start over."

I hesitate long enough for him to continue.

"No brooding or cryptic one-liners. I'd like to have a real conversation. If you'll stay."

It's the first genuine thing he's said all night. And it hits harder than all the flirting and silence combined.

The scent of cardamom and smoke lingers, and I draw in a breath. My gaze meets his, coffee-black and shining. I chew the inside of my cheek, the resolve I'd mustered faltering.

Maybe I'm not the only one pretending. Maybe

we both showed up tonight as shinier, more seductive versions of ourselves designed to photograph well but not fit into the real world.

Rolling my shoulders back, I meet his gaze head-on. "Then we're doing something I want to do."

Declan's brow lifts, intrigued but cautious. He starts to speak, then stops. His chiseled jaw flexes, hands sliding into his pockets as he rocks onto the balls of his feet before settling onto his heels. A man used to giving orders, not taking them.

"What do you have in mind?"

"Something fun." I lift my chin. "And witchy."

His mouth curves, warmer and looser at the edges. "I'm game."

A thrill races through me, part fear, part possibility. I hold out my hand, palm up, pulse loud in my ears.

"Let's see if the universe is too."

FOUR

"Your palm," I say, nodding toward my outstretched hand. My purse is hooked over one shoulder—half security blanket, half escape plan. I'm still ready to bolt the second he stops being amenable and falls back into acting like a fuckboy.

His gaze drops, and he stares at my fingers like they're a test he didn't study for. "My palm?" he echoes.

"How else am I supposed to tell you your destiny?"

He studies me for a beat, unreadable emotions flickering behind his eyes. The tension between us is veering dangerously close to real vulnerability, and my pulse is doing things I do not trust. I need a minute to recalibrate, so I lean into the one thing that feels safe—performance.

The lines around his eyes feather with a smile, but he doesn't move right away. "I got the sense you were witchy, but I didn't think you…"

I cock my hip. "Didn't think I what?"

Declan lifts one broad shoulder. "*Practiced.* If that's the right word."

"It is, and I am well-versed in many forms of witchcraft. Including palmistry. So, come on." I wiggle my fingers. "We had a deal."

Declan's skeptical expression doesn't shift, but he extends his hand, palm up between us. His fingers curl into a loose fist, then unfurl again. There's a mountain range of calluses along the insides of his fingers, and a thin, pale scar traces the curve of his thumb.

"Rock climbing."

The words barely register. I'm too busy staring at his hand—long fingers, rough palm, a knuckle that looks like it's been broken and reset.

"I'm a rock climber. *Used to be*..." There's hesitation in the way he says it. A fracture, almost. Like something about it still stings. "I *used to be* a rock climber."

"What happened?"

His fingers twitch. "Aren't you supposed to be telling me my future?"

"Okay, *secrets*."

"Some things are better learned slowly." His voice is low. Not a warning, exactly. But not an invitation either.

My heart gives an unhelpful little stutter. "I think that qualifies as a cryptic one-liner."

He exhales softly, nearly a laugh, and his smile this time is real. It changes his whole face. Makes him look almost reachable.

I cup his hand, warm and heavy in mine. His skin carries its own current, lightning pacing beneath the surface, looking for somewhere to land.

My skin tingles. My pulse spikes again. A spark of heat moves up my arm.

Declan inhales sharply, his gaze snapping to mine.

My smile wobbles. I am not going to make this into a *thing*. That jolt? That magnetic pull that just shot up my arm? That's just me being touch-starved and too hopped up on nerves and alcohol to think straight. He's not staring because he felt it too. He's only staring because I'm practically drooling into his hand.

Focus, Amanda.

I hover over the curve of his heart line with my index finger. "Whoa, this is rare."

Declan doesn't blink. "What?"

"You have a double heart line."

"I don't know what that means."

"It means you're generous, sensitive. You're passionate. Well, you will be when you find the right person." I hum under my breath. "You're going to fall hard, Mr. Thorne, and when you do it'll be full-on emotional combustion."

His nostrils flare.

A beat of silence stretches between us.

He's staring at me like I just said something loaded.

Shit. No. Abort.

I sputter on an exhale, suddenly unable to breathe.

He probably thinks I'm projecting, outlining our possible future. I don't want him thinking I'm building some whirlwind romance starring the two of us in my head. Or that I'm not capable of keeping this light, surface-level, safe.

I know this is a flirty little game.

And I am not fantasizing about how Declan Thorne

might love. If he's truly like me and put up a strong, confident front online and is really just squishy scared bits on the inside. I'm not imagining what it would feel like to be chosen by a man like him.

Definitely not.

"What else do you see?" he asks, voice rougher now.

I could lie. Could say something cheeky. But his hand is still in mine, warm and open, and for a split second, the air between us feels like the quiet before a storm.

Work. I need to switch to work. Work is safe. Work is boring. Work is not located anywhere near my vagina.

I clear my throat again, but my gaze snags on the lines of his palm I'm trying to ignore. Before I can stop myself, my fingers hover back over them, tracing the air above the creases.

Declan's voice drops, soft and smoky. "Well?"

He's watching me like he wants to be read like a smutty little book, and I do that shit for a living.

Another pulse of heat rolls through me, blooming beneath my skin.

I pull back, adjust, pretend to examine a different part of his palm. "Actually, this area has a lot to say." I swallow, aware that my voice is an octave too high. "Your career line. Very robust. Very…virile."

Dear God. *Virile*?

I want to climb into my purse and zip myself inside.

I bite my lip, cheeks flushing, and risk a glance up at him.

Declan's looking at me, one brow raised, his expression caught somewhere between amusement and heat. "You were telling me about my heart lines."

I let out a strangled laugh. "There's a lot going on here."

The weight of his gaze presses against me as I stare back down at his palm and gesture vaguely.

"This line here is your creativity," I ramble. "It curves upward, which usually means you have a great imagination, which, same. I used to steal my mom's bodice rippers and rewrite the endings so the heroine saved herself and the storyline with the hero was just frosting. Then I'd hide them under my bed. My mom thought I was writing erotic fan fiction."

I blink up at him and then over his shoulder, suddenly unsure where to look.

"So you're a writer."

"I'm a wannabe editor." I shrug. "I also make witchy content, sell moon-charged things, give workshops no one signs up for."

"You read palms in fancy lounges."

Smiling, I glance at him. "What about you, former rock climber turned venture capitalist?"

He pauses, tugging his bottom lip between his teeth. "There's no money in rock climbing," he says finally. "No prestige. At least, not the kind you can put on a résumé or talk about over Sunday-night family dinners."

My brows lift. "You have dinner with your family every Sunday? I can't remember the last time my mom even wanted to hang out with me."

"It's really not as great as it sounds. It's less being a family and more like a weekly performance review."

I let out a surprised laugh. "That's bleak."

"That's being a Thorne," he says, and I catch something in his expression that feels honest.

It makes me hesitate. Makes me want to stay for longer than just tonight. For a second, I even consider setting my purse down—physically and metaphorically.

Then he nods toward his palm. "What else do you see?"

"Right." I clear my throat. "So this little break in your head line usually means a shift in perspective. Like you're changing how you think about your life. Or your future. Or your whole identity."

"You think people can change like that? Shift perspective or make a choice and become a different person."

I meet his eyes, and for once, I don't dodge. The weight of his gaze is steady, searching, like he's not truly asking about *people*—he's asking about himself. "When I figure that out, I'll let you know."

He watches me for a beat too long, mouth parting like he's about to speak. Then he shuts it again. With a slow shake of his head, he shifts his attention back down at his hand.

"And this..." I follow the slashes etched into his palm, my fingertip hovering just above his skin. "Well, it's clear you don't let people in easily, but when you do—"

My voice falters. A blush creeps up my neck as I clamp my mouth shut, teeth sinking into the inside of my cheek.

Stop talking, Amanda.

He leans in, closing the small space between us. I catch the smoky edge of liquor on his lips, the faint spice of his cologne threading through it, and it's suddenly hard to remember how to breathe.

"But when I do?"

The crackle of his words against my temple sends heat flaring through me. My pulse pounds in my fingertips, in my throat, in places I'd rather not think about right now. The steady pulse of music from the dance floor fades to a muffled hum, every nerve tuned only to him—how close he is, how easily he could close the distance.

"They don't forget it."

I can't resist. I press the tip of my finger to the curve of his love line. He jumps at my touch. The spark is immediate. A searing surge of heat races up my arm. My breath escapes in a rough exhale. Touching him feels like touching a live wire. Something inside me is waking up, one nerve ending at a time.

I pull back, but I don't have space to process it. My side is hot. Like, really hot.

Declan's gaze flicks down.

"Your purse," he says slowly. "It's…smoking."

Hazy orange light hisses out from between the teeth of the zipper, curling toward the ceiling.

"I don't have anything flammable," I mutter, half in denial, half trying to logic my way through something that I can't actually cxplain.

I fumble the zipper open, fingers flying past lip gloss, a half-melted honey throat lozenge, my phone, to my Break Glass in Case of Emotional Instability kit.

Heart thudding, I grab it and my phone before the heat can warp the case. The kit's button is hot under my thumb as I unfasten it. The satin edges of my tarot pouch glow like lit coals.

Heat sears my palm as I reach for it. I yelp and jerk it free, pinching it between two fingers and holding it at arm's length like it might explode. Gray tendrils curl off the singed corners like breath from a dragon. The fabric is scorched, radiating waves of heat that prickle against my skin.

Inside, my tarot deck sparks, tiny arcs of light zapping in and out like fireflies.

Declan's hand hovers near my arm, ready to snatch me back. "What the hell is that?"

I throw it onto the table like it's cursed. It detonates in a flash of heat and light. A pop echoes off the booth as the pouch bursts open, and a gust of hot air hits my face. Cards whip upward in a spinning cyclone, their gilded edges slicing through the low light like shrapnel.

They twist and cartwheel above us, flashes of color and arcane symbols blurring into one impossible kaleidoscope before the whirlwind collapses. The deck rains down, cards slapping against leather seats, skidding across the table, tumbling to the floor.

One lands at our feet.

The Wheel of Fortune.

For a second, I can't breathe. My heart hammers so hard it hurts. The smell of burnt fabric and ozone fills the air, and I can't tell if I'm seconds from fainting or laughing.

"This isn't happening," I whisper. My voice sounds too small, too human for the moment. I squeeze my hands into fists, nails biting my palms, and try to take deep breaths so I can think straight. "Static electricity. That's all. And faulty craftsmanship."

Declan steps closer, jaw pulsing at the temples.

I force out a shaky laugh even as I follow his gaze down to the tarot card and the images that are...*moving*?

The gilded wheel at the center spins. Its middle glows white-hot, light pulsing outward in steady, golden rings, radiating like a star on the edge of collapse. Framing the wheel, the angel, eagle, bull, and the lion chase each other in a game of otherworldly tag. The background shimmers with inky starlight. It glows, deep and vast and impossible. I hold my breath and squat down to pick it up.

Crack!

A jagged bolt of lightning rips across the top of the card, splitting the wheel clean in two.

The shock hits me. It races up through the soles of my feet, seizing my calves, crawling higher until it's in my chest, my throat, my teeth. Light shines from the card and pulses in time with my heartbeat, each thud sending another burst of electricity through my veins.

A rumble swells from deep beneath my feet, the earth clearing its throat. The floor shudders. The room trembles. Behind the bar, bottles crash against one another as bulbs strobe violently, throwing out craggy, stuttering shadows. Heat surges up from the floor, prickling every inch of exposed skin.

The door slams open with a gunshot-loud bang, and a blast of dry, searing air tears through the lounge, carrying the sting of sand. It whips my hair across my face and steals my breath.

Declan surges toward me, hand outstretched. "Amanda—"

He doesn't get the chance to finish.

The wind roars, swallowing sound. The lights flare, then shatter, bulbs bursting in fireworks of glass and sparks.

A shockwave of hot air ripples out, and the room

detonates around us in a blaze of fire. For a single, suspended heartbeat, everything is light and heat and the sensation of falling.

Then we're gone.

FIVE

Sand explodes around me and coats my sweat-slick skin. The impact of the ground against my back knocks the breath from my lungs, dust flooding my mouth before I can gasp.

I groan. Limbs splayed, skin scorching, spine sinking into heat-packed grains. The sky above is so aggressively blue it looks fake, like some divine being cranked up the saturation. The clouds are wispy and few, painted on like set dressing.

Desert wind blows over me like an oven door swinging open. Whatever bullshit people say about dry heat doesn't mean it's not fucking hot. It's a mouthful of cotton. A fever that's impossible to sweat out.

I try to sit up, but my head pounds—an internal warning bell clanging hard enough to rattle my teeth—and I crash back into the sand.

I crane my neck. Nothing but dunes.

Gone are the candles.

Gone is the night.

This isn't Ember. This isn't even New York.

I scrunch my face, shut my eyes tight, and tense every muscle in my body one at a time, just like my former therapist used to tell me to do when I needed to ground myself in the here and now.

I release slowly, blowing out a steady breath, keeping my eyes shut as I wait for the sounds and smells of Manhattan to knit themselves back together around me.

But there's no car exhaust. No blaring horns, or distant shouts. Just heat, silence, and—

A shadow moves over me.

My eyelids fly open.

A figure bends, their outline haloed in a spill of sunlight.

I blink hard, but my vision swims. All I can make out are the dark shape of a robe shifting in the wind and two eyes glowing like hot coals pressed deep into shadow.

Dazed, I squint up and croak, "Who are you?"

It's quiet; there's only the hiss of sand sliding over itself. Then her voice drifts down—light and airy, curling around the syllables like smoke. "It has been so long since I have had a name."

"I'm sorry, what?" I lift a hand to shield my eyes, trying to push myself upright, but the world tilts violently. Nausea swells in my throat, and I collapse back against the sand.

"Fate has led you here," she says. "To us. To me. But why? I cannot remember."

"I don't understand," I say, heat drying my tongue. "There's something wrong. I don't… I don't know where I am or—"

"I have kept the wheel turning," she interrupts, her voice carrying over the wind. "Counted the cycles. Lit the path for those who will choose change. For those who will risk everything to step beyond what they know."

A familiarity in her words snags in my chest, pulling me back to the card that's been stalking me for weeks.

She straightens, the sun flaring behind her so bright it blots out detail. Even as she tips her chin toward the sky, her features stay hidden, swallowed in shadow as if the light itself refuses to touch her.

I repeat her words under my breath. "The wheel… The path for those who will choose change."

I groan again, the sound scraping up my throat. "Of course my brain would conjure a tarot card hallucination."

Her fiery gaze snaps back to mine. The shift is sudden enough to make me flinch. "I am as real as you are."

The words ignite the flicker of heat in my chest. It builds, an urgent, insistent force that thrums so loudly I swear it's echoing between us.

I grope at the sand for anything with weight, anything that could prove that this is real.

"Seriously…" My voice is thin, breathless. "Who are you?"

"I have told you." Her eyes burn hotter, twin flames fixed on me. "I am—"

The word blossoms in my mind before she can speak it. It's there all at once, as familiar as my own name.

"Fortune."

We say it in unison, the syllables hanging in the air like they've been waiting for us, heavy on my tongue like a truth I've always known.

I push up onto one elbow, sand cascading off my

arm, trying to get closer, to see her clearly, but the world lurches sideways. My vision narrows at the edges, black creeping in. My ears ring like struck bells.

Memories flash uninvited—the Wheel of Fortune card landing at my feet, heat flaring up my legs, the crack of lightning splitting the wheel in two. Declan's hand reaching for me. The rush of wind, glass shattering, the world going white—

"I think..." My voice shakes. "I think the universe was trying to tell me you were real. Or that I was supposed to find you."

Her head tilts, assessing.

"Not *find*," she murmurs, her voice crackling like fire through dry wood. "*Remember*."

From somewhere nearby, Declan groans like he just got hit by a truck.

I twist toward the sound, the motion setting off a brief wave of vertigo that tilts the horizon and makes my stomach pitch.

He's sprawled in the sand a few yards away, one hand braced against the ground, swearing under his breath.

When I glance back toward the possible figment of my imagination, she's gone. Vanished without a trace. No footprints. No distant receding figure. No proof she was ever there at all.

"Shit," I grumble. "I'm losing my mind."

That awareness slips through the cracks in my hazy thoughts, slowly at first, then crashes in all at once, an avalanche of wrongness that threatens to bury me.

Golden dunes ripple around me like frozen waves. At my back, silk tents bloom across the sand in shades of red, orange, and yellow. Smoke coils from bronze torches spiked with lit incense and tucked between tent aisles, perfuming the air with earthy, spicy scents. Heat wraps around my legs, crawls up my spine, licks at my neck with greedy fingers.

I'm in…the desert?

"This isn't real," I whisper, swiping the sweat from my brow, panic prickling beneath my skin as I stand.

A camel lumbers out from between two tents, completely unbothered. "Nope. No. No way. This is a hallucination. A stress response. My brain hit overload and now I'm trapped in a Sahara-themed metaphor for my relationship issues."

The camel slows beside me, one massive glossy eye blinking down at me. It lets out a deep, guttural bellow then sneezes a wet spray of camel snot and desert dust directly in my face before plodding toward the dunes.

Declan fails to hide his chuckle behind a cough as he rises to his feet.

"You're seriously laughing at me right now?" I throw up my hands. "This is *my* hallucination. Is it too much to ask my own brain to give me a little more Prince Charming?"

"I'm…appreciating the spectacle." He dusts sand off his black velvet jacket. Against the riot of silks and firelight colors behind him, he looks like an inkblot on a painting. "This isn't a hallucination." He straightens to his full height and stretches out his back with a faint wince. "Pretty sure hallucinations don't hurt. And I'm very sure they can't be shared by two people. Not on this level."

"So, we're actually here?"

Neither of us speaks as we both take in the scene—the

curve of desert dunes, the scent of spice and smoke hanging in the heat, silks rustling in the breeze.

"Yeah," he says finally, his tone unreadable. "We are exactly where we are."

For some reason it was better when I thought this was all in my head. Eventually I'd wake up in a hospital bed with Gemma hovering, ready to hear my wild, delirious story about the flaming space-time portal and the camel snot and the fact that Declan hadn't once tried to save me.

But with no modern medicine about to surge through my veins and fix this, I'm left with a familiar question: What the actual fuck am I supposed to do?

Something catches my eye in the sand—my things, partially buried in glittering drifts. My purse lies on its side, the zippered mouth gaping open. A few feet away, my ritual pouch pokes out of the sand.

I snatch it up, clutching the warm fabric to my chest before scrambling to my bag. I yank it open and drop to my knees. Lip gloss, mascara, receipts, protein bar wrappers. I shove it all aside in my hunt for the one thing that might actually help.

My phone isn't here.

"Shit, shit, shit."

I stand again, purse and ritual pouch hugged tight, spinning in a frantic circle.

"What are you doing?" Declan calls.

"Trying to get us out of here. Wanna help?"

Something shiny catches the light near a dune. I dive for it. My fingers close around a card, sand spilling away to reveal the ornate gold edges of the Wheel of Fortune.

I brush it off and run my finger over the arcane

symbols stamped into the center of the wheel. If this isn't a hallucination then that woman, *Fortune*, wasn't a hallucination either.

Nope. Too much. My brain is already a jumbled tangle of panic and heatstroke. I am not unpacking that right now.

I shove the card into my bag.

"Looking for this?"

I turn to see Declan holding up my phone, shaking his head.

"You don't have any service."

I rush over and snatch it from him. "It's incredibly rude to go through someone else's phone."

"I wasn't going through it. You can see the bars from the lock screen."

Ignoring him, I clutch my phone tighter, thumb already jabbing at the screen.

"Oh no no no no no. Please work. Please connect. Please do literally anything." I hold it up and angle it toward the sky like that might do the trick. But he's right. There are no bars. No hope.

"Do you have any service?" I ask, whirling around to face him. "Please tell me you have some sort of signal."

He wrinkles his nose in a way that would be endearing if I weren't on the edge of a full-blown panic attack. "I don't have my phone."

"What?"

"I left it in my office. At Ember."

"What do you mean *you left it in your office*?" My voice pitches so high I wouldn't be surprised if a pack of wild dogs appeared. "Who just…doesn't have their phone?"

He shrugs. "I thought it would be rude to check it while I was trying to give my date my full attention."

"That should be the most charming thing anyone's ever said to me, but right now it makes me want to strangle you."

With shaking hands, I dig through my emergency ritual pouch, whip out the chunk of rose quartz, and press it to my chest.

"Okay, deep breaths. Deeeeeep breaths," I coach myself. "I need grounding. I *am* grounded. I am so grounded I'm practically dirt."

I nearly upend the vegan leather mini bag grabbing my affirmation deck. The matchbook sized cards stick to my sweaty fingers as I shuffle and draw one at random.

You are exactly where you're meant to be.

With an outraged gasp, I shake the card at the sky. "Oh, that's hilarious."

Declan exhales sharply through his nose. "You done?"

"No, I'm not *done*! We just got magickally thrown into a Burning Man meets Ren Faire hellscape." I gesture wildly at the silk-draped tents and endless dunes. "And you're standing there like it's just another day."

The sun beats down on us as Declan slides off his black jacket, hooks it on one finger, and slings it over his shoulder. "I've had worse first dates."

"If you were one of my clients, I would tell you that this situation requires energetic recalibration," I continue, voice rising with each word, "major chakra balancing, some sort of divine offering, not...*dissociation*."

"I'm not going to start panicking, Amanda."

"Well, good for you, *Declan*. I guess I'll panic for both of us."

I hurl my crystal down in a burst of melodramatic rage, immediately regret it, and dive into the sand after it.

"Somebody's gotta lose their shit while the emotionally unavailable hero with the perfect jawline makes unhelpful little quips and stares out at the horizon," I mutter, digging frantically through hot, grainy earth.

Declan crouches beside me with aggravating grace, then plucks the rose quartz from the sand with two long fingers. "I would hand this over, but you insulted my emotional depth."

"It's not an insult," I grind out, snatching it from his grip. "It's a coping mechanism."

We're nose to nose now. A dry breeze drags hot fingers across my skin. Sweat soaks through his button-down, and it clings to his chest, outlining the smooth slopes of muscle. Not that I notice. I don't. I'm not looking. He's the worst. The absolute worst.

He tilts his head, his throat moving with a swallow. "You're scared."

"And you're not?" I fire back.

"I don't have the luxury of fear."

"Oh, puke." An incredulous bark of laughter flies past my lips. "That has to be one of the most emotionally constipated lines I've ever heard. You're literally proving my point in real time," I say, jabbing a finger in his direction. "I thought we got past all this bullshit, but I suppose that was just a continued effort to get into my pants."

"It didn't seem like I would have to make much of an effort."

My jaw drops. "You know women are allowed to change their minds between hot DM banter and the actual act, right? And maybe I wouldn't have if you hadn't been so, I don't know..." I shrug and tilt my chin. "Impossible to talk to."

I drop back onto my heels, scrubbing a hand down my face. "There was a second at Ember when I thought we were the same. That you were nervous about seeing me, about everything going perfectly. That you and I were just two kind, sweet people hiding behind hyper-confident personas we built to survive dating apps."

Wind tugs at my hair as I shake my head. "But I was wrong. You are exactly how you seem online—intense and damaged and moody—which is great for a fantasy and great for a meaningless fling but not great for this."

His dark eyes narrow, brows knitting. "Not great for what?"

"For actually finding a solution," I snap. "For talking through something. For doing more than growling and glaring and moving your eyebrows in place of real communication."

A muscle ticks in his temple. "You say you're kind, Amanda, but you're not. All you've done since we landed...wherever this is, is tell me what a dick I am."

"I wouldn't tell you what a dick you are if you weren't being such a dick."

"That's exactly what I mean."

"Same."

The sky is an impossible stretch of color, but I can't look away from him. Our breathing syncs in ragged pulls as we stare each other down. A bead of sweat slips along the hollow of his throat, tracing a path along his skin before vanishing beneath the open edge of his collar.

Bastard.

"This is a test," he says, rising to his full height and looking down his ridiculously straight nose at me.

The wind stirs, lifting a curtain of saffron silk from a nearby tent. It twists overhead in a hypnotic spiral, gliding through the dry air like a warning inked in color.

I rise too, a little less gracefully, my heels immediately sinking into the sand. "A test," I deadpan. "Right. What kind of test physically snatches you off your feet and spits you through a flaming portal into…whatever the hell *this* is?" I fling my arms wide. "Face it, Declan. The universe has kidnapped us."

His eyes narrow. "Are you listening to yourself?"

"Are you looking around? That is a camel." I motion to the snotty animal leaving fat footprints in the sand. "*A camel.* The universe is mad at me and—" A terrible thought slams into me, and my stomach flips. "Oh shit," I whisper, clutching the rose quartz to my chest. "This is a test."

He exhales, voice flat. "The universe is probably trying to see how long it takes before you manifest a nervous breakdown."

"See? You're a dick. That is dickish behavior. Which is really hard for me to say out loud because I'm all about love and light."

"That was hard for you?"

"Yeah. Really, *really* hard. Had to work it around in my mouth for a while before I could get it out."

Declan smirks. "I'd like to see what else you can work around in your mouth."

"Ugh. Gross. And typical. Gross and typical." I roll my eyes, but the protest sounds flimsy even to me. We've said filthier things to each other over DM back when it was a game, a fantasy I invited.

But somewhere between the Wheel of Fortune stalking me and watching my own patterns play out at Ember, I've figured out that there's a lesson to be learned here. Maybe if I'm a better person—less impulsive, less chaotic—it will finally stop shitting all over me. So I'm making a quiet little vow to act like the kind of person good things happen to. Fake it till I fucking make it.

His expression shifts, the humor on his lips flattening into a thin line. "Typical?"

"Yes. Typical."

"You knew exactly who I was on the app." He takes a step closer. "I never once promised you anything else, and now you're pissed I'm not handing you some different version of myself because we're finally standing in the same place."

I open my mouth, but he cuts me off with a curt, "It's *my* turn."

"Your turn for—"

He presses a finger to my lips like he's hitting a mute button.

Rude.

"To read you. To tell *you* what *I* see."

Before I can protest, he catches my hand, yanks me closer, and unceremoniously lifts my palm.

"You liked the fantasy. No." He drags his finger along the line that swoops down beneath my index finger and trails all the way to my wrist. "You begged for it. For me."

My throat tightens. "I didn't—"

"It's still my turn," he cuts in, gaze pinned to mine.

I go quiet, the words dying in my mouth.

"Now we're here, in person, and suddenly you're furious I'm not soft. That I'm not sweet. You want to punish me for being the man you wanted when it was safe, when it wasn't real."

Heat prickles across my skin as he drags me closer.

"But here's the thing. The 'universe'"—he lifts his free hand and makes actual air quotes—"doesn't give handouts. You can tell yourself you're changing or evolving, being a better person to reap the rewards, but it's all bullshit. You're lost. Waiting for someone else to decide for you."

My skin goes hot, shame rushing up my neck like a rash. I've spent years building this glossy, mystical armor he's ripped off in one motion, leaving me exposed… pathetic.

My vision tunnels. My ears buzz. I can't breathe past the thick knot in my throat.

"You're not some empowered woman, Amanda. You're a scared little girl."

The slap cracks through the air before I register raising my hand.

Decan exhales through flared nostrils and takes the blow, nodding like it confirms something he already suspected.

I yank my other hand from his, drop to my knees, and start scooping my things from the sand. All of it is gritty and sun-scorched and mostly useless.

"I'll figure this out myself," I mutter, half to him, half to the blazing, sandy nothingness that stretches away from the tents. "I don't need you. I'll figure out where we are and how to get home. *Alone*."

I clutch my bag to my chest and pivot toward the row of tents when a dark shape slips between those farther down the stretch of sand. Another follows, drawing closer.

Someone's coming.

I freeze, my hot skin cooling with an icy rush of adrenaline. My fingers tighten around my bag as my heart kicks my ribs.

I glance over my shoulder at Declan. He stiffens, jaw tight, body coiling with tension. Without a word, he jogs forward and steps into the slim shadow of a nearby tent. He lifts the edge of the silk, gestures once, and disappears inside.

I duck in after him just as voices draw closer and footsteps crunch over sand.

The silk rustles on the far side of the tent. A shadow looms tall and thin, pausing just outside the entrance. The fabric twitches, and a hand slips in, fingers adorned with thick gold rings.

"Let us see what the sands have delivered."

SIX

The tent flap twitches. Gold rings flash as the man tightens his hold on the silk. Then, his nasally voice pipes up, "Do you want them alive?"

My stomach drops. My grip tightens on my bag, knuckles white. I can't move. They're going to come in, find me, and…and…

Declan's hands clamp around my waist. His bruising grip yanks me deeper into the shadows.

The movement breaks through my freeze response. "Seriously?" I hiss, elbowing him. "I can move backward without being manhandled."

"You weren't moving at all," he whispers. "And they're going to kill us."

I try to shrug away from him, whisper shouting over my shoulder, "I was assessing!"

"You were a statue."

"I was processing," I say through clenched teeth, clutching my bag to my chest while attempting to wiggle out of his grasp. "Some of us like to take minute before leaping straight into action-hero mode."

"Some of us like living."

"I like living too." I slap his hands off me without turning. "I do have survival instincts, you know."

"Then use them," he says, low and dry next to my ear.

A long-suffering sigh floats in from outside the tent. "Yes, Tarek. I want them alive. How else will the spies be questioned?"

My mouth goes dry. Spies. They think we're spies. What does this place do to spies?

"Just checking!" Tarek chirps, drumming his fingers on the fabric. "You are often quite dramatic and kill-y. I never know which version of you I'll get."

"Tarek," the other man grates out, "must you continue to trample on my lines? I put quite a bit of thought into these."

"Apologies," Tarek says sheepishly, and the silk stills. "They were fine lines, truly."

"Chilling, if I do say so myself."

"Most chilling!" Tarek agrees. "Gooseflesh up and down my arms. I only... Well, I didn't wish to assume the degree of violence you intended."

A silence falls, thick enough to chew on. My argument with Declan has evaporated, but my elbow still hovers near Declan's chest, his palm halfway up my arm like we're two dolls caught mid-motion. Neither of us moves. Neither of us dares to breathe too loudly.

"Ruin one more entrance, I swear by the sun, Tarek, I will bury you up to your nose in the sand."

"Classic!" Tarek crows. "A classic punishment! Love that."

The tent flap parts another inch.

Declan raises his hands in silent surrender and eases deeper into the shadows.

"Thank you," I whisper and begin to follow when the pointed toe of my shoe catches on the lip of something hard.

Copper singing bowls crash into each other, tumbling across the sand-speckled rug in a clanging cascade that rings out like an alarm.

With a sigh, Declan closes his eyes and shakes his head slowly.

The silks fling open, and sunlight pours into the tent like a spotlight.

Well shit.

Two robed guards close in. They're draped in layers of crimson and molten-orange fabrics that shimmer like fire in the sunlight, the hems heavy with copper coins and ruby beads that chime softly as they move. Broadswords hang at their hips, hilts wrapped in crimson leather, the pommels shaped like flames.

They look like characters out of a fantasy epic filmed on an unlimited budget. Also like they're absolutely about to murder us.

"I knew it," Not Tarek growls, stomping forward, hand on the hilt of his blade. "Saw the sand burst all the way from the other side of camp. Only spies would have the gall to lurk this far from the stage during rehearsal. Have you traveled here from Cups like the others?"

Declan and I shake our heads in unison.

"Pentacles, then." The guard's bushy eyebrows furrow like two angry caterpillars.

Declan looks at me. I look back.

"No," we say together. At least we see eye to eye on something.

"Swords?" he tries again, the thick ropes of beads and amulets around his neck clinking together like wind chimes.

"Wait." I tilt my chin. "Are you listing tarot suits?"

If so, that's weirdly on brand for the way my week is going.

"We're not spies," Declan says, stepping squarely in front of me like some kind of tall, sweaty, muscled human shield.

"I can speak for myself."

He doesn't look at me, but the tension in his shoulders ratchets tighter.

"They do not look to be spies," Tarek offers cheerfully from behind the lead guard.

"And how are spies meant to look?" the other guard growls.

Tarek shrugs. "Not like them."

"We're not spies," I repeat, rising onto my toes to peek over Declan's unnecessarily broad shoulder. "We're from Manhattan."

"*Manhattan*?" the first man repeats, rolling the syllables around his tongue like loose marbles.

"Oh!" Tarek brightens and snaps his fingers, jeweled cuffs glinting on his wrists. "Dav, I would wager these are the new performers!"

"*Tarek*," Dav groans, dragging a hand down his tanned face.

"What?" Tarek blinks, wide-eyed and unfazed.

"If they *were* spies, they would now know to say they are the new performers."

"Well," Tarek responds with a helpless shrug, "they said they weren't."

"And we're not," I reiterate with all the confidence I can muster while covered in sand in a world I don't recognize, and half sheltered behind a man I technically met an hour ago.

"We shall see about that," Dav mutters.

With a sharp jerk of his wide chin, we're flanked—him in front, Tarek bringing up the rear like a kid on a field trip—and herded out of the tent.

We're led through the heart of the camp, flames leaping from massive copper braziers lining the path and casting our shadows like spindly monsters against the silk walls. Wind snaps the fabric canopies. Incense winds through the air in thick ribbons while somewhere in the distance, drums pulse a slow, ominous beat.

"I take back what I said before. *This* is kidnapping," I hiss under my breath.

"This is your fault," Declan mutters back.

"My fault?"

"You were the one who wanted something witchy."

"Oh, I'm sorry." I scoff. "Was magickally landing in the desert not your idea of the perfect first date?"

He doesn't answer, but I catch the slight flex of his jaw like he's fighting the urge to argue. It's the smallest chink in that polished exterior. *Victory*.

Performers part for us in a stream of moving color—dyed feathers arranged like wings, carmine and tangerine silks that ripple with every step, bronze beads that shimmer in the sun. Their faces are painted in slashes of red and curls of yellow. Some have tiny mirrors affixed to their foreheads, catching and throwing the light like otherworldly third eyes.

They glide past like living illusions, all shimmer and sparkle. But up close, the cracks show—hollow eyes, smiles stretched too wide, shoulders, jaws, fists tight and locked in place.

One woman in a corset of obsidian beads and citrine gems catches my gaze as we're led past. She's perched on a barrel outside a tent, reading from a curled scroll. Her painted face is split down the center, one half in warm oranges with feathery lashes, the other stark white with a single teardrop drawn beneath her eye.

"Where the hell are we?" I murmur under my breath.

Her head snaps up, and in one fluid motion she springs from the barrel, landing in front of me light as a sprite. She tilts her head, studying me like a bird.

I clutch my purse tighter as she blocks my path, cutting me off from the guards and Declan.

"It's all for show," she murmurs, her voice thin and papery. "No one listens unless it sparkles." Her smile sharpens as her fingers twitch in the air, jerking like puppet strings pulled too tight.

"Back to your script!" Dav's bark cracks across the sand. "Know your place."

The woman flinches and scurries away to her tent.

My stomach twists. I wrap my arms around my middle and hurry to catch up.

We need to get out of here. Figure out where *here* even is.

I adjust the strap of my purse and glance sideways at Declan, voice pitched low. "Aren't you supposed to do something? Like Hulk out or brood our way to freedom? Me, Declan. Me knock other man on head with stick. Me win woman."

Declan doesn't even blink. "Do you want me to lean into the heteronormative bullshit, or do you want me to be in touch with my emotions, Amanda? Pick a fucking lane."

Shit, he's right. He's right and I hate it. But I will never admit that out loud.

"You pick a lane," I grumble, squaring my shoulders.

He mimics me in a high-pitched falsetto. *"You pick a lane."*

I whip my head toward him. "Real mature, Declan."

Ahead of us, Dav turns with an exhausted sigh, his robes jingling with the motion. "Quiet," he snaps. "We have arrived."

He parts a deep-crimson silk curtain. Sunlight knifes through the opening. Without an explanation, he shoves us forward.

As I stumble through the curtain, a hand tugs on my purse. I whirl around, palm itching for another slap. Tarek's eyes are wide and apologetic as he eases the strap from my shoulder.

"Forgive me!" he says quickly, holding it up like he's fending off an attack. "I ought to have done so sooner, but… Well, you did not strike me as the sort to bear weapons."

I glower but let him take it.

"Come along!" Dav barks.

I squawk as he grabs my arm and yanks me forward.

We're marched up a steep wooden ramp, the boards groaning beneath our feet, then shoved onto a raised platform that sits at the center of the camp like the bright, burning heart of the sun. Gleaming obsidian pillars encircle the stage and the crowd. They stretch up from the sand and reach for the sky, their blunt tops reflecting the sunlight so fiercely they look as if they're holding up the sky itself.

Beyond them, silk-draped tents burst out from it in every direction like flame-colored rays. The crowd surrounds us in a dizzying circle—onlookers draped in sun-bleached linens, embroidered tunics, and metallic accents that glint and flash in the harsh light.

Cases line the back of the stage, their glass fronts warped and rippled. Each holds what looks like relics of past performances—faded masks, hoops blackened and charred at the edges, costumes reduced to delicate scraps of silk now pinned in place like butterflies in a display box. Each is labeled like an artifact in a forgotten museum.

An elaborate open tent rises across from us, terracotta and ruby silks draped to shade the section of ornate seats elevated on a crescent-shaped dais made of gleaming black stone. Two women recline at its center, unmistakably regal. Flame-shaped crowns perch on their heads, all sharp points and scarlet glint. Their robes shimmer like liquid copper, and thick, dramatic eye makeup fans out toward their temples in wings of glittering fire.

People fan out around them, dressed in robes and jewels with flame-shaped collars and pinched faces.

It feels ceremonial. It feels claustrophobic. It feels exactly like the kind of place where people get publicly executed.

Above, birds wheel through the sky, their cries carrying faintly. My gaze follows them up, then out until it catches on the horizon and the nothingness of endless dunes.

The beat of drums vibrates the platform beneath our feet as more guards arrive, weapons drawn, flanking us in a semicircle of steel. We're forced to the center, directly under the relentless eye of the sun. Giant brass braziers blaze along the edge of the stage, flames licking skyward.

Declan stands beside me, tall but extremely silent. Like he thinks if he's quiet and grumpy, this will all resolve itself. Maybe the guards will be so overwhelmed by the sheer breadth of his shoulders that they'll just let us go.

He is insufferable. Meeting him in person is every bit the disaster I knew it would be.

"If you want something done right, you have to do it yourself," I grumble.

I clear my throat and step forward. The guards respond instantly, swords lifting, the line they hold behind us inching closer.

"Hi," I say brightly, even as panic sparks beneath my skin like static on a sweater. "So...slight misunderstanding."

"State your names," one of the crowned women snaps. Her voice cracks through the heat like a whip as she straightens her shoulders and cranes her long neck.

I glance at Declan, who remains frustratingly silent. He's calm, cool, and collected. A statue with high cheekbones and the emotional range of granite.

"I'm Amanda," I say, voice catching. "This is Declan. We're not spies."

"Do tell me and my dear queen sister who you are and what you are doing in our great kingdom," the second crowned woman demands. She's younger than the first, her coal-black hair piled high beneath a crown that juts out like rising flames.

"We're travelers." There's a knot in my throat, and I start cycling through affirmations like radio stations. *I am calm. I am grounded. I am definitely not about to die.*

"My sister and I are of the same mind," the first resumes, brushing her corn silk curls from deep-umber shoulders. "You have not, however, told us what you are doing within the bounds of our Kingdom of Wands."

"That is a good question." I draw out each syllable while turning to glare at Declan in hopes of lighting him on fire.

"We're passing through," he says. "If there's nothing else, we'll be on our way."

Relief flickers through me. He's finally saying something, finally *doing* something. Then he takes a step toward the ramp, and the guards lunge forward in unison. The flames in the braziers encircling the stage flare. The stifling heat cinches around my chest.

The dark-haired queen fixes him with a narrowed gaze. "Members of the masked guard from the Kingdom of Cups also claimed they were not spies when they crossed into our lands. Do you wish to know their fate?"

"I think I can infer," Declan says evenly.

The flames crack. The wind hisses.

"They are dead. Burned at the stake. That is what my sister and I do to spies."

"Understood." Declan lifts his hands, a calculated gesture of surrender, but his voice never loses its cool edge. "But we are not spies. We are travelers, unarmed, caught in circumstances beyond our control. I believe there's an opportunity here to turn a chance encounter into something mutually beneficial. My companion and I have skills, resources, knowledge—"

I elbow him, and shoot him a warning look, equal

parts panic and please-shut-up-before-you-overpromise-and-get-us-killed.

The queens shift, the smallest flicker of intrigue.

Declan presses forward, sensing an opening. "We would be honored to put them to use in service of your kingdom. My family has built alliances across continents—mergers, rescues, profitable turnarounds. I can recognize an opportunity when it appears."

The dark-haired queen arches one brow and lifts her pointed chin, bidding him to continue.

"As I'm sure you both do as well," Declan adds smoothly. "This is a chance to strengthen your rule, to take some weight off your shoulders. I imagine a kingdom like this must be overwhelming for two women to manage alone."

The shift is immediate. The crowd tenses. I flinch, every nerve on edge. Somewhere behind me, a guard sucks in a sharp breath through his teeth.

Declan stiffens, then pushes forward, words tumbling out faster. "That—uh—that came out wrong. I didn't mean it's overwhelming *because* you're women. I only meant ruling an entire kingdom is difficult for anyone. The fact that you've managed it so well is proof of your strength, not a criticism of it."

The queens' expressions remain stony.

Declan swallows, his tone softening as if he can easily fix what he just damaged. "Any man would have broken under half the weight you carry."

A nod from the golden-haired queen summons Dav forward, sword flashing. The flat of the blade presses to Declan's throat, not drawing blood but making his next swallow audible.

This is exactly what Declan did in Ember when I tried to walk out on our date. He pivoted the moment his charm started to slip. But this is life-and-death, and no amount of smooth confidence is going to save him from two queens who look ready to order him to death.

Think, Amanda. Think.

"No one listens unless it sparkles," I mutter. My stomach flips. "I'm a story witch!" I blurt. "And I—I apologize for speaking out of turn."

I attempt a curtsy, but it comes out more like an unbalanced lunge.

There's a beat of stunned silence. I brace for impact. Any second now, I expect the guards to seize me, swords drawn. For the queens to shout *Off with her head!*

Instead, the queen with golden hair arches one perfectly painted brow. "Continue."

"I, uh, I use the magicks all around us to…channel tales," I begin, every bit more word-salad-y than the last. "It's, um, emotionally charged performance art that is… spiritually guided."

Sweat slides down my back as I wait for approval or a death sentence.

Actually, now that I think about it, that might be something: *Divine improv*. That's a brand idea, isn't it? I could work that into my online course offerings.

"And your partner?" the other queen asks, flicking two fingers toward Declan, who, for the first time, has the sense to look genuinely uncomfortable. Probably because of the broadsword pressed to his throat.

"He's—he's my brooding costar," I say quickly. "My muse. My…bodyguard. He doesn't talk much, but when he does, it's very dramatic."

Slowly, Declan slides his gaze to me, eyes filled with disbelief and the kind of murderous calm I assume men like him employ before launching a hostile takeover.

I smile sweetly at the queens. "We're part of a sacred act. Art. Performance. Cosmic storytelling."

The golden-haired queen leans forward. A slow, delighted smile curves her lips. "Then perform, you will. Tonight. Before my sister, me, and our esteemed court."

"Oh, no. We couldn't possibly interrupt whatever beautiful, er, situation you have planned." I sputter, shaking my head so hard hair whips my neck. My hands flap wildly as I gesture to the stage, the guards, the silent crowd watching. "We're happy to just watch. Or leave! Honestly, leaving sounds great." I force a laugh that comes out high and unhinged. "If you could point us to the nearest, uh, bus stop? Or crossroads? Maybe fiery interdimensional portal?"

A soft wave of laughter rises from the crowd, amused and tinkling like wind chimes in the sun. They think I'm joking.

I very much am not.

"Seriously," I say, pushing through the panic rising in my throat, "we can just be on our way. If you wouldn't mind—"

"We would," interrupts a sharp voice from stage left.

A woman steps forward, draped in layered orange silks. Her face is bare, save for a slash of red paint across her eyes.

"You'll perform at tonight's Festival of Flame as the queens have ordered," she says, already turning on her heel.

Dav removes the blade from Declan's throat with a

grunt and shoves him toward the wooden ramp at the side of the stage. The guards close in without a word, boxing us in on all sides. I glance at Declan, who's too busy brooding to be remotely helpful, and then follow. What other choice do I have?

The air behind the stage shimmers with heat. Gold draperies hang from the rafters, threaded through with bronze chains. Copper lanterns line the narrow corridor, their flames captured behind glass etched with symbols. The scent of smoke and sandalwood clings to everything, heavy and sweet.

Tarek approaches sheepishly and holds out my purse. "Apologies."

Before I can answer, the woman in charge flicks her wrist, and the guards scatter. Only Dav lingers.

"I don't like the look of this one," he mutters, jerking his chin toward Declan.

The woman doesn't even turn. "It's a good thing I have yet to consult you."

He bristles, opens his mouth to speak, but she steps toward him.

"More to say, *guard*?"

"No, that is all." Dav falters and bows his head slightly. "Apologies, Player."

He turns to leave, slamming his shoulder into Declan on the way out. Declan—an immovable wall of muscle wrapped in sweat-slick heat—doesn't even blink.

"Enjoy your last sunset," Dav sneers.

Declan mutters something under his breath, jaw flexing, but falls silent when the Player pivots toward us, her tawny gaze raking over every inch.

"You'll perform tonight," she says. "Or else."

"Then we'll perform," I say. "If that's what keeps us alive."

Declan folds his arms across his chest. "You're certain this is the right move?"

"No," I admit. "But it's the only one we've got."

He dips his chin, brow furrowed as if there's another option we're not seeing.

"You tried to negotiate with the queens and get us out of this. It didn't work. So now we fake it."

He nods slowly. "We fake it."

The Player watches us, a slow smile unfurling across her pale face like smoke. "The two of you shall fit right in. Everyone here knows how to lie pretty."

SEVEN

Torchlight dances across the walls of the tent the Player leads us to, throwing shadows over a woven rug on the sand and the massive bed—yes, *bed*, singular—that takes up most of the space. Lazy spirals of incense curl up from a copper dish in the corner next to a red velvet screen held in place by a gilded frame. The whole space smells faintly of fire and clove.

"You shall find both costumes and props there," the Player says, nodding toward a domed trunk at the foot of the bed. It's carved from dark wood and banded in copper. Its surface is etched with spiking flames and dotted with yellow and orange gemstones that wink like warning lights.

"The Festival of Flame begins at sunset," she continues. "A guard will be sent to collect you. If you are no longer here..." Her voice hardens enough to make a lump of nerves form in my stomach. "There is not one of us who could or would protect you from your fate when you are found."

She turns to leave.

"Wait," I blurt. "We'll perform. That's fine. But we need to get home. We don't belong here. We're not even sure where *here* is. The Kingdom of Wands, yes, but..." Words fail me as I try to form a question that won't undo the lenient sentence we're serving.

The Player's gaze finds mine, steady and full of something I can't quite name. "Why, you're in Towerfall. Within the bounds of the greatest kingdom of the realm. It seems fate has led you here."

With that, she steps out into the heat, the tent flap whispering shut behind her.

No matter how much I want to, I can't keep my hands from shaking. I just lied to royalty to save us from death, and even with the information the Player gave us, I'm still not sure where we are.

"Well..." I swallow past the lump in my throat and turn to face Declan. "I suppose all that's left to say is *you're welcome*."

He presses a long finger to his chest. "What exactly should I be thanking you for?"

"For saving you from becoming a kebab. Or did you miss the part where they were about to flambé your ass because you didn't know when enough was enough?"

"Didn't realize you were looking for a thank-you."

"Oh, screw you."

"Tempting."

I throw my hands up. "You're impossible to pin down, you know that? It's...it's...*obnoxious*."

"That's rich, coming from the woman who improv-ed a story-witch persona in front of two queens with a fondness for public executions."

"It worked, didn't it?" I snap, then inhale through my nose. "Okay, no. No more bickering. That's clearly not helping, and wanting to strangle you isn't going to get us back home any faster."

He doesn't reply. He just stands there, arms folded, taking up too much space without even moving, which only makes me more annoyed.

My heels stab divots into the rug, and I kick them off with a frustrated grunt. The plush weave beneath my bare feet is surprisingly soft as I shrug off my purse and toss it onto the bed. Shoulders tight, I fumble through its contents for my ritual pouch. I pull out a chunk of rose quartz and balance it in my palm as I whisper a soft chant. "You're safe. You're resourceful. Everything's going to be okay."

I can feel him watching me, and I squeeze my eyes shut, willing myself to sink into the words. *Be one with the present. Centered. Peaceful.*

Even with my eyes closed, his gaze burns hotter than the sun, needling me and undoing every breath I try to steady.

"What?" I snap, lids flying open.

Declan's gaze flicks to the crystal in my palm. "That's your plan? Whisper to a rock until someone rescues you?"

"It's a crystal, and many people believe they reduce stress. Excuse me for needing a little help bringing down my blood pressure." I wrap my fingers around the quartz and squeeze. "And I am by no means waiting for someone to rescue me. I can do that myself," I say, although I'm not sure which lie is greater.

His mouth curves faintly. "I'll give you this—you're committed to the bit."

I close my eyes and exhale slowly, reminding myself that chucking this crystal at his head is the opposite of the love and light I'm desperately trying to channel.

"Say whatever you want. I refuse to stoop to your level." I flash a saccharine smile and flutter my lashes. "Which, I just have to add, is that of an annoying twelve-year-old boy."

"Noted." He slips his hands into his pockets and tilts his head. "Next time I'll try a strategy that doesn't work quite so well on you."

With a stifled grunt, I turn my attention back to my items and start to line up the contents of my pouch across the silk sheets: crystals marred with scorch marks, a partially melted bottle of rosemary and lavender air-cleansing spray, the mini affirmation deck—

I run my thumb along the scorched edges of the cards. "Everything is burnt."

Declan moves closer, squinting down at the bed. "Right. Your purse was practically on fire. What exactly do you keep in there?"

Ignoring him, I dump the rest of the pouch on the deep persimmon bedsheets. My breath catches when I spot the one thing undamaged.

The Wheel of Fortune.

Its edges are smooth, gold-dusted, untouched by flame or smoke. Not a single singe mark.

I hold it up. "You don't think the card has anything to do with this?"

He scoffs. "Honestly, I've been wondering if my bartender slipped something into our drinks."

"And now we're trapped in a shared trip?" I shake my head. "We've already established that hallucinations don't work that way. Plus, I don't know about you, but I'm not having a very groovy time."

Declan arches a brow and brushes a streak of grit from his sleeve. "You know drugs exist outside of Woodstock and that whole *groovy* decade?"

"I wouldn't know." I lift my chin, clutching the rose quartz tighter. "I don't do drugs. I'm high on life."

Shaking his head, he blows out a breath and plucks the card from my hand. His fingers brush mine, and I hate that I notice how warm his skin is. For a second, he just stares at the card, his expression shifting, curiosity sharpening into wariness.

"Is this design solar powered?" he asks.

My stomach drops. "Why?"

He flips the card so it's facing me. "The picture. It's moving."

Before I can respond, the flames in the lanterns shoot higher, and a hot gust of wind blasts through the tent. The flap tears open with a snap. Sand rushes in, stinging my cheeks and burning my eyes.

I dive for my purse, fumbling for the hair clip I know is buried in there somewhere. "Ow—shit—sand in my mouth—hold it shut!"

"I *am* holding it shut!" Declan grits out, wrestling the silks.

I rush to help him, balling the fabric in my free hand as I struggle to clamp it shut with the other. Just as I fasten the hair clip into place, a sheet of parchment whips through the gap and smacks me square in the face.

Cursing, I peel it off, the paper warm, rough with grains of sand, and hand-painted in furious strokes of burnt orange and bloodred.

At its center is an unmistakable image. An image I know all too well.

A wheel.

Its spokes gleam a metallic gold. The same gold as the Wheel of Fortune. This wheel's outer ring is charred on one side, and behind it is a faceless figure wrapped in robes of flame, arms outstretched.

Along the bottom, scrawled in a looping script with familiar curves and slants that pull at the edges of memory like an itch I can't scratch: *REMEMBER*.

My throat tightens.

It's *her.*

I am as real as you are.

It's Fortune.

And now she's painted on a flyer that literally slapped me in the face. This message is meant for me.

That strange knot forms in my chest, like fate is clawing its way out of my very soul.

"This is a sign from the universe," I whisper, voice thin and breathless. "It has to be."

I've said that before. Hundreds of times, probably. To the camera. To myself. Usually it's just code for something good will happen if I want it badly enough. But this feels different.

With a sigh, Declan pinches the bridge of his nose. "We should take a moment to—"

"No, listen. This woman—" I shake the parchment in front of his face, the metallic paint catching firelight. "She was here the second we landed. She came to me. She knows something. She can tell us what's going on." I glance down at the flyer again, conviction sparking. "She's probably my Wise Woman. I've read about them.

And this place seems like they'd have Wise Women, right?"

Declan blinks like I'm speaking in tongues.

"My mentor," I clarify.

"Oh." His mouth curves. "Your Obi-Wan."

I smile. "Declan Thorne, are you secretly a nerd?"

He doesn't answer, but it doesn't matter. A *Star Wars* nerd won't get us home, but I know who can.

I rip off my makeshift tent closure and throw open the flap. Heat slaps me in the face, the air scorching as sunlight pours in. A white glare burns across my vision, turning the world into one overwhelming blaze.

I stumble forward, sand already searing the soles of my bare feet, and plow directly into something solid. Copper-threaded fabric. Immovable muscle.

The impact bounces me backward with a startled yelp. My heel catches on the threshold of our tent, and I nearly go down before a thick hand clamps around my arm, steadying me with far more force than necessary.

Dav looms above me, lips curled, brown eyes burning beneath the fringe of his sideswept hair. "Going somewhere?"

"I didn't realize we were on house arrest," I snap, yanking my arm from his hold as I glare up at him.

"Course not." The words are delivered flatly, but an unspoken threat simmers just beneath them. "But you're not performers either. And I have a duty to protect my queens and kingdom."

The fabric of the tent rustles behind me, and I feel Declan before I see him—his presence a low, controlled shadow in my periphery. His hand curls around my arm.

What is it with men thinking they need to touch me to make a point? I don't need to be claimed to exist.

I jerk free, heat flaring in my cheeks. "I've got it," I hiss, snapping my attention back to Dav. "We want to see Fortune."

He blinks once. Then snorts. "You seek fortune? So you admit to being promised riches when you report back to Cups?"

"Not *fortune*. *Fortune*," I say, gesturing to the page in my hand. "As in, capital F. A woman. Big, flowy robe. Sort of spoke in riddles. You know—*Fortune*."

Dav raises a thick brow and glares over my head at Declan. "Your woman cannot handle her ale."

"What, no, I'm not…" I pause, then exhale.

Love and light. Love and light.

I try again. "She's real. I saw her just like I'm seeing you. She told me her name was—"

"Yes, *Fortune*. You said." He crosses his meaty arms and throws another look over me at Declan. "Do you know this woman of whom she speaks?"

"I'm the one who saw her, and he doesn't need to back up what—"

"I do not have time for your lies."

"Or manners, since you keep interrupting—"

Dav takes a step forward, crowding into my space. "Get back in the tent, *spy*."

He jabs me in the shoulder with one thick finger.

I stiffen, rising like a cobra, and jab him right back. "I." Poke. "Am not." Poke, poke. "A spy!"

His eyes go wide before narrowing into slices, his hand moving to his side. Steel sings as he yanks his sword free. The blade glints in the light. My breath catches in my throat, stomach plummeting into my ass.

Before I can so much as scream, Declan steps between us and clocks Dav, a sharp crack of knuckles to jaw. Dav's head snaps to the side, his grip loosening on the hilt of his sword as it falls to the sand.

Dav stumbles back, hand flying to his jaw, shock and rage twisting his features. He spits a mouthful of red-streaked phlegm at Declan's boots. "You'll pay for that," he snarls. He retrieves his sword and sheathes it with a vicious snap. Then he turns on his heel and stalks off, favoring his jaw, and muttering a fresh string of curses with every step.

A bottled breath whooshes from my lungs, and adrenaline buzzes beneath my skin like bees in a jar.

Blood drips from the split in Declan's knuckles and spatters the sand at his feet, bright against the sunbaked ground. His injured hand remains curled into a fist at his side even as he shakes out his shoulders and rolls his neck like stepping in to defend me was nothing.

It's not nothing.

"Come on," I say, quieter than I mean to. Reaching for his uninjured hand, I tug him back into the tent.

I drop to my knees beside the trunk at the foot of the bed, fingers diving into silk and gemstones, beaded masks and braided belts. I dig until I find something soft. A velvet scarf the color of spilled wine.

"Sit." I nod toward the edge of the bed.

He follows my direction, folding down onto the bed the way a big cat crouches to observe a mouse. There's tension in him still, muscles coiled tight beneath his skin.

I kneel in front of him and reach for his hand. His skin is warm. The blood is sticky.

I start to wrap the velvet scarf around his knuckles, trying to focus on the task. But my fingers tremble. I tell myself it's from nerves. My brush with danger. The adrenaline crashing through my system. Anything but simply feeling his hand in mine.

After all the irritation and arguments, I shouldn't care that he's this close. I shouldn't register every inch separating us like it matters. But I do.

"No one's ever punched someone on my behalf before," I say quietly, gaze fixed on the makeshift bandage.

He lets out a breath that sticks somewhere between a sigh and a laugh. "I've never had to punch someone on a woman's behalf before." A pause. "Doesn't feel as great as I thought it would."

He flexes his fingers and winces. There's a jagged split along his middle knuckle, an inky stain blooming against the deep velvet as I finish tying the bandage.

My lips curve. "Well… Thank you."

He doesn't reply right away. And when I finally look up, he's watching me. The flames in the lanterns pulse a slow, flickering rhythm, and the heat in the tent spikes. Or maybe it simply feels hotter under the weight of his eyes on me.

The moment stretches. One breath. Then another.

His coffee-black gaze is steady. He's looking through me, not at me, peeling back the layers I've added to keep myself safe.

My throat tightens. Declan's hand is still in mine, my thumb smoothing over the velvet as he looks at me like I'm a question he wants to find the answer to. And I suddenly, *desperately* want him to try.

I'm aware that I've fully become a cliché. One punch

and my ovaries are ready to hand over the keys to the kingdom. All because someone other than me made me feel protected.

My foot is falling asleep, so I shift, rising onto my knees to let the blood flow back to my extremities. If I'm lucky, it'll also move to my brain. But since when have I been lucky?

As the space between us shrinks, Declan's breath catches. Or maybe that's mine.

The torches flare as his eyes drop to my mouth, and I swear he starts to lean down, to eliminate the gap of air between us, to bring his lips to mine.

My heart is a drumline in my chest, loud and powerful. I want Declan to *try* to reach me, but I'm not ready for him to succeed.

I pull my hands back quickly, fingers slipping free from his, and rise to my feet so fast I'm dizzy.

"We still need to find Fortune." I scurry back toward the trunk, hands already digging through fabrics, desperate for a task to busy my mind. "And I need more practical footwear."

"How are we supposed to find her?" Declan's voice is low, thoughtful. "Assuming that guard wasn't entirely incompetent, he genuinely didn't know who she was. Does that mean she's not local?" He pauses, eyes unfocused, tracking some invisible calculation. "If she isn't from here… That might complicate things."

The bed frame creaks as he leans back, long legs stretching out over the silk cushions. One arm hooks behind his head, the motion pulling his wrinkled button-down taut across his chest. He drags his bandaged hand along his jaw. "How big do you suppose this kingdom is?"

A chime punctures the air, and I yip, dropping an armful of clothes. My gaze snaps to the corner of the tent where a small bronze bell I hadn't noticed before sways on a cord.

From outside the tent, someone clears their throat.

Declan pushes up from the bed, his injured fist clenched, ready to fight Dav if he's come back for more. The sight sends a hot pulse through me, and my traitorous mouth tips into a grin.

Ack, no! I do *not* get turned on by potential displays of violence in defense of my honor.

"*Declan*," I start, but it comes out in a nasally maternal tone that makes me wince.

He ignores it and yanks back the flap.

Tarek stands there, head cocked, arms folded in front of him. "Supplies have arrived from the Everspring along with goods from Pentacles. There are many camels to unload, and Dav volunteered you."

"Of course he did," Declan mutters. He glances back at me, a ghost of a smile creasing the corners of his eyes, and warmth rushes under my skin. "Ready to get sneezed on by another camel?"

I glare, mostly to cover the way my stomach swoops.

Tarek sets the pace, cutting a smooth path through the narrow aisle of tents as Declan and I fall in behind him.

"Getting sneezed on by a camel is a great blessing!" Tarek calls back over his shoulder.

Declan huffs a laugh. "Hear that, Amanda? A *blessing*."

"And here I thought I was just unlucky. Guess I've been wrong this whole time."

"You said it, not me." Declan winks.

The caravan hums around us as we wind between

the tents. Bells jingle from awnings, each with a slightly different pitch that makes the campground sound like it's singing. Smoke from the roasting of peppers and meats coils through the air, tangling with the earthy bite of incense. Performers brush past, their laughter sharp as broken glass. Two children chase each other around a dozing donkey, shrieking with delight until their mother snags them and ushers them inside.

Tarek points out the community bathing area and the healer's tent. "Over there"—he points at the spacious section of yurts surrounded by guards—"is where the sister queens reside, as well as the Great Families."

Declan walks close enough that his arm brushes mine whenever people pass by. Tarek glides ahead of us, his shoulders relaxed, his cheery whistle catching on the breeze. Dav loomed like a guard dog, all threat and jagged corners, while Tarek practically bounces along the path.

"The tents are beautiful," I say as a couple slips into one, their conversation still clearly audible behind the fabric, "but silk doesn't exactly make solid walls. Doesn't everyone hear every private moment?"

Tarek shrugs, casual as ever. "What sorts of conversations would neighbors need to keep from one another?"

A shiver slides down my spine. I lean closer to Declan, whispering, "So basically everybody's always listening?"

His jaw ticks as he scans the rows of tents. "Then we need to be careful with what we say."

I nod. "I'm sure they'll be listening to us, especially since they believe we're spies."

"Always assume they are," he says quietly. "A place like this— We don't know the hierarchy, the rules, or who answers to whom. Until we do, we keep our heads down and blend in."

His gaze remains trained forward as if mapping escape routes. It's unsettling and steadying all at once.

"I like it better when we're not arguing." His hand brushes against mine as we walk, fingers grazing like it's an accident, but then he lets the contact linger, warm and steady. "Leaves room for other things to happen."

The words sink straight to my veins, so distracting that I trip over my own feet. I stumble, heat rushing to my cheeks, and cover it with a snort. "Don't flatter yourself."

We round another corner, and the aisle opens into a wide square. Camels kneel, allowing members of the kingdom to unload their packs. Baskets of figs and pomegranates land with heavy thumps onto the sand. Sacks of wheat lean against one another, stalks spilling from the open tops, their feathery golden heads swaying in the breeze. Amphorae are stacked carefully beside the tents, and a few of the camels carry bundles of dazzling maroon and gold fabrics with glints of golden pentacles and gleaming candlesticks tucked among their loads.

Actual treasure, my brain shrieks. Like, glittering-loot-you'd-hide-in-a-chest kind of treasure. Land pirates. What's the word for that? Highwaymen? My inner preteen—the one who used to spend entire summers rewriting dog-eared bodice rippers—lets out a full-body scream.

"Oi, you!" Tarek calls, already halfway to a line of stacked amphorae. He jerks his chin toward a crate filled with iron tools, heavy enough to bow the boards. "Bet those arms are more than decoration."

Declan straightens, almost eager, rolling his shoulders

as if lifting something backbreaking is exactly the kind of distraction he's been waiting for.

I take the moment of freedom to drift toward one of the camels, silk spilling out of its pack in waves. The maroon folds gleam like wine in the sunlight, rich and heavy, the scent of cinnamon and cloves baked into the fabric as if it's been marinating in spice the whole way here.

"Don't even think about it," I warn. "One of your brethren already blessed me with a face full of snot."

The camel blinks slowly, unimpressed, lashes thick as fans.

A woman in a headscarf approaches, one arm hooked around a woven basket of figs. She nods at the camel's pack. "Hand, please?"

I reach up and help her unclip one of the treasure-stuffed packs from its harness. "Is all this for the tents?" I ask, eyeing the silks and gleaming candlesticks.

She puffs out an incredulous laugh. Gesturing to the shimmer of gold peeking out from the bundle, she says, "These items are not necessary goods. They're meant for our performances. For show. Any who want them are able to trade for them at the market."

"So you only get to use these things while you're performing? Not to decorate your personal space?"

Her thin mouth twists into a smile. "What with rehearsals and performances and the work of tending to the kingdom, I spend so little time in my personal quarters, there would be no use in decorating it."

"Where does all this come from?"

"Our queens send their court to Pentacles at the turn of each season," she explains. "We bring spices and glasswork. In return, they give us metals, gold, fabrics. Enough to dazzle the crowd during our nightly performances."

"I didn't realize everyone performed as their job." I say, shifting the pack into her grip.

Again, she laughs softly, the sound like sand running through fingers. "No Festival of Flame, no applause. And what's the point of life without applause?"

The camel snorts as if to agree.

I hesitate, my fingers tracing the edge of one of the silks spilling from the bundle. "Do you know of a woman named Fortune?"

Her brow furrows.

"She's..." I falter, searching for the right description. "A performer, maybe. Someone important."

"An unusual name...one I would remember." She gives a small, regretful smile. "Can't say that I have heard of her. But I hope you find who you're searching for."

The woman steadies the pack against her hip and moves back toward the tents.

Something tugs at the back of my dress. I glance down and nearly shriek.

A miniature donkey stares up at me with enormous brown eyes rimmed by long lashes. The skirt of my dress is clenched between his teeth, silk drooping out of his mouth. He chews happily, unbothered by my horror, his jaw working in slow, contented circles.

Perched on his back, like a queen on her throne, is a cat with lemon-yellow eyes and smoke-gray fur, sleek and gleaming despite the desert dust.

"Hey!" The donkey tilts his head, long ears turning toward me. I yank the damp fabric free, and strings of spit plop onto the sand. "Absolutely not. Do I look like your salad bar?"

The cat flicks her tail and curls it neatly around her paws as she sits on her steed, and my annoyance dissolves in an instant. "Oh my goodness," I gush, reaching out in what I'm sure is a universal gesture of *can I pet you?* "Aren't you gorgeous?"

The cat slowly raises one paw. Holds it there. Then—*whap*. A hiss slices the air as her claws skim my knuckles.

I jerk my hand back with a gasp, staring at the faint red lines blooming across my skin.

Tarek jogs over with Declan close behind. Declan drags a forearm across his brow, wiping sweat from his face, then runs his palm down the back of his neck. His black button-down is plastered to his chest, clinging to every line of muscle. In the sunlight, the damp fabric gleams like ink poured over steel. For one delirious second, I completely understand straight men's fascination with wet T-shirt contests.

"I see you met Cinder," Tarek says cheerfully, interrupting my mental drooling. "Keeps the caravan clean of pests. But she is rather..." He tilts his head from side to side as if weighing his options. "*Picky*."

"Picky?" I echo in time to watch Cinder abandon glaring at me to launch straight into a purr when Declan reaches out. She presses her head into his palm like they're old friends.

I scowl. Cats like me. They always like me. In third grade, my next-door neighbor's Maine Coon used to follow me to school every single day and wait for me to get out. I was basically "Mary Had a Little Lamb," only "Amanda Had a Very Large Cat."

The donkey brays softly and butts his wet nose against my thigh.

"Oh no you don't." I sidestep quickly.

Tarek grins as he scratches the donkey behind the ears. "And this is Fennel. He chooses his friends wisely."

Declan chuckles, stroking Cinder's back. The cat all but liquefies under his touch, eyelids closed in bliss. "Guess this smart girl can tell who the difficult one is."

I frown. "Ass."

Fennel brays loudly.

Tarek claps his hands together, loud enough to make me jump. "On to our next task!"

Before I can ask what it is, he takes off toward the stacked amphorae. He hauls one up with ease, then thrusts another into my arms. The clay is cool against my palms but heavy enough that my knees wobble.

"Each of you delivers one, and then there will be no need for a second trip. Teamwork!" He grins and claps me on the back. Water sloshes over the rim of my urn and splashes my feet.

"Delivers one where?" I demand, hugging the amphora tight to keep from spilling more as Declan takes his without complaint and holds it with one strong arm like he was born to be a farmer.

"Why, the market, of course!" Tarek calls, already marching down the aisle.

We follow him to another stretch of open sand where silk ripples overhead in shades of scarlet, saffron, and vermilion. The air here in the market is hazy with smoke from stalls offering hand pies, spiced meats, and roasted vegetables. At the center of the market, a circle of musicians weaves a lively rhythm from drums, lutes, and the high, reedy trill of a pan flute.

A stall keeper stirs bubbling pots, the broth spitting and hissing as it splashes onto open flames. A glass-blower blows molten orbs into beads that glow like captured suns. One stall is stacked high with rugs in every pattern and hue imaginable, while another gleams with the same golden candlesticks and pentacles I helped unload earlier. At a stall overflowing with dates, figs, pomegranates, prickly pears, and apples, Tarek waves us over.

Behind us comes the steady clop of small hooves. I don't have to look to know Fennel has followed, Cinder perched on his back, the donkey's cat-clad shadow following mine.

"Ever heard of personal space?" I mutter over my shoulder. Fennel edges closer until his flank brushes my hip. "Unbelievable," I grumble.

The handles of the amphora dig into my arms, water sloshing over the rim as my feet sink into the sand. My shoulders ache, and my grip slips. There's no way I can make it another five feet, much less fifty, without losing more of its contents.

Declan strolls up beside me, not a hitch in his breathing. He eyes the damp streak running down the front of my dress and smirks. "I'm surprised there's any water left in there."

I shoot him a look. "This thing is half my size."

Without asking, he dips down and takes the urn from me like it weighs less than a purse. My arms, suddenly empty, feel like wet noodles at my sides as I trail after him toward Tarek.

"Set them here," Tarek instructs cheerfully, plunking his own down onto a woven mat.

Declan lowers both of ours while I pretend I'm not panting.

"I appreciate it," I say, swiping the spilled water from my arms.

He brushes off his hands and flashes a perfect white smile. "I wanted to take it from you from the start, but I figured you wouldn't like that."

"Yeah, I, uh, I probably wouldn't have."

We stand there awkwardly, not making eye contact, the silence stretching taut while I scramble for something to say next.

I'm saved by Tarek, who vaults between us right as a vendor's fan comes down hard on his shoulder. "Ow!" he cries, rubbing the spot. "No fighting in the market, Sasha!"

The woman running the stall leans over her table of fruit and swats the air with the same closed fan. "And what of stealing, Tarek?"

Stolen apple in hand, he clutches his chest. "You wound me, madam. I haven't stolen a thing." Then, grinning from ear to ear, he takes a massive bite and blows her an exaggerated kiss.

We drift away from the fruit stand and weave through the crowd.

A frown creases Declan's forehead as he toes the sand. "Where does all the produce come from? It can't be easy growing things in this."

"The Everspring." Tarek holds up the partially eaten apple as evidence. "It's an oasis a bit of a distance away from camp, but its forest is thick enough to get lost in, soil soft as silk, with fresh, cold springs that bring water up through the ground." He stares off wistfully before taking another bite and talking around the mouthful. "My favorite's the lagoon. Perfect for soaking tired muscles after a long day."

"Help me understand, because from a cost perspective, it doesn't make sense. All this effort moving goods and people back and forth when you could centralize at the Everspring," Declan remarks.

"The Everspring is not what it once was. Legend says it used to stretch as far as the sand touched." He sweeps his arm wide, his gesture taking in the camp. "Great obsidian columns larger than those around the stage stood at its center, and there were no queens, no kings. No one person in charge. Can you imagine?" Shaking his head, he takes another bite. "Who ran the kingdom? The camels? Absolute camelarchy!"

I blink. "Camel *what*?"

"*Camelarchy*," he repeats proudly, a goofy grin plumping his cheeks. "A fanciful tale, of course. Fireside fancy. But pleasant enough to ponder."

His grin falters, and his brow pinches. "That part about the Everspring stretching on and on, however, that's no tale. I've watched it dwindle in my lifetime. Each year the sand creeps farther, and the green yields a little more. One day, it will be gone." He crunches into the apple, speaking around the mouthful with forced cheer. "But I try not to dwell on such things."

A sudden swell of whooping and hollering pulls the market's attention. Two performers burst into the square. Yellow ribbons unfurl from their hands laced with gold coins that chime and clatter as the strands crack the air in intricate, hypnotic patterns.

The Player strides between them, her blunt black bob stark against the painted slash of crimson across her face. She flicks her wrist and the crowd parts instantly, her frolicking entourage swirling around her like sparks kicked up from a fire. At a spice stall she pauses, selects a small bundle of saffron threads, trades a few clipped words with the vendor, and tucks the prize neatly into her pocket.

Tarek leans in, lowering his voice like he's sharing a secret but still grinning as if it's gossip. "The Player was tasked by the queens with running the troupe. Performers regard her almost as highly as they do the crown."

I crane my neck, rising onto my tiptoes for a better look.

"So they're scared of her?" I ask. "Dav looked like he'd rather swallow nails than cross her."

"Fear, respect—two sides of the same coin, eh?"

The crowd surges back as one, pressed by the Player's movements through the market, and bodies jostle against mine. I step to retreat only to collide with Fennel's broad, stubborn bulk. His portly frame takes me out at the knees and sends me pitching backward.

The donkey brays. Cinder yowls, launching herself from his back in a streak of gray before disappearing into a nearby stall with an indignant hiss.

I flail, cursing gravity and the universe for conspiring in this series of mortifying spectacles when Declan's arm slides firmly around my waist. In one effortless motion, he hauls me against him, my palms braced against the wall of his chest. Heat radiates through his sweat-damp shirt, my body slotting against his like this was the plan all along.

Neither of us moves as the market goes on around us, but it all blurs into static. The only thing I can feel is him. The solid press of muscle beneath fabric, the rise and fall of his breath, the steady thrum of his pulse against my hand.

Declan dips his head, his lips grazing close enough that his words skim the shell of my ear. "If you want me to touch you," he murmurs, voice low and rough, "all you have to do is ask."

Sparks crackle up my spine as I inhale the salty sweet tang of his skin.

Then an elbow jabs into my ribs. I jolt and spin around to find Tarek grinning like he's just caught us making out behind the bleachers. "Feigning a fall to draw eyes before your performance? A bold tactic."

I force a laugh, trying to shake loose the butterflies flapping in my stomach. "So, um, Tarek, about our performance..." My gaze lands on the Player, all sharp angles and painted red slash, cutting through the market with her retinue like a blade. "What happens if it doesn't go well?"

"The queens see to it that the audience's attention never wanders," Tarek says easily as we give the Player's crowd a wide berth.

"That's...cryptic."

Declan's mouth quirks. "She doesn't like cryptic."

But Tarek doesn't elaborate. Instead, he tosses his apple core into a brazier, wipes his hands on his trousers, and keeps walking. "All are born to perform, save those the queens—or their ancestors—have chosen another path for. That was the Player's fate." His teeth flash in a cheesy grin. "And, as luck would have it, my family's as well."

Declan's attention is fixed somewhere behind me, and he tears his gaze away long enough to ask, "You hungry?"

Before I can answer, my stomach growls loud enough to earn a laugh from Tarek. Declan's already moving, striding to whichever stall piqued his interest without waiting for verbal confirmation.

I fall into step beside Tarek. "Somewhere along the way it was decided your family line was best suited to guard the kingdom?"

"The line of Duggermore, at your service." He straightens, chin high, palm resting on his hip in mock formality. His eyes go wide. He opens his mouth, shuts it again, and spins in a circle. When he comes back around, his smattering of freckles stands out like dots of ink against his ashen complexion.

"What's wrong?" I ask. "Did you lose something?"

"My sword!"

"Your sw—"

"Can the two of you find your way back to your tent and ready yourselves for tonight's performance?" Tarek blurts, voice jumping an octave with panic.

I open my mouth to protest—I have *no idea* where our tent is—when Declan reappears at my side with two steaming hand pies. He presses one into my palm. "I've got the sense of a homing pigeon."

"Good," Tarek says distractedly, scanning the crowd. "I'll fetch you at sunset. And perhaps keep quiet about my…misplaced weapon." He dashes off, muttering to himself.

I look down at the warm pastry. "What is this?"

"Try it," Declan says, already taking another bite of his.

I sink my teeth into the golden crust. Buttery flakes give way to a filling that's both savory and sweet, spiced with cinnamon and cumin, the vegetables tender enough to melt on my tongue.

My eyelids flutter shut, and before I can stop myself, I let out a contented hum.

When I open them again, Declan is watching me. His gaze lingers on my mouth, and heat crawls up my throat.

I snap my gaze back to the pie, pretending sudden fascination with its crimped edge. "I've eaten Michelin-starred meals that didn't taste half this good," I mutter, the words a little breathless despite my best efforts.

Declan's smile deepens, but before I can read anything more in it, Cinder lets out a throaty trill and twines herself in figure eights around his ankles, tail flicking high, her purr loud enough to rumble above the market chatter.

Declan crouches, tearing off a bit of his hand pie and offering it to Cinder. She takes it delicately, a queen accepting tribute. He straightens and holds another piece out toward Fennel.

"Don't feed him," I scold, narrowing my eyes. "He'll never leave, and I have no idea what to do with a donkey."

Declan quirks a brow and pops the bit into his own mouth. "Pretty sure he has no intention of leaving anyway."

"Why don't you flex those pigeon muscles and lead us back to our tent?"

He turns smoothly, guiding the way out of the market

as if he's got a compass wired into his brain. The moment his back is to me, I slip Fennel a piece of my pie.

The donkey eats noisily as I stroke his fuzzy forehead. "Dusty little menace."

Fennel brays happily, loud enough to echo down the aisle as we leave the market.

EIGHT

"I'm all for putting on a show," Declan begins when we're back in our tent, "but do you have any idea what you're going to say when we're onstage?"

Fennel and Cinder are firmly banished outside, and I'm elbow deep in the trunk at the foot of the bed. I pull out a gauzy, bronze dress that looks close enough to my size to work and a pair of strappy gladiator sandals that would have been helpful a few hours ago when I was trekking barefoot through the desert.

"Something witchy and storylike." I shrug. "I'll improvise."

He raises a brow. "Are you good enough at improv to bet our lives on it?"

"Fair point." I chew the inside of my cheek.

"You are an editor," he says, peeling the bandage from his hand. "And we both know you have a way with words."

My cheeks heat, and I focus on smoothing the fabric

of the bronze dress like it's the most interesting thing I've ever seen. "Assistant editor," I murmur, mostly to myself.

"Then you've probably read more books than your boss. Isn't that how it works? The lower you are on the totem pole, the more work you actually do?"

"You've never been the low man on the totem pole, have you?"

"Not exactly," he admits. "Nepotism has its perks."

"Maybe. But you also work hard. How long does it count as nepotism if you keep earning your place?"

He tilts his head. "Are you giving me a compliment?"

I ignore the question entirely. "You are right about one thing. I've read *a lot* of books, and I'm betting most of them don't exist here."

"Meaning?"

"Meaning," I say, closing the trunk, "I can borrow from them. Use pieces to craft something that sounds allegorical and wise. No one here will know the difference."

"You're going to plagiarize your performance?"

"*Plagiarize* is such an ugly word." I smooth the fabric between my fingers. "I prefer *reinterpret*. Plus, I'll change the names."

"This isn't a documentary." He laughs. "I don't think that'll count."

"Do you have a better idea?"

He considers that for a moment. "You could create your own story."

I sigh. "I don't know. I've spent years rewriting other people's words. The only ones that are mine are those I post. Even those don't sound like me. They're written for the algorithm. Although, that doesn't seem to be working. Plus, they're not stories so much as…products."

His brow furrows. "But you believe in what you're selling."

"Well, yeah," I say, easing down onto the edge of the trunk, the bronze dress pooling across my lap. "I believe in the effects of positive thinking. In ritual. In the power of small things—candles, crystals, meditation, spells—as a way to focus and shift perspective. It's something I've always been drawn to and love learning about. But actual magick?" I shake my head, a small, rueful smile tugging at my lips. "That part I'm not so sure about."

He studies me for a long moment, quiet and unreadable. "Then what brought us here?"

I look away, fingers tracing the gauzy folds of the dress. "That," I admit, "is a big question. And one I can't answer. Which is why I'd really love to find Fortune."

"I asked that stall vendor, the one selling hand pies, if he'd heard of her," Declan says. "He hadn't."

I exhale through my nose. "Yeah... I had the same luck."

"I guess getting sneezed on by that camel wasn't quite the blessing it was rumored to be."

I grab a cushion from the bed and lob it at him.

With a laugh, he ducks and moves to jump on the bed.

I point the second cushion at him like a weapon. "You cannot get on that bed in those grimy, sweaty clothes."

He lifts his hands, dark eyes glinting with mock innocence. "So you'd rather I take them off?"

Slowly, he pops open the first button.

"Declan."

Pop. Another button.

"That's not what I meant."

He pauses just long enough for a sly smile to lift his cheeks before the third button pops free, revealing a strip of bronzed skin over smooth, lean muscle.

"Just following orders." He shrugs, fingers moving to the next.

"You're more of a menace than Fennel." I fling the cushion, and he catches it midair.

The shirt parts wider, baring the ridges of his abs, the breadth of his chest, and those solid muscles I've already felt pressed against me twice in reality and countless times in my head. Heat floods me so fast, it's dizzying, a hot rush straight to the pit of my stomach.

His mouth moves, lips parting like he's speaking, but I'm too deep in the mental gutter to catch any of it.

"Yes. No, wait," I blurt and tear my gaze away, fanning myself with the flimsy dress. "Sorry, I was just, uh, thinking about…costumes. And performance structure. Blocking. You know, theater things."

Declan's gaze narrows, and that slow, devastating smirk spreads like wildfire across his face. "You're fantasizing about me, aren't you?"

I nearly inhale my own tongue. "What? No. Absolutely not. That's ridiculous."

"Mm." With a wink, he pops another button. "I know when I'm being eye fucked, Amanda."

My cheeks burn. "You are mistaken."

"Am I?" He takes a step closer, close enough that the air between us hums. "Don't forget I was on the other end of all those messages you sent."

"Being physically attracted to someone is very different from having actual chemistry with them." I cross my arms, pretending not to notice how my pulse stutters.

"If you were half as smooth as you think you are, we wouldn't be arguing about it."

He leans down. "Who says I'm trying to be smooth?"

"If this is you *not* trying, I'm terrified to see what happens when you put in effort."

Almost on cue, Fennel brays from outside so loudly it rattles the tent poles.

I suck in a breath and stand. "We should get ready. Figure out what we're going to say. It'll be sunset soon."

"Yeah." Declan rubs a hand across his jaw. "And Tarek wasn't exactly clear about what happens if we don't show."

Gathering the dress and the sandals, I slip behind the velvet divider. "I feel like the murkiness was its own kind of clarity."

The trunk creaks open, and metal clinks softly as he rummages through it.

"So, Story Witch, what book are we reinterpreting tonight?"

I exhale, shifting my weight as I think. "Something popular. Something we both know." I unlace my corset dress and let it pool at my feet. "Are you a reader?"

There's a pause. Then a strange, squeaky sound.

I frown. "Declan?"

"Yeah. I, um, yes. I can read."

"I know you can read." I laugh. "We've been DMing each other for weeks. What books have stuck with you?"

He mutters something I can't make out.

"What was that?"

Another mumble, lower this time.

I clutch the dress against my bare chest and poke my head around the divider. "Use your words, Thorne."

He scrubs a hand over his face. "*Twilight*, okay? I've read all the books. Twice." He shakes his head, a gentle wash of color rising in his cheeks. "Four times."

My grin is so big it hurts. "Nothing to be embarrassed about. Sparkly immortals, doomed loved, teen angst. It's practically a classic." I disappear back behind the divider and tug the bronze dress over my head. "*Twilight*… I wonder if we can get some body glitter."

NINE

The sun melts behind the dunes, turning the sky the color of overripe peaches. Wind slithers through the Kingdom of Wands like it's hunting, snapping silk against tent poles and lifting sand in tight, angry spirals. Torch flames carve through the twilight, casting the world in glints of gold, flickers of red, and trembling shadow.

This time, we're led deeper into the open-air backstage area. Performers dart between embroidered silk screens that divide the space into narrow lanes. Low tables overflow with makeup pots, bowls of pigment, and trays of polished gemstones. I pace a strip of carpet worn bare by nervous feet, clutching my affirmation cards in a death grip. Each one is a neon pop of glossy lamination. They're supposed to calm me, center me, but instead I'm one deep breath away from projectile vomiting.

I chose these instead of pulling from my tarot deck for one very specific reason: I cannot, under any circumstances, deal with being harassed by the Wheel of Fortune right now.

Declan saw the image move too. The wheel turned, the flames shimmered, the figures chased each other around the edges. I know what I saw. I know what *we* saw. I've also built my entire adult life on ritual and energy and manifestation, but always within the realm of metaphor. *Symbolic* magick. Not fire portals and kingdoms that shouldn't exist.

The most terrifying thing is that, if the Wheel of Fortune actually brought us here, then I've been messing around with forces I don't completely understand.

A hush ripples backstage, followed by the sharp crack of a staff against the boards. The Player strides out from one of the narrow alleyways past the curtains in a sweep of crimson silk, bell sleeves spilling down her arms like fresh blood. "Prepare yourselves. Your queens are waiting."

"Shit," I whisper, pressing a shaky hand to my chest as she disappears around the next curtain. "Okay, okay. You've got this." I force air into my constricted lungs. "You can do hard things. Everything you want is on the other side of fear."

I keep breathing deeply, struggling against the fact that it feels like I'm not getting enough oxygen. My fingers flex around the deck, and its laminated corners dig into my palm, leaving tiny divots in my skin.

"You look nervous."

Declan's voice jolts me. He leans against a screen post, arms folded, jaw set. He left his shirt unlaced, the open V stopping in the middle of his sternum, and his loose sleeves are rolled up to the elbows.

Not that I'm keeping track of how much skin he has exposed.

He shifts, and his forearms flex with the movement.

I didn't know forearms could be sexy. Like, *deliciously* sexy. Like I want to lick the ridge of that tendon, taste the sand and the salt.

I have absolutely no business staring, so naturally, I can't look away.

"Isn't public speaking the number one thing people are afraid of?" he asks, voice like a splash of cold water on my tendon-licking fantasy. "Even above death?"

I let out a shaky laugh that's barely able to escape my body. "Lucky us. Looks like we'll get to experience both public speaking and a flaming hot death."

The corner of his mouth lifts. "We'll be fine."

"That's not helpful." My hands won't stay still, nails tapping against the cards.

"Is it helpful to know that I'm not worried?"

"No," I say flatly. "Not even a little."

"Then honesty it is." He drags his hand through his hair, tugging lightly on the ends. "Normally, I'd say the queens have already made their decision. That this"—he gestures in direction of the ramp leading to the stage—"is just optics. They're not looking to be impressed. They're looking to feel correct, and that it's all about confirmation bias."

"But…?" I prompt.

He exhales. "*But* this is not a dinner meeting at Oma, and I have no fucking clue what's about to happen out there."

"In some weird way, that actually does make me feel better. A teensy tiny bit." I hold up my thumb and forefinger with only a small gap between the two. "But better. Sort of."

Declan flashes me a white-toothed smile. "Amanda Ward, are we becoming friends?"

The question makes warmth spark deep in my chest. I refuse to let it show. "Don't ruin it," I mutter, rolling my eyes and pulling an affirmation card from the middle of the stack. Before I can read it, the wind snatches it out of my hand and carries it into the dark.

"Ominous," Declan says as we both watch it disappear.

I try to shrug it off, even though my nerves are eating a hole straight through my stomach. I want to concentrate on something simple, something manageable. A mantra that'll drown out the sound of musicians tuning their instruments, the audience's applause, the Player's directions, and my own thoughts trying to outpace them all.

I shuffle through the stack with trembling fingers and pull another card.

I trust the winds of change to carry me where I'm meant to go.

I lift my chin, close my eyes, press the affirmation card flat against my chest, and take a deep breath, letting it out slowly, the way every audio meditation app insists I should.

I trust the winds of change to carry me where I'm meant to go. I trust the winds of change to carry me where I'm meant to go. I trust the winds of change to carry me where I'm meant to go.

The words run on a soft, rhythmic loop inside my head, smoothing the edges of everything sharp inside me. Each repetition packs another feeling away—fear, doubt, the creeping sensation that the air around me has started to shift. I keep breathing, keep reciting, tucking the mess of what I'm feeling and what's actually happening into a neat little box labeled *Later.* Or, ideally, *Never*.

"I trust the winds of change to carry me where I'm meant to go."

Tent flaps rustle. Torches hiss. Sand whips around my ankles.

A smoke-filled gust slams into my chest and knocks me back a step.

I open my eyes in time to see Declan push off the screen post. His brow is furrowed, mouth parted like he's halfway through a thought. His eyes track me slowly, head tilted the smallest fraction, dark hair falling across his brow.

More smoke barrels toward me. It rips the cards from my hands, yanking them skyward in a shiny cyclone of neon confetti.

I shriek as they whip around me, catching in my hair, smacking my cheeks, laminated points biting my skin.

The ash-thick wind howls, wrapping around me in a twisting column of pressure and movement—tugging, yanking, *lifting*.

My feet hover off the ground, and suddenly, I'm airborne.

The cyclone whirls around me in a cloud of smoke and sparks. I flail, limbs flapping. My skirt whips my thighs as the tunnel of firelit haze drags me through the backstage maze and up the ramp. The roar of wind fills my ears, and hot air claws down my throat as I'm spat forward, flung through the curtain with zero regard for my dignity.

I slam down flat on my ass in the center of the stage, the impact rattling my spine hard enough to make my teeth clack.

Coughing, eyes streaming, I paw at the top of my dress to make sure my nipples aren't peeking out at the crowd. My fingers snag on sweat and static cling as I rake them through my hair and plaster on a smile even though I'm sure it looks like I've been licked by Clifford the Big Red Dog.

Torchlight halos the crowd, every expression wide-eyed, stunned. I wheeze and scramble to my feet, legs shaking. Somewhere in the audience, a child starts to cry.

Declan's boots pound the ramp, his stride just shy of a run as if he's desperate to reach me but hell-bent on not looking like it. His brows lift enough to crease the space between them, lips pressed into a tight line, jaw tense and twitching like he's biting back ten different versions of *what the fuck happened?!*

From the center of the windswept stage, I give him a tight, frantic smile and a helpless shrug that says, *I don't fucking know!*

The audience stretches out before us, seated cross-legged on vibrant rugs and patchwork quilts spread across the sand. Through the shifting smoke, they look less like people and more like undulating dunes scattered across a desert of color.

At the very back is the queens' platform. Dozens of flame-shaped lanterns sway gently around it, while braziers pour out so much resin and dried herb smoke that it looks as if the platform itself has created its own atmosphere.

The queens sit there like two treasures unearthed from the sand. The golden-haired one wears an elaborate mantle of copper chains and hammered coins. Her ivory gown is stitched with threads of reddish-orange that wink like glitter the firelight. The dark-haired queen is crowned in a circlet of polished opals and draped in a lavish burnt sienna and carnelian gown, her wrists wrapped in bangles that flash whenever she moves her hands. Their high-backed thrones are decorated with gilded accents and velvet cushions that spill over with honey-colored tassels.

A clear, cool voice slices through the thick haze of incense and the dramatic entrance I've managed to stage without even trying.

"A superb start." The golden-blond queens claps from her velvet-draped dais. "To what promises to be a most *eventful* evening."

A smattering of applause rises from the audience, building into cheers. Someone in the back even lets out a high-pitched *woo!*

I blink into the torchlight. They're cheering. For *me*.

So this is what it feels like to have more than two people join a livestream.

I smooth my skirt, lift my chin, and raise both hands dramatically in the air like I've rehearsed this moment a hundred times—which, to be fair, I kind of have. Albeit, usually in the shower.

"Yes," I say, loud and proud. "Thank you. I am the Story Witch, and this is my brooding assistant…Mister, uh, Thorne."

I gesture to Declan with a little flourish. He bows, and a few of the women in the audience resume their cheers.

"Tonight," I continue, "we bring you an enchanting story filled with…enchantment and…and…"

My brain blanks.

"Adventure?" Declan offers.

"Thank you, Mr. Thorne. Yes, and *adventure*," I repeat, sweeping my arms overhead again like maybe a bigger gesture will summon actual words.

But nothing comes.

A few murmurs ripple through the crowd. The silence that follows is heavy, suffocating, humiliating.

My mouth goes dry, tongue stuck to the roof like I've just swallowed a fistful of sand. The crowd is silent. Scores of people staring at me from their rugs and pillows, their faces coming in and out of focus behind veils of smoke.

Every eye is on me.

And my mind is a snow globe that's been shaken too hard—flakes of panic swirling, no single thought landing long enough to hold.

What even is a Story Witch? What the fuck was I going to say? Holy shit. What have I done? I'm going to get us both killed.

My chest tightens, heat crawling up my neck. The silence thickens, heavier with every second, my lips pressing together more firmly, locking around words that don't exist.

Someone coughs. A baby fusses. The fire from the torches crackles louder than seems possible.

"Once upon a time," Declan begins, saving me from myself, "there was a girl who moved to a damp and gloomy kingdom where everyone was pale and mysterious."

The crowd leans forward.

"Yes!" I cry, nodding like this was the plan all along. "And Bella—uh—*Beulah* was terribly clumsy, but luck had gifted her with the ability to narrowly escape death's sharp scythe."

Declan glances my way, the faintest smile tugging at his mouth.

"Unfortunately," I add, "she was also deeply committed to poor decision-making and was in desperate need of help to sort out her life."

Several people in the audience nod in understanding.

"Then, one day, Beulah met a man who sparkled in direct sunlight." I lift my arms dramatically. Declan steps forward, tugging open the unlaced collar of his shirt to reveal his glitter-dusted chest.

The crowd breaks into delighted *ooohs* and *ahhhs*.

"Ed…mund was a brooding immortal with severe boundary issues and a strange fixation on watching Beulah sleep."

The audience erupts into boos.

"Look at him!" I shout over the noise. "So tall! So handsome! So strong!"

Declan flexes. I lean in and whisper, "More chest," and he obliges, lifting his shirt to show off his washboard abs in their full, shimmering glory. The women in the front row shriek and wave their scarves.

"You can see why Beulah was so taken with Edmund," I say. "But do we want the story to end with them simply riding off into the sunset together?"

More boos, louder this time.

"Enter, Jacobius!"

Declan spins, smoothing his hair down, then flashes a charming grin at the crowd.

"Jacobius enjoyed long runs on the beach and occasionally turning into a very…large…*wolf*."

With a playful growl, Declan tears open his shirt, howls to the sky, and leaps off the stage. The crowd goes feral.

"Beulah was torn between her glittery stalker and her golden retriever wolfman," I say once they settle. "So naturally, she did what any young woman in love does." I pause for effect. "She jumped off a cliff."

Gasps pop through the audience as I press the back of my hand to my forehead and swoon dramatically at the edge of the stage. Declan lunges forward, catching me before I can hit the ground, just like we rehearsed in the tent. Even with the practice, my stomach somersaults, and when his arms cradle me, relief floods my chest.

"Magickally," I proclaim as he lifts me back onto the stage and climbs up after me, "Beulah survived! And when she washed up on shore, she realized something profound."

The crowd leans in, and the golden-haired queen calls out, "What realization did our Beulah come to?"

"That maybe—just maybe—she didn't need Edmund or Jacobius to fix her life. That she didn't need to find someone else to save her. She needed to learn how to save herself."

A thoughtful hush falls.

"And while Beulah worked on herself, Edmund and Jacobius realized they didn't actually like fighting over the same woman. What they wanted was each other."

Declan turns his back to the crowd, wraps his arms around himself, and mimes a steamy, over-the-top embrace. Cheers and laughter explode through the audience.

"The two men opened a charming seaside bed-and-breakfast," I finish, "where they lived happily ever after."

The whole crowd bursts into applause. Cheers, whistles, and elated chatter roll over the stage as we bow.

I grin, wide and breathless, and turn to Declan. "I think we did it."

Smoke curls around us, and the warm air whips into a sudden wind that lashes the stage. Incense stings my throat. Heat pricks my skin. The audience gasps.

Something flutters through the haze, tumbling from above like a leaf caught in the breeze. It slips down my arm, brushing my skin with the faintest electric tingle.

I snatch it before it hits the ground, my fingers stinging from the contact.

The wind dies, plunging the kingdom into a silence so sudden it makes my ears ring. I stare down at the card.

The Wheel of Fortune.

My breath catches as the painted image shifts. The wheel turns. Its figures move in an endless loop, no longer paint but flesh and bone caught in perpetual motion, alive in my hands.

Out of the corner of my eye, Declan leans toward me, trying to see what has me gaping. Only, he's moving strangely, slowly as cold molasses. His hand stretches toward me, then stalls halfway, suspended in midair.

"Declan?"

He doesn't answer. Doesn't move at all.

My gaze jerks to the crowd.

Every single face turned toward me is perfectly still.

A woman's scarf is frozen mid-flutter, fabric caught in the gentle breeze like a picture. A man's mouth hangs open around a gasp that never lands. One child's fruit-filled hand is locked halfway to his lips.

The entire world has stopped.

I stumble backward, sweat beading along my hairline. "What—what's going on?"

Tendrils of smoke curl in the torchlight, the flames and I the only things left moving. It softens the world into a dream while the tarot card pulses against my clammy palm.

A woman steps from the shadows like she's been waiting there all along, and I feel it again, that same low hum beneath my ribs that I felt when she and I first met. Her hood is lowered, casting shadows across her face so deep I can't make out the contours of her appearance. Copper threads are braided into the long chestnut coils of her hair draped over her shoulders. The hem of her robe trails through the sand behind her like a brushstroke.

"It's you." My mouth is dry, but I manage to push out the words. "Fortune."

The flames from the torches at her back lean toward her presence, crackling louder, brighter, licking the air like they recognize their maker. She stops short of the stage. Her shadow-darkened face lifts, and her eyes, still the only features I can see through the shadows, lock onto mine like hot coals.

My grip on the card tightens as it finally sinks in—Towerfall's magick is real.

"It is a shame." She's not loud, but her voice slides through the space like molten glass. "I thought you would be ready."

The flames ringing the stage respond before I can. They leap high and wild, burning orange flares of heat that sear the air and snap hungrily at the sky.

I flinch, instinctively shrinking back, from the fire as well as the certainty in her voice and the disappointment she doesn't bother to hide.

"I wonder then," she adds, head tilting slightly, "why the Tower chose you now. It should have waited."

"The Tower…tarot card? Is that what you're talking about?"

Her vibrant eyes flick to the card clenched in my hand.

I swear it pulses harder, as if it feels her watching.

"The wheel is preparing to turn," she says, her voice dipping to a whisper. "Remember, or it shall not be gentle."

"Remember what?" My chest heaves, breaths rough and uneven. "I don't know what you want me to remember. I don't know what I've forgotten or what any of this means. I don't know why I'm here."

Her gaze burns through me as she lifts her right hand. From fingertip to elbow, it's encrusted in rubies. Embedded like scales, they shimmer when she moves, catching the light like a living torch.

Heat radiates from her palm in slow waves, warping the air between us. The space crackles. The scent of singed dust and something older—iron, ozone, scorched earth—fills my lungs.

My skin prickles, flushed and burning. Sweat slides down my temples.

The Wheel of Fortune hums, a low, vibrating thrum against my palm like it's answering her—like it knows what's coming.

For a heartbeat, I think she's going to touch me. Leave some mark. Pass ancient and irreversible magick—*real* magick—into my bones.

I don't mean to lean in, but I do. Drawn to her like a moth to flame, like a lost thing hearing its name for the first time. Something inside me, something buried and aching, pulls taut in her presence. As if her stillness speaks a language my chaos has always longed to understand.

The heat of her outstretched hand flares so close to my cheek my skin threatens to blister.

My breath hitches. Tears sting my eyes.

And then she withdraws.

The heat vanishes with her, a candle snuffed.

Fortune turns with a finality that makes the wooden planks of the stage feel less solid beneath my feet and strides away. Smoke clings to the hem of her robes. Ash kicks up in small spirals behind her, tiny fire ghosts vanishing before they land. The flames along the path bow as she passes. She disappears into the veil of smoke and flickering torchlight, swallowed by shadow and flame. Gone, as if she were never really here at all.

I rub my cheek where the heat lingers, skin tender and stinging.

The crowd's unblinking eyes cling to me like spotlights. But I barely feel them now. I'm too stunned. Too rattled.

And I need answers from her before I can even start to piece together what's happening—why the crowd is frozen, why Declan and I were pulled here, why the Wheel of Fortune card suddenly feels like it's lighting a fire inside me.

What does it want from me?

What does *she* want from me?

What do I need to remember?

...why the Tower chose you.

The words echo in my chest, louder now that she's gone.

I stumble forward a step. "Wait," I call out, my voice cracking. "I need your help!"

The words hang in the air, unanswered.

My heart lurches.

I slide off the stage, the Wheel of Fortune card still clutched tight in my hand, edges digging into my palm, and chase after her. My silk skirt drags across the sand, my lungs burning, smoke and ash painting the back of my throat. The path she walked is still visible. Embers glow faintly in the dust, the air around them rippling with leftover heat.

The wheel only turns when something is about to change. It brings upheaval, transformation, consequences—good and bad. It doesn't ask for permission. It just moves. And once it does, nothing stays the same.

The heat thickens the farther I push into camp, weaving between tents. The air shimmers before me, rippling with heat as if reality is warping at the edges.

My sandals crunch over charred earth as I chase Fortune's path. The faint scent of ozone and scorched sage curls into my nose.

Up ahead, the singed edge of her robe flutters around the last line of tents, trailing her like a dying comet.

"Please," I shout. "Just tell me what I'm supposed to do. How I get us home?"

I round the corner, heart in my throat…

But she's gone. All that's left is her heat, distorting the air in uneasy waves.

The scorched black path opens onto endless dunes, edges softened by wind and moonlight. No footprints. No sign of her. Like she walked into the desert, and it swallowed her whole.

The card thumps against my palm like a cursed heart. It brought me here. It tore my life wide open. It's the one constant in a series of events I don't understand, pulling me toward something I begged for a thousand different ways—only to realize too late I might not survive it.

Like Fortune said, the wheel is set to turn. I just have to remember…

A shout echoes behind me. Then another and another, rolling into a rising clamor.

I spin, skirts tangling around my legs, heart lurching against my ribs.

The stillness is broken. Whatever magick this world has that took effect when Fortune appeared and held them all in place has snapped, leaving panic in its wake.

When they realize it looks like I simply vanished into thin air, maybe—hopefully—it'll add to the Story Witch mystique. If I can't control the story, I can at least let them believe the magick is mine.

TEN

I sprint through the maze of tents and burst out in an aisle directly behind the audience.

A man in the crowd spots me. He stands, his voice cutting through the confused chatter. "There she is!"

Heads whip toward me at once.

The golden-haired queen surges to her feet with a delighted squeal. "What a show!" she cries, clapping so enthusiastically her bracelets jangle. "Did you see her vanish, Solara? And now she has reappeared! Oh, that was splendid indeed!"

Her sister, Solara, rises more gracefully, offering a cool, approving smile. "It is a great honor to earn such high praise from Zephara. I, too, was quite entertained." She begins clapping, and soon the entire court follows suit. The platform erupts in applause. The crowd joins in, cheering and stomping their feet until the air feel like it's trembling.

Declan stands at the center of the stage, eyes fixed

on me. His expression mirrors the sinking feeling in my gut—bewilderment, unease, the shared understanding that whatever just happened wasn't part of the act.

For what seems like the hundredth time today, I have no idea what just happened.

The card burns against my palm, its edges biting into my skin as if reminding me it's still there.

People leap from their rugs and cushions, swarming toward me. Questions volley faster than I can breathe.

"How did you vanish?"

"What inspired your story?

"Are you and Mr. Thorne betrothed?"

I lose sight of Declan in the crush. Perfume, sweat, and incense press in as hands reach for my sleeves, my hair, my skirt.

"Stay back," Dav booms, his voice cutting through the din. He carves a path through the people encircling me and plants himself at my side with one hand hovering near his sword.

Tarek bounds through the crowd behind him, a grin plumping his round cheeks. "By the sun, that was magnificent! We thought the gods themselves had swallowed you whole! And then your return…as if conjured from thin air. What drama! What theater!"

Declan muscles through last, shoulders squared, jaw tight. "Glad we could entertain," he mutters, nodding to the crowd as they gawk at him and hurl questions and compliments. His dark eyes snap to me. "Are you all right? What happened out there?"

I shake my head quickly, forcing the words through a tight smile. "Not here."

My pulse thrums against my ears, the applause and

chatter blending into a single, roaring blur. I can still feel the heat of Fortune's presence clinging to my skin, the shimmer of magick thick in the air. My fingers ache from gripping the card, its edges digging into my palm.

It's proof. Terrifying, impossible proof.

The Wheel of Fortune isn't metaphor or coincidence—it's real. And if this place holds that kind of power, what else might it be capable of?

I can't catch my breath. I can't begin to explain.

Beneath the confusion is fear tangled with awe so potent it almost hurts. I've spent years hiding behind the idea of magick, treating it like armor. Something to sell, to believe in just enough, to hold between myself and the world. But now that it's staring back at me, alive and undeniable, I feel small. Naive. Afraid of what it might want from me.

The circle parts again, and the crowd quiets as the Player glides forward.

"The queens are most pleased," she says, gaze flicking between us. "You will perform again tomorrow night. As you see, the people hunger for another tale."

My throat dries out. "Tomorrow? I thought we could leave—"

"And journey where?" Her smile is all edges. "Back to Cups?"

"Why would we return to the lesser Kingdom of Cups," Declan replies smoothly, "when we have clearly come here to share our gifts with Wands?"

She inclines her head. "Well spoken, Mr. Thorne. Yet mark my words—so long as you dwell beneath our sister queens' favor, you *will* perform each night. It is the custom of this kingdom, and no soul stands above its law."

Dav barks at the gawking onlookers to clear a path, and he and Tarek guide us through the narrow lanes of tents. The cheers fade behind us, swallowed by the hiss of the torches and the thrum of blood in my ears.

Questions radiate off Declan like heat, but he keeps them behind his teeth, both of us silent until we duck inside.

A platter of food waits on the low table near the bed—bowls of roasted vegetables glistening with oil, charred flatbread, figs split open and glistening like jewels, and a small pot of something that smells like honey and spice. I barely register it before throwing the tarot card onto the bed, half expecting it to burst into flames or suck us into another realm.

"It was Fortune."

He glances back at the seam of light along the ground, then takes my hand and draws me to the tent's center, away from the walls. "They can hear us."

I swallow. "She was here," I whisper. "On the stage. She—she stopped everything. Time. The crowd. You." My throat tightens, the words spilling out too fast. "It was like the world froze, except for her and me. She said the Tower chose me, that I wasn't ready. Then she left. I chased her all the way to the edge of camp, but she disappeared."

Declan studies me in silence, his brows drawn tight, the flickering lanterns throwing shadows across his face. "You're sure it wasn't—"

"I know how it sounds. But magick here… It's real. I saw it. Felt it. There's no logical explanation for what happened. The Wheel of Fortune card… It's alive somehow. It's what brought us here."

He rubs the back of his neck. "If that's true…" He exhales slowly. "Then is she the key? Does Fortune control it—the magick?"

"She has to." I sink onto the edge of the bed and tear the flatbread in half. "She literally stopped time," I say around a mouthful. "She has to be the one who can send us home."

Declan picks up the rest of the flatbread and folds it in half before taking a bite.

I pop a roasted chunk of carrot into my mouth as I trace a finger over the card's gold edges. "I don't know how to pretend this is normal." I shake my head and shove the card out of view under the nearest pillow. "Every time I think I've caught my breath, something else happens."

Declan stops in front of me, his shadow falling across my lap. "We'll find her again," he says firmly. "Fortune is drawn to you. You've seen her twice in less than a day. Meanwhile everyone else we've asked hasn't seen her at all."

He lowers himself to one knee in front of me and closes his hand over mine where it's fisted in my lap. The heat of his palm quiets the restless tremor buzzing through my body. He's close enough that I can smell the salt of sweat on his skin and the faint earthy tang of dust and smoke clinging to him.

"But until we do," he continues, voice quieter now, "we keep acting the way they expect us to. We perform, we stay alive, and we figure out how this place works."

I force out a small, wobbly smile. "Right. Think positively. We can do this."

"That's the spirit." His mouth curves, and he squeezes my hand before releasing it and rising back to his full height. The space between us fills with cool air, and I hate how quickly I miss the solid warmth of him—the quiet steadiness he carries while everything around us continues to spin.

"You were really good onstage," I say. "Like, surprisingly good."

He shrugs, eyes darting anywhere but mine, and in the low, flickering light I swear there's the faintest flush creeping up his neck. "I may or may not have been Edward one Halloween," he says, voice dry but softer than usual. "And Jacob the next."

A laugh bursts out of me. "So this performance was years in the making."

"Something like that."

I open my mouth to tease him again, but a yawn steals the moment.

"We should wash off this glitter and get some sleep." He crosses to the trunk, rummages through it, and pulls out two silk robes—gold for me, deep burgundy for him.

"Is it too much to hope that we'll each get our own private shower?" I ask, clutching the gold robe.

Declan parts the tent flap, the corners of his mouth twitching. "In a kingdom where everyone performs for a living? I wouldn't count on privacy being part of the package."

The bathing tent sits a few aisles over, humming with voices and candlelight. People slip in and out, wrapped in robes, steam curling around them. The air smells faintly of myrrh and citrus.

Inside, the ground is packed, wet sand that shimmers

with leftover suds. Barrels line the perimeter, each brimming with water and fitted with ladles that glint in the steamy air. Smaller amphorae wait nearby, their clay mouths chipped from use, and soft towels hang from carved wooden racks.

The tent is empty, and we claim a spot in the corner. Without prompting, Declan turns his back to me and positions himself between me and the rest of the tent, broad shoulders angled just enough to block the view if anyone should enter.

My fingers fumble at the ties of my dress. The fabric slides down, whispering against my skin before pooling at my feet. I peel off my underwear, kick the pile of clothes aside, and try not to think about the fact that my heart is pounding loud enough for him to hear.

He peels off his shirt, and a fine dusting of glitter drifts from his shoulders like starlight. I try not to stare at the way the muscles shift beneath his skin as he takes off his pants, the play of light across his shoulders, the faint trail of glitter clinging to the curve of his spine and shimmering down his ass.

I fail spectacularly.

"Are you going to keep watching," he asks over his shoulder voice, teasing but careful, "or help me get this glitter off?"

"Bossy," I mutter, rolling my eyes even though my face is on fire. I grab a rough cloth from a nearby rack and dip it into the soapy water. Bubbles burst between my fingers as I wring it out and step closer.

I move slowly, dragging the suds across the wide span of his back, following the ridges of muscle, the slope of his shoulders. Soap and glitter swirl together, sliding down his skin in iridescent streaks.

He exhales, a soft sound that curls low in my stomach.

When he starts to turn, I spin around so fast I nearly lose my balance. My blush creeps down my neck, my chest, my entire body burning.

"You missed a spot," he says behind me, his voice rougher now.

Before I can muster any syllables, he takes the cloth from my hand. His broad palm glides down my back, across my shoulders. I close my eyes as he works the suds over my skin, gentle but thorough, his fingertips catching in my damp hair.

Clay scrapes softly against the sand as he lifts one of the amphorae. A moment later, cool water spills down my back in a steady, glistening stream. It runs over my shoulders, between my breasts, down my stomach. I gasp, the sound catching in my throat as his hand follows. Rough fingertips trace the water's path. He brushes away the last of the suds, each touch leaving heat in its wake, a trail that lingers long after he's moved on. The rhythm of his movements becomes hypnotic, soft and careful in a way that makes my heart beat faster.

Then his fingers slip into my wet hair, combing through it with intimate tenderness that steals thought. My body moves before my mind can catch up—a soft sigh, a small surrender—until I'm leaning back into him. His warmth presses along my spine, the steady rise and fall of his chest syncing with my own uneven breaths.

He brushes my hair aside, his fingers grazing the sensitive skin of my neck. The air shifts as he leans closer.

His breath ghosts over the damp curve of my shoulder, sending a shiver down my spine.

Every nerve in my body strains toward him, caught in that fragile place between impulse and restraint.

My pulse stutters in the hollow of my throat, begging for him to act first, because I can't seem to move. His nearness is its own gravity, holding me in place.

It feels like the whole world has gone quiet, just the sounds of water pattering against sand and the faint rasp of his breath behind me.

Laughter ripples outside the tent. Then footsteps, closer and louder, as reality rushes back in.

Declan moves first, reaching for a towel and wrapping it around me. His hands linger a moment too long at my shoulders before he lets go, and the loss of his touch leaves the air feeling colder.

"Th-thank you," I manage, voice barely above a whisper.

When I turn, his own towel is slung low around his hips. Droplets slide down from his temple, tracing the line of his jaw. I reach up and catch one with the edge of my towel. The brief touch sparks through me like static before I drop my hand.

I clear my throat, trying to sound casual and failing completely. "We should, um, go back to the tent. Get some sleep."

Neither of us says anything as we walk back to the tent, robes clinging to our damp skin, the night air cool and heavy around us. The camp hums softly around us, but it all feels far away, muted by the pulse drumming in my ears.

Inside, my gaze drifts to the single bed waiting for us, its embroidered cushions piled high.

"You take it," Declan says as he crosses to the trunk and pulls out a pair of loose, harem-style pants. "I'll sleep on the floor."

I busy myself fluffing the pillows, rearranging them into neat rows, pretending that the single king-sized bed doesn't suddenly feel too small.

Declan joins me, gathering the pillows I threw at him earlier.

"You don't have to—" I start, then meet his gaze.

He's looking at me with an intensity that feels like a touch. Heat blooms low in my stomach as his eyes trace the bare stretches of skin peeking out from my robe.

"I do," he says softly. He drags one of the blankets off the bed and lowers himself onto the rug.

When he settles on the ground, long body stretched across the floor, I move to the trunk and rummage through the items until I find a red slip threaded with gold embroidery. I duck behind the screen and put it on before blowing out the candles and crawling into bed.

Below, close enough to touch if I only reached down, I can hear Declan shift—cloth rustling, the slow exhale as he settles in.

For a long time, I lie there staring at the tent ceiling, pulse still uneven from the stage, from the bathhouse, from him.

I turn onto my side and slip a hand beneath the pillow. My fingers find the card. Its edges are warm against my skin.

The wheel is preparing to turn. Remember, or it shall not be gentle.

"For what it's worth," Declan says, voice breaking through the silence, "if I had to be trapped in another world with someone, I'm glad it's you. I couldn't imagine a better *Twilight* partner."

Tension loosens inside me. The ache of the day, the fear, the strangeness, all of it dissipates into a feeling close to comfort.

"Night, Declan."

"Good night, Amanda."

ELEVEN

"Again!" The Player's clap cracks across the sand as she paces where the audience will sit come nightfall. "But this time, with *passion*."

Declan exhales through his nose, while I clutch my script, if my frantic scribbles about *Fourth Wing* can be called a script. We're halfway through our retelling, or at least my very loose interpretation of it, and apparently we're failing to convey the life-or-death yearning of dragon riders in love.

The Player sweeps up the ramp, crimson sleeves whispering against the planks. "Story Witch," she declares, "you speak of their love, yet it sounds as though young Xavier and Viola are merely trapped within the same verses. And Mr. Thorne"—her gaze flicks to him—"you must *want* her words, not merely endure them."

"I'm trying," Declan says flatly.

"Try *harder*." Her bracelets clink as she gestures

between us. "When the Story Witch breathes, your eyes should follow the air itself. When she speaks of suffering, you should ache for her. When she looks at you—"

"Burst into flames?" he mutters.

A delighted smile curls her painted mouth. "Now that would be a show worth watching."

After another hour of acting notes and critique, the Player finally dismisses us with a regal flick of her wrist and an instruction to "find the thread between story and soul."

As we move through the bustling backstage, Declan leans closer. "Do you have any idea what she was talking about?"

I inhale like I'm about to deliver something profound, then sigh. "Nope. Although I do feel like we just went through couples counseling."

Declan murmurs his agreement as we push through the curtain and are immediately intercepted by Dav, sword at his hip, expression carved into its usual scowl. A dark bruise shadows the edge of his jaw right where Declan hit him last night.

"You can take your next meal in the market while tending one of the food stalls," he barks.

Declan tilts his chin. "You volunteered us for another job, didn't you?"

Dav's mouth twitches. "Consider it an opportunity to make yourselves useful instead of ornamental."

Declan smirks and motions toward the bruise. "How's your jaw?"

"Move." His nostrils flare as he jerks his head toward the path.

I yawn so hard my eyes water. "I am way too tired to

run or fight anyone off today, so maybe try not to get us into more shit than we're already in."

"I didn't sleep well either." He pulls his lower lip between his teeth, a slow drag that makes it hard to remember what breathing is. His gaze finds mine, dark and burning, and holds.

Heat flares beneath my skin, memory crashing over me in a rush of rough hands and cool water and what would've happened if he hadn't slept on the floor.

"I kept thinking about—"

"Our performance tonight?" I cut in quickly. "Yes. Me too."

"Sure," he says softly. "Our performance."

We brush against each other as we step into the market stall. Even through the fabric of my dress, the contact sends a shiver up my arm I pretend not to notice.

The stall's table is stacked with honeyed fruits, smoked meats, and small loaves of crusty bread. Declan and I drop onto a narrow bench. Fennel spots us from across the market and rushes over, Cinder clinging to his back like a furry pirate captain.

Declan starts picking at the offerings, eating figs and slices of cured meat with his fingers, while I tear off bits of bread and assemble apple, pear, and meat finger sandwiches like it's a spread for adult Lunchables.

Fennel collapses half under the table, half in the sun, snoring contentedly with his head on my foot. My toes go numb, but I don't have the heart to move him.

Dav prowls a few paces away, scanning the market like everyone's a potential assassin. A boy no older than ten wanders too close to a spice stall, fingers hovering over a pyramid of garlic bulbs. Dav barks a command harsh enough to make the kid flinch and nearly topple the whole display.

"My queen," Declan murmurs and lifts Cinder onto his lap. Immediately, she starts purring and licking honey from his shirt. He strokes her head with a gentleness that makes me wish I could curl up in his lap too.

Cinder rubs her sticky head under his chin, and he laughs. It's a low, rumbling sound that sends my pulse skittering.

I tear off another piece of bread, more forcefully than necessary. "We need to talk about what we're doing," I say under my breath, keeping my smile pasted on for anyone who might be watching. "We can't just wait around for Fortune to reappear."

Declan leans forward, elbows braced on his knees, voice pitched low enough to hide beneath the market chatter. "Maybe there's a way to speak to the queens. They have influence, power. If anyone else knows how magick works here it's them."

He reaches for another fig, and a glob of honey plops onto Cinder's head. She blinks up at him, offended, while he chuckles and wipes her fur clean.

A blur of silk skirts and jangling beads barrels toward the stall. Three girls no older than sixteen skid to a stop in front of me, breathless and wide-eyed.

"Oh, by the gods, it's her! You are truly spectacular," the one in the middle gasps, clasping her hands like I just descended from a cloud. Her cheeks are flushed pink from running, her crystal-blue eyes glittering like chips of polished quartz. Gold bangles slide down her wrists, clinking as she bounces on her toes.

"The Story Witch," the girl on her left breathes,

her round face framed by golden curls she immediately wraps nervously around her finger. The cluster of freckles scattered across her nose crinkle with her wide grin. "We saw you at rehearsal, but we couldn't speak then. As soon as we were released, we had to come find you—the brilliant storyteller!"

Their adoration lands like glitter bombs, and suddenly I'm sparkly, dazzling. My chest fizzes and warms like I just chugged a bottle of champagne.

"Who, me?" I scoff, batting at the air with theatrical modesty. "No way!"

"Celine!" the girl in the middle shrieks, seizing the third one by the shoulders. "Celine! I have forgotten my question. What was my question?!"

Celine shrugs her off and smooths her sleek black braid over one shoulder. Her gaze slides past me to Declan, and she leans across the counter, lashes fluttering. "So, you're *the* Mr. Thorne."

Declan freezes. Color drains from his face. He looks at me, then at Cinder, who is shooting glowing yellow daggers at the young woman. "I—uh—" He clears his throat. "I should probably see if I can't arrange an audience with the queens."

"Wait, we haven't—" I start, but he's already charging across the market, waving down Dav with Cinder draped across his broad shoulders like a smoky cape.

"Oh, wait! I remember now." The girl at the center claps her hands together. "The vanishing act. How did you do it? You were there, and then—*poof*—you were gone."

"Nessa has *not* ceased speaking about it," the one on the left says, still fiddling with her curls.

"*Romy*," Nessa whines, jabbing her friend in the side with her elbow.

"Ow! What? It's true. You've spoken of little else. I think it was wondrous too, but honestly, it's all you've spoken about since last night."

Celine, lips tilted in a pout at Declan's escape, pushes off the counter and folds her arms over her chest. "It must have been some trick built into the stage. Not true magick. No one possess real magick anymore. It's all misdirection and illusions."

"And what of the storm of smoke that carried her onto the stage?" Nessa demands, one hand on her hip. By Celine's exaggerated eye roll, I can tell this isn't the first time they've had this argument. "Do you suppose she used great hidden fans?"

Celine purses her lips and blows out a sharp exhale through her nose.

Nessa spins back to me, her whole face brightening again. "Can you teach us? *Please*? We wish to learn your Story Witch ways."

"Yes!" Romy blurts, nodding so hard her heavy gold earrings slap her cheeks. "It would make our performances that much better! Everyone would turn their heads from the same old fire tricks to watch us."

Celine shrugs, inspecting her braid as if she's only partially invested. "I suppose there is always room to improve. The queens do not look kindly on stale acts."

I straighten and brush the crumbs from my lap. "You want me to…teach a class?"

"Yes!" Nessa squeals, clasping her hands like she might explode if I say no. "Please teach us."

Heat swells in my chest, bright and buoyant. After

everything that's happened, it's a relief to have someone look at me like I'm actually in control. Last night's performance might have been built on a borrowed plot and magick that I had nothing to do with, but these girls don't care. To them, I'm powerful. I'm the Story Witch.

And maybe I've tripped and fallen directly into my calling.

"I can't teach the disappearing act—"

"I thought as much." Nessa nods gravely. "You'd want to keep that one and the smoke cyclone for yourself."

"Yeah..." I clear my throat, trying to sound mysterious instead of panicked. "But I can teach you about something else. A class I've been working on. It's about using manifestation and scripting to shape the energy around you," I continue, slipping into my practiced cadence, "so you can move through the world protected by intention and what you choose to project."

This is a chance for me to perfect my newest class offering. More than that, it'll truly help these girls stay positive and put the kind of armor in place that people like to see, that they expect. Our worlds are different, but I know that the messy softness—the kind that's real, the kind that hurts—is best kept hidden no matter where they are.

Romy's freckled cheeks flush pink as she leans closer, eyes bright. "And the way you speak. I want to learn of that too. Being from Cups, you and Mr. Thorne sound differently than we do here in Wands, and you use such curious words."

Heat prickles along my neck, and I let out a strangled laugh. "Sure, I can teach you some words."

Nessa seizes Romy's hand, then snags Celine's,

tugging them into a chain. She and Romy squeal in unison, bouncing up and down. Celine rolls her eyes and lifts her limp arm in solidarity and mutters an unconvincing, "Huzzah."

Their laughter bubbles over the stall like soda foam, until Nessa blurts, "When can we start? Now? Tonight? How many lessons will it take? Every day, perhaps?"

I bite my lip, stalling. "I'm not sure how long we'll even be in town—"

"The market's closing," Nessa insists, already gesturing around us. "The timing is wonderful."

I glance around. Vendors are shuttering stalls, loading up crates, folding bolts of cloth. Across the sand, Declan and Tarek are helping a woman wrestle massive rugs into rolls, both of them sending up clouds of dust with every move.

"I don't know..." I hesitate.

That's all the opening they need. Nessa leans forward, pleading. Romy clasps her hands like she's praying at an altar. Even Celine, halfhearted though the motion is, tilts her head and tosses her braid as their chorus of begging rises up.

"Okay," I say, a little breathless. "Let's do it."

I pluck an orange tasseled cushion from a nearby stall and settle down on it in front of my teenage audience. Nessa, Romy, Celine, plus a handful of other curious girls, crowd in close, skirts pooling around them in a kaleidoscope of silks and beads.

At the very back, Dav looms like a human exclamation point, arms crossed, jaw hard, sword gleaming at his hip. Tarek, in contrast, plops down at the end of the front row with all the enthusiasm of a puppy. Declan sinks onto the rug beside him as Fennel joins and Cinder curls into a smoky comma against his flank. The donkey stares at me adoringly, and I can't help but smile at him.

"Welcome everyone," I begin, voice wobbling before I catch it and push the sound into theater-kid projection. "I am so pleased you enjoyed our performance. I hope you also enjoy this lesson."

The girls clap and squeal. Tarek whoops loud enough to make Cinder flinch.

"First," I say, lifting a finger like a professor, "affirmations. They're not spells so much as reminders. We repeat them to align our energy with what we want and how we want to be seen by the people around us."

"Like scales for the voice," Nessa offers eagerly, her bracelets chiming as she jots down notes on parchment.

"Exactly." I snap my fingers, seizing the metaphor. "Except instead of do-re-mi, it's *I am worthy*."

I stand and pace in front of them like I'm leading a seminar at some chic Manhattan coworking space instead of a patch of desert sand. "Okay. First rule of affirmations: no hedging. No *I hope*, no *maybe*, no *someday*." I sweep my hand in a decisive little chop. "The universe is not your flaky boyfriend. It doesn't respond to wishy-washy. You have to talk to it like it's already listening."

Nessa leans forward, eyes shining. Romy scribbles furiously on her paper. Even Celine tilts her chin, pretending not to care while clearly taking notes when she thinks no one is looking.

"Second," I say, "it has to be *present tense*. Not I *will be* brave. I *am* brave. You perform without fear. You command the stage and captivate the crowd. Speak as though it's already happening."

Nessa looks up at me like I have all the answers, like every word coming out of my mouth is sacred text. And maybe I actually am helping. Someone like this, like me, would've helped me when I was younger. If someone had told that girl she could change her life just by changing her language, by scripting a better story and wrapping herself in intention until she believed she was untouchable… Maybe she wouldn't have felt so invisible. So unchosen. So small in rooms where no one cared to see her. Maybe she wouldn't have handed herself over to every boy who noticed her.

My chest warms, my spine straightens, and for once in this sand-scorched circus I don't feel lost. I *am* exactly where I'm supposed to be.

"Now, once you've written it, you speak it. Say it like you'd bet your life on it. That's how you align your energy."

Romy bites her lip, nodding so fast her curls bounce.

I sweep my hand like I'm conducting an orchestra. "Go on. Get to crafting your affirmation."

For five minutes, the empty market fills with the scratch of writing and murmured affirmations. Nessa mouths her words over and over, adjusting her phrasing until her lips form a triumphant grin. Romy keeps scratching lines out and rewriting, her curls bouncing with every shake of her head. Celine sighs like this is beneath her, but her hand moves steadily across the page anyway.

I float among the girls, dropping encouragement: "Yes, that! Say it louder." "Good but make it more you. Less apologetic." "Perfect. Own it."

"Is it time to speak them aloud?" Nessa asks.

"Yes, whenever you're ready."

She straightens her back, rolls her shoulders like she's stepping onto a stage, and declares, clear and sure, "I am worthy of being seen."

"I am chosen," Romy says, chin tugged higher by invisible thread.

"I perform without fear," another girl murmurs, fingers clutching her parchment.

"I am a glorious warrior!" Tarek bellows, pounding his chest for emphasis.

From the back of the class, Dav throws up his hands and mutters something unfit for young ladies' ears.

Declan laughs, claps Tarek on the back, and says, "Yeah you are, buddy."

We move from affirmations to scripting, where I teach them how to describe what they want out of life so they can work on manifesting that reality. Before I know it, an hour has passed. The class winds down in a flurry of parchment scraps, charcoal dust, and squealing voices. The girls compare lines, trade compliments, and recite drafted manifestation scripts to each other with the urgency of people convinced they've just discovered the secrets of the universe.

I bask in it. In them. Their energy is giddy, golden, infectious. They hang on every word I say, their eyes wide as if I'm Prometheus and have handed them fire. I'm so damn proud of myself and of them I could burst.

I wave as the last cluster of girls drifts away from the market square, their laughter trailing behind them like ribbons. Nessa lingers, shifting from foot to foot, her bangles clinking softly in the quiet.

"Is everything all right, Nessa?"

"You've already taught me more than I dared hope for," she says quickly.

"But…?" I prompt.

She lifts her chin. "But I think I want more than some of the others."

My brows rise. "More?"

"I want to be part of the queens' court," she says, the words tumbling out in a rush. "I can feel I'm meant for it. Perhaps I could even stand where the Player does now. Or make a place of my own beside the queens." Her crystalline blue eyes gleam, already seeing herself on that smoke-wreathed dais. "Can what you're teaching me lead there?"

I draw in a slow breath. "How do the queens choose their court? Tarek told me a little, but it's *different* from anything I'm used to."

Nessa nods. "Oh, yes. Each kingdom within Towerfall is quite different from the next. Here, there are seasons when petitions are heard—solstices, equinoxes. The Player sponsors performers. The guards sponsor those fit to rise within their ranks. The queens themselves sometimes choose from the floor, though rarely. Still…" Her voice tightens, determination lacing every word. "They cannot pass me by if I am exactly what they seek."

She reminds me of me at sixteen—desperate for more, for someone to see me, to choose me. Back then, I believed if I could just be perfect enough, pretty enough, quiet enough, accommodating enough, someone would finally decide I was worth keeping. I wish I had my rose quartz palm stone now, something cool and smooth to press against my heart, to remind me that these roiling feelings clawing their way up are just energy that needs redirecting. That I can alchemize ache into purpose if I just breathe and believe hard enough.

"If I am perfect," she continues, "they will have no choice but to choose me."

Perfect. That cursed word. The one that drove me to crash diets and spending money I didn't have. The word that dangled a carrot in front of me my whole life and left me starving for approval.

"There was a business course I took that called it 'building a pillar,'" I tell her, smoothing confidence over my voice. "With your goal, your pillar would be one bold transformation that no one can ignore. What's your work-in-progress?"

"I've been working with the fire dancers. Not simply twirling torches or juggling flames—that's child's play. I'm learning to take the flame into myself. To eat it." She lifts onto her toes. "If I can swallow fire and breathe it back out for the queens, they'll see I'm not like the rest. They'll see I'm fearless. And fearlessness is surely needed amongst their court."

"Good," I say. "But *great* is a piece that scares you a little. That's when you know it really hits."

Nessa's hands tremble. "Very well," she murmurs more to herself than to me. "Then I shall make it so."

"That's right you will."

Nessa beams, cheeks flushed, before dashing off to catch up to her friends.

Across the square, Declan and Tarek are talking, their laughter low and easy. I brush sand off the cushion I borrowed, tuck it under my arm, and start toward the stall.

Dav's shadow falls over me, and I groan. "I'm putting

it back." I hold out the cushion as evidence as I turn to face him. "I'm not stealing it."

He folds his arms, his thick forearms crossing like stacked logs. "Boldness is admirable. Recklessness is not."

"I didn't tell her to be reckless," I shoot back, clutching the cushion tighter.

"I am aware."

Declan breaks from Tarek, striding toward us. His shoulders are squared, his dark eyes sharp with intent, and something low in my stomach flutters. He's ready to throw a punch. Again. For me.

The thought makes me queasy and hot all at once. It's brutish and gross and infuriating and, Lord help me, so fucking sexy.

Dav doesn't notice Declan, or pretends not to, his gaze pinning me to the spot. "Until your next performance, you will keep to your tent unless escorted."

"Because, despite everything, you still believe I'm a spy?"

His stare is granite. "Because you are a variable."

Tarek lets out a snort that doesn't lighten the tension. "He means you make things happen."

"No," Dav corrects, his eyes never leaving mine. "I mean she makes things *change*."

A chill snakes under my skin despite the desert heat. My instinct is to flinch, but I square my shoulders instead. "I thought this kingdom liked spectacle."

"It does..." Tarek says carefully.

"Until it doesn't." Dav doesn't miss a beat. He turns on his heel and stalks off.

Tarek gives me a quick, apologetic shrug before jogging after him and motioning for us to follow.

“Whatever he said isn’t worth listening to.” Declan bends to pick up Cinder. “He’s pissed he can’t prove we’re spies.”

Fennel noses insistently at my hip. Without thinking, I dig into my pocket and slip him a carrot stub I took from the stall.

“Yeah, thanks.”

But my gaze lingers on Dav’s back, his words hanging in the air like smoke. And where there’s smoke, there’s fire, waiting for the chance to burn everything down.

TWELVE

The sky is a white-hot sheet of sunlight when we finally manage to slip out of our tent without being spotted. It's been five days since we landed in this kingdom. Five days of performing, pretending, and trying not to die. And this is the first time we've been allowed to wander unaccompanied, and by *allowed* and *unaccompanied*, I mean Dav is presumably off terrorizing some other poor soul with his trademark brand of aggressive chaperoning and unwavering eye contact.

"I give us fifteen minutes before he pops out from behind a barrel and makes good on one of his many threats to end you," I say, squinting into the heat shimmer that blurs the path winding through camp.

Declan strolls beside me, hands tucked into the pockets of the harem pants he dug out of the bottom of the trunk back at our tent, radiating an obscene level of unbothered for a man trapped in a desert dimension with zero air-conditioning.

"Don't worry about Dav," he says, bumping his elbow lightly against my arm. "We'll be back before he notices we're gone. Actually, if your plan goes the way we want it to, we'll be out of this world for good."

He scratches at the stubble darkening his jaw, and heat flushes down my spine. My brain, traitorous as ever, supplies a flash of how it would scrape against my cheek, against my thighs, rasping sandpaper over soft skin—

"What's the chance we end up in a different world that isn't home but also isn't this one?" he asks.

"About the same as hitting a bull's-eye in the dark."

Declan frowns.

"I have no idea how we got here, so I don't know how to aim us back home. But I *do* know that the Wheel of Fortune card is our best lead, especially since Fortune hasn't reappeared and your attempts to talk with the queens have gone nowhere. It's the one consistent variable."

"What I'm hearing is that we should take more time. Run an experiment, or five. Otherwise, best case scenario, we spend the rest of our lives dimension hopping."

"This"—I hold up my emergency bag of witchy essentials—"*is* the experiment."

He looks doubtful, which is not the vibe I need.

"We need high energy, positive thinking, maybe even a dash of delusion, if this has any chance of working."

Rounding the next bend, I spot the woman I helped unload the camels with before. She's kneeling in front of an open tent, quick fingers tying together bundles of dried herbs. Her gaze flicks up as we pass.

"Hi again!" I wave and veer toward her before I can talk myself out of it. "Could I ask you another question?"

"You are quite curious." She takes a deep breath as

she winds twine around the thick branches of rosemary. "Ask if you must."

"I can come back if you're busy."

"You're here now." She wipes her palms on her apron and settles back on her heels.

"Thank you." I bend down, lowering my voice. "I'm wondering if you've seen a woman—dark robe, copper threads in her hair. And this part is going to sound strange, but one of her arms looked like it had rubies and red crystals, I don't know, *fused* into it…"

"I do not know this woman," she says flatly.

"Are you sure? She—"

The woman rises swiftly, bundles clutched tight. "Too many questions call forth trouble. Curiosity often marks you as other than you are." She glances over her shoulder, then lowers her voice. "Better to be overlooked than remembered."

Before I can press her, she ducks into her tent, the flap snapping shut behind her.

Declan rejoins me, arching a brow. "She didn't seem too interested in being friends."

"No," I say, unsettled. "She didn't."

Something about what she said scratches an in itch in my brain, a suspicion that's been growing since we arrived. Layers beneath the pageantry, this kingdom is hiding a truth. And I want to be far, far away before it cracks open—because things like this never stay buried. Secrets are like cards in a tarot deck—they can be shuffled to the bottom, far away from the next draw, but sooner or later they will reach the surface.

The strap of my bag bites into my palm as I tighten my grip. I've been chewing this theory to death, tugging threads from every occult book I ever dog-eared, every WitchTok video I let worm into my brain at two a.m. And the truth is, my plan isn't just wild guessing. The wheel is the through line—the only thing that makes sense. If it brought us here, it can send us back.

If this were a story I'd devoured under the covers in my childhood bedroom, I'd scrawl a furious note in the margin about how the heroine should've just trusted herself, how she should've spoken the truth before Act Three forced her hand when her beloved's life was dangling in the balance.

Which means I don't get to hold back now.

"I might not know how to do actual magick, but I've read enough books about it to have some idea where to start," I finally say as we resume our trek and pass a woman in full gold face paint leading a camel draped in a silk cape. The camel looks majestic. The woman looks exhausted. "I understand tarot, and this is basically tarot on steroids. In tarot, and here in Towerfall, wands is the fire suit. It's all about willpower and drive and creative potential, which seems to be the entire foundation of this glittering desert circus we've landed in.

"Fire as an element equals energy, passion, volatility. A spark that becomes a blaze that becomes, apparently, mandatory community theater." I gesture toward a shirtless man twirling a flaming hoop over his head.

"And you think that plus your bag of tricks gets us home?"

"I think I understand the concept that got us here. Although, maybe not exactly *how* it happened."

"Ah, yes, very reassuring. Every great escape plan starts with *I understand the concept*."

"It does when you're working with elemental theory and archetypal symbolism."

He lifts a brow.

"I've created a theory—no, scratch that—it's the only logical explanation based on observable tarot phenomena and energetic principles."

"Tarot phenomena," he repeats.

"You don't have to say it like that."

"Like what?"

I stop walking and stare up at him. "You're patronizing me."

"No, I'm not. I—" He scrubs a hand over his jaw, frustration edging his voice. "I'm not patronizing you, Amanda. I'm trying to—God, I don't know—engage? Tease? Flirt, maybe? Except every time I open my mouth, you take it as an insult."

"When were you flirting?"

He groans. "I don't know how to do this, okay? When it comes to talking to you, I'm shit. I keep putting my foot in my mouth. It's that way with pretty much everyone here except Tarek, which… I'm not sure if that's comforting or terrifying. Fuck, I almost got us killed because, since the moment I met you in person, I've been off my game."

I open my mouth to respond, but he continues.

"I'm better at being a mirror than a window," he mutters.

I wrinkle my nose. "I don't think that's the saying."

Declan throws his hands up, pacing a step ahead before wheeling back to face me. "I am great at projecting what people want to see. That's what makes me so good at my job—so good that it's become my whole fucking life."

He shakes his head and drags on hand down the back of his neck. "And my parents, especially my dad, they expect—no, they *demand*—a certain level of success."

He exhales sharply, gaze fixed somewhere over my shoulder, like eye contact might break whatever dam he's barely holding together.

"I can talk down hostile investors, restructure eight-figure portfolios, and negotiate buyouts with billionaires in boat shoes..." His voice cracks on a bitter laugh. "But when it comes to a normal conversation with someone I actually—" He cuts himself off, the thought hanging unsaid between us. His fists curl and uncurl restlessly at his sides. "I say the wrong thing, you take it the wrong way, and then I fall into CEO-speak or turn into a fucking Chad as a defense mechanism.

"And yes," he adds, "I know it's annoying. For both of us."

I study him in the golden light of the sun. "I thought you were just being a dick. Waiting for everything to sort itself out the way it always has for you."

He lets out another short, humorless laugh. "That's not how my life has gone."

He stares out at the sea of glossy scarlet and tangerine tents, jaw pulsing as he clenches and unclenches his teeth like he's weighing whether to bother saying the rest aloud.

"When you're in full-on save-the-day mode, I don't know where I fit. I've tried everything—talking to the locals, digging for information about Fortune, even finding someone who might get us in front of the queens. Nothing works. I hit a wall at every turn, and I don't know how to push past it."

His shoulders sink, the fight draining out of him in a single reluctant breath.

"I can't remember the last time anyone tried to save me from anything. Ever." He looks down at his hands, flexes them once like they might hold an answer, then lets them fall uselessly to his sides. "And I'll admit, there's a part of me that doesn't know what to do with that. A part that doesn't know how to exist if I'm not the one driving forward. It's…messing with my pride."

Words bottleneck in my throat, and my thoughts swim in a disorienting loop. Declan has been nothing but composed and infuriatingly calm since the second we landed in this tarot-themed kingdom. But now, with the sun baking us in his admissions, and his voice rough around the edges, he looks less like the untouchable CEO who steamrolls boardrooms and more like…a man. A man who doesn't have all the answers, who doesn't always know what to do, who's just as scared and lost as I am.

My mouth goes dry, and I'm all too aware of how close we're standing. How his dark hair curls slightly where it's damp with sweat. How the sun makes his eyes look almost amber around the edges. How I could maybe fall for him—the *real* him—if I let myself.

Declan drags a hand through his hair, leaving one dark strand tumbling across his forehead. It clings stubbornly to the sweat beading at his temple. I reach up, brush it back, my fingers lingering against the heat of his skin.

"You can let it go. I'll be your knight in shining armor."

His jaw flexes, then his calm facade slips. His eyes lock on mine, and the shift there guts me. "That's not how this is supposed to work," he says, voice low, rough. "I'm the one who's supposed to protect you."

"I think we've both seen how well that's gone," I tease gently, but my heart squeezes.

I pull back, and he catches my hand as it falls away. He lifts it and presses a kiss to the pad of my thumb. The warmth of his mouth lingers, and when he draws in a breath against my skin, I'm dizzy.

"You don't know what that means to me," he murmurs against my fingers.

But I think I do. Because the ache in my chest is reckless and unguarded and reaching out to him.

A shadow wheels over us. A bird circles high, its wings cutting feathery brown pinwheels into the sky. Declan looks up and winces, rolling his neck.

"Everything okay?" I ask, tucking my hand against my stomach, holding his warmth for as long as I can.

"Thirty-five is too old to be sleeping on the ground." He rolls his shoulders until the joints pop. The motion makes him wince, pain flickering across his face before he tries to smooth it over with nonchalance. "Tarek took me to see the healer, which sounded promising until she gave me honey drops, a clay jar of balm, and told me to lie on a piece of charred wood to draw out the bad spirits."

I choke on a laugh and, before I can stop myself, loop my arm through his as we continue walking. His body is solid and warm beside me, the kind of anchor I've always wanted.

"I think I have something that might actually help."

"Oh yeah?" He waggles his brows. "Is it in your bag of tricks?"

"Even better." I give him a playful shove. "You can sleep in the bed."

His arm stiffens against mine.

Ever since that first night when getting into the same bed would've been a fun but disastrous idea, he's made a point of bedding down on the floor like it's some kind of moral duty. And every night since, I've caught myself wondering what it would be like to tell him not to.

"Are you sure?"

"I'm sure," I say, not sure at all.

I feel his gaze on me, the slow curve of a grin tugging at his mouth. It's the kind of look that would melt me on the spot if I let it. Which is exactly why I don't look up. Because if I do, I'm not sure I'll remember why keeping my distance ever felt like the smart decision.

THIRTEEN

We pass the final row of tents at the outer edge of the kingdom's caravan where the desert unrolls in an endless carpet of ecru dunes stacked like waves on a sunburned sea. Heat rises in silken sheets, warping the horizon until sand and sky bleed together in glistening golds.

Declan halts beside me, hands on his hips, eyes scanning the landscape. "That's a lot of nothing," he mutters.

"Not nothing." I swallow, throat dry. "This is where Fortune disappeared. Where the world unfroze. There has to be something out here I'm meant to find. A spark of magick I'm supposed to channel."

If I can just figure out how.

Hot sand bites through the thin fabric of my dress as I kneel and shrug off my purse. Declan leans over my shoulder, his shadow falling across my hands.

"Need anything from your knight-in-training slash extremely supportive sidekick?" he asks, giving my shoulder a nudge.

Despite the heat and the pressure I've put on myself and the fact that I'm kneeling in a desert about to attempt fire magick for the very first time, my lips quirk into a grin. "Think happy thoughts."

"Noted. Less brooding, more believing. It'll mess with your energy if I stand here cataloging how this could go sideways." He sobers a beat. "For what it's worth, I do believe in you. And in this."

"Then here's hoping the portal opens gently and we can walk through instead of being dropped from the sky."

"As long as we don't land in the Hudson, I'm flexible." He taps two fingers to the citrine in my palm, giving it a tiny blessing, then steps back to allow me space.

I open my purse and pull out what I packed this morning: a small bag of crushed cinnamon bark I bartered for at the market from a spice seller in a bejeweled vest in exchange for an eighty-dollar impulse buy highlighter brush; the chunk of raw citrine I keep in my bag next to the other crystals I use for emotional stability; and a single strand of red silk thread torn from the hem of our bedsheets. Symbols of fire, clarity, and intention—anchors to help me draw down whatever magick Towerfall and the Wheel of Fortune are willing to lend, to shape it, to guide it, and maybe, just maybe, to get us home.

From the purse's depths, the Wheel of Fortune pulses against my fingertips. A slow, steady throb. A heartbeat that's not my own.

I slide my fingers along the worn edges, pulse hammering, anticipation building in my chest. The card hums against my skin, heat gathering. It's alive, expectant.

I draw it out.

My breath stalls in my lungs.

It's blank.

The tarot card is blank.

The wheel, the figures, the shifting spokes—they're gone. Wiped clean. It's just a sheet of glossy cardstock catching the sun, smeared with my fingerprints.

"What the—" The words rasp, dry and cracked, sticking to the back of my throat.

Panic spikes. I'm dizzy, ribs locked tight around my lungs. Heat flashes down my arms, then cold, leaving my fingers trembling around the useless slab of cardstock.

This was my proof, my tether. This was the one thing in this world I could hold on to. The one thing that could get us home.

And now it's nothing.

My stomach lurches, hollow and heavy at once.

Breathe.

I squeeze my eyes shut, drag air into my lungs until it hurts, and force it out slowly.

Maybe blank isn't empty. Maybe it's a door.

The thought steadies me, calms the frantic flutter in my chest. I've read enough books about the tarot to know that the cards speak in riddles, not direct answers. Maybe whatever magick dragged me here isn't finished yet. Maybe the wheel is still turning, waiting for me to remember what Fortune said I've forgotten.

I press my thumb against the slick white face of the card.

"I hear you," I whisper. "I'm listening. But you have to give me a little more."

I glance over my shoulder, hoping Declan didn't notice the stampede of dread that just barreled through me. He gives me two very enthusiastic thumbs up.

I respond with a crooked smile and turn back to the spell that is not going to plan.

I close my eyes. Let the sand warm my shins. Let cinnamon sting my senses. Let the dry air catch in my lungs.

"I'm not asking for much," I whisper to the fire that's claimed dominion over this realm. "Just a nudge. A flicker. A sign."

I've never cast a spell before. I've never believed in this type of magick enough to try. But, ever since I've been here, things have been different. There's real magick here. At times, I can feel it smoldering in my chest. This world is not mine. Towerfall is truly magickal.

I draw a breath, open my eyes, and blend my writing skills with what I've learned about spellcasting.

"Fire that cleanses, fire that knows…"

Slowly, I wind the red silk thread around the chunk of citrine, knotting it tight, anchoring the energy like muscle to bone.

"Spark the truth this desert shows."

I press the stone into the sand.

"Find the path—the place to start."

I empty the cinnamon into my palm, inhale its spicy heat, then draw a circle around the stone.

"Reveal the way…" I lower my hand, pressing it to the stone. "Send it straight to my heart."

The sand beneath my palm trembles. Then buckles. The ring of cinnamon spits and flares, a lit fuse racing around my hand. The red thread writhes as it lengthens, slithering out from the citrine to coil around my fingers. The stone pulses, its glow swelling until it burns like a miniature sun. Jagged seams of light crack through the sand, splitting outward in lightning-fast veins.

I try to yank my hand back, but the thread has already tightened, binding me to the stone. The citrine is locked fast in the sand, immovable no matter how hard I tug.

"Okay," I breathe, my muscles tensing. My voice comes out high, panicked. "Okay, I'm listening. What do you want me to know?"

The sand beneath me shudders, then softens. Heat rises in waves. The surface bubbles, simmers, then gives way.

"Declan!" My scream rips out as the sand grabs my thighs, swallowing my legs.

The thread surges higher, twisting up my arm, tightening around my wrist, and with a violent yank it drags my hand beneath the surface.

He's there in a heartbeat, grabbing my arms just as I sink deeper, sand gurgling around my waist. "Can you stand?"

I try to kick my legs, to wiggle free, but every movement drags me deeper and tightens the thread's grip around my arm. "This isn't normal quicksand, Declan. This is magick murder sand! Do something!"

He plants his feet in the soft slope around the sudden pool of quicksand and crouches low. He leans in and slides his arms under mine like we're about to hug. "Stop thrashing," he grunts. "You're making it worse."

"Shut up and pull!"

His arms tighten around me, trying to keep me from sinking deeper, from going under. Despite Declan's best efforts, I continue to sink deeper. Liquid sand sloshes around my chest like wet cement.

"While I *love* that the magick is finally trying to communicate with me," I gasp, sand sucking at my ribs, "we are *not* on the same page right now! Use your words and *let me fucking go*!"

The dune convulses. With a violent lurch, Declan yanks me free. We tumble backward, momentum sending us crashing through a nearby tent.

The door explodes, splinters of wood spinning as we slam through. Dust billows. We hit cool stone in a heap of limbs and grit and frantic breathing.

Beneath me, Declan groans, arms still cinched around my waist. "Well," he pants, "that escalated quickly."

"You think?" I wheeze.

His mouth tilts into that barely there smirk I'm starting to recognize as a hazard to my mental health. "For the record, I not only saved you, but I managed to save your purse."

He tilts his chin in the direction of my sand-crusted purse. I try to sit up, but his arms stay very firmly around my waist, his thumbs tracing idle circles along my sides. One hand slides higher, heat trailing over my waist, the ridge of my ribs, the slope of my shoulder and arm resting against his chest. He sweeps a line of grit from my jaw, then brushes sand from my temple.

"You've got a little…" His voice is quiet as he continues to clean the sand from my cheek. "Everywhere."

"I'm a mess," I mumble, cheeks blazing for reasons unrelated to the desert heat.

His hand lingers, thumb ghosting the curve of my mouth. "No," he whispers. "Not a mess." His gaze drops, settles on my mouth, and stays there—heavy, hungry, pulling the air from my lungs.

My throat tightens. I swallow, and without thinking, I flick my tongue across my lips.

Declan's body goes rigid beneath me. His chest rises sharply against mine, breath catching in his chest.

I hold the moment, aware of every racing pulse in my body. Then I decide. Slowly, deliberately, I drag my tongue over my lower lip.

His fingers flex at my waist, beneath my jaw, gripping me tighter. A groan escapes him. The vibration rumbles through his chest into mine like we're strung together.

My hands twitch on his thick shoulders, desperate to move. To chart the hard lines hidden under his soaked shirt, to memorize the muscle, the heat, the feel of him.

His palm cups my cheek, callused and hot, thumb glossing over my damp lips. My world funnels down to his touch. His breath. The thick, sparking current tethering us closer with every heartbeat.

My hips shift and suddenly I feel him. All of him. The hard press of his body against mine, sliding into place so easily, so perfectly it steals my breath. My skirt has ridden high, bunched at my waist, and the red silk panties tied at my hips may as well not exist. Every rigid line, every stuttered inhale, every inch of aching want between us burns through the thin barrier.

When his eyes finally lift from my mouth, they carry a storm—dark, unguarded, flashing with a question I don't know how to answer.

His fingers slip into my hair, threading gently at first, then firmer, guiding me down. The space between us collapses into a single suspended heartbeat. The pause—the breathless sliver right before—feels impossibly intimate, more than any kiss I've ever had.

I want to fall into it.

I want to run from it.

I want to burn alive inside it.

The realization sears through me, a match dropped

into oil. I shiver, and my thighs tighten around him as goosebumps race down my arms.

A cool breeze ghosts the sweat at my nape, and I shiver again.

Wait. Cool breeze? Ten minutes ago, the sun was set to broil, and now the space around us is cold as steel.

My head snaps up. "Declan."

"Yeah?" His voice is thick, gravelly, lost in the moment.

"Do you feel that?"

"Oh yeah." His gaze dips to my mouth again. His hand flexes at my waist as he starts to lift up, eyelids lowering.

"The air, Declan." The words tumble out. "It's cold."

I scramble off him, legs shaky, pulse still galloping.

We're not in a silk tent like the others that make up this firelit kingdom. We're inside four stone walls and the shattered remains of a door—not a flap of fabric but a wooden door.

"It's cold." I rub warmth into my skin, breath fogging faintly in the quiet, subterranean chill.

Dust hangs in the air, turning to gold flecks in the soft flicker of torchlight. Shelves line the walls, bowing beneath the weight of ancient scrolls and brittle, yellowed pages. A heavy trunk squats in the center of the room, brass edges scorched, leather straps curled with age. Next to it, a narrow desk lists under documents and wax-sealed envelopes.

Declan brushes sand from his pants, his narrowed gaze sweeping the room like he's scanning for other exits. Or threats. "What is this place?"

I turn in a slow circle, attention catching on the soot-streaked torches smoldering in their brackets, strange runes carved into the stone walls, piles of parchment scattered across the floor as if someone left in a hurry. This doesn't feel random. It's a place someone wanted hidden.

"Fortune wasn't leading me out there," I say slowly, tasting the truth of it as I speak. "She was leading me here."

Pressure tightens beneath my sternum, a string pulled taut. A quiet, insistent tug.

I drift forward, feet carrying me toward the trunk like it's magnetized and I'm nothing but a scatter of iron filings. The closer I get, the stronger the pull—the knowing in my bones that I'm meant to be here. Fortune didn't abandon me to the sand. She pointed me toward this. Toward answers.

"There's a lot in here," Declan says behind me. "What is it she wants you find?"

I hear him, but it's distant, muffled, like his voice is coming from underwater. The rest of the room blurs at the edges as I wade through it to the trunk.

And then I hear it.

No, not hear. *Feel.*

The faintest tick of unseen gears. A mechanical beat that rises from the earth.

Click.

Click.

Click.

A slow, certain progression.

The wheel is turning.

Declan is talking again. I think he's saying my name, but the world is thick and syrupy around me. My body moves without my direction, drawn forward in a steady, inevitable glide. Spellbound, I kneel in front of it.

The trunk is massive, its dark wood swollen and warped with age, banded in copper that glows dully in the dim light. Intricate flame etchings curl along the edges. At the center of the lid, a copper wheel is mounted and quartered, each wedge branded with an elemental rune.

"Amanda." Declan's voice cracks through the spell like a whip.

I blink, shoulders jerking, hands frozen above the trunk. Awareness slams back into me all at once. My vision spins before it steadies, the pull receding just enough to let me fully come to inside my body.

Declan crouches beside me, worry furrowing his brow. "Where did you go? I was talking to you, and it was like you couldn't even hear me."

I shake my head and rub my temples. "I don't know. This trunk—"

"You want to go back to the tent? See the healer?"

A hollow laugh breaks out of me. "A plank of burnt wood isn't going to fix whatever's going on here. I need to open it."

His jaw ticks. "Then take a second. Let me try first."

He curls his fingers under the edge of the lid, muscles in his forearms flexing, shoulders braced. "I have a feeling this is going to get weirder."

The hum inside me swells, vibrating against my ribs. And over it, a voice—clear, crisp, undeniably Fortune's:

He can't open that.

I draw in a breath. "You won't be able to open it."

He gives me a look. "Why not?"

I shrug. "It's not meant for you."

Declan grunts and strains anyway, teeth bared, but the lid doesn't so much as creak. Finally, he exhales and leans back, shaking his head. "I defer to you, oh wise Story Witch."

I roll my eyes, but a smile slips free anyway. It's getting harder to pretend he's irritating. Harder to pretend I don't like the way he looks at me when he steps back, like he actually trusts me with this. Harder to forget that real people, real relationships, are messy, complicated, doomed to fail no matter how many affirmations I arm myself with.

I step forward. The copper wheel glints, the scorched runes shifting under my gaze. A prickle rides my spine. My fingers tremble as I lift my hand and hover it above the wheel.

The second I do, the air thickens. Heat and static press in. The room itself seems to lean toward me, waiting.

A whisper of *yes*, Fortune's whisper, rises from the center of my being and fills me with knowing. It's a knowing that says I was always meant to find this place. To land in Towerfall. To change.

I splay my fingers wider, draw a breath deeper.

"I think you were right." My voice is unsteady as I glance up at Declan. "This is going to get way weirder."

FOURTEEN

I run my fingers over each of the four runes in the copper wheel: water, earth, air, fire. The brands drink in the warmth of my palm and give it back in a steady, glowing pulse that stirs an ancient ache deep in my chest. It hums beneath my skin and welcomes me with a slow build of heat.

I glance over my shoulder. Declan's watching, arms crossed, gaze sharpened by caution and something else. Something protective. Like he's ready to drag me out of danger again, whether I ask him to or not.

"When we first landed in this kingdom," I say, voice quiet but steady, "you said I was scared."

He glances down at his borrowed sandals. "I said a lot of things."

"True. But you weren't wrong about that one." My pulse echoes in my ears, in my chest, in the pit of my stomach. "I've been scared this whole time."

He lifts his chin, those dark eyes pouring fire into mine. "So have I."

A crooked smile tugs at my mouth. "We don't have to be afraid of this."

His brows draw together, the smallest flicker of uncertainty flashing across his face. "What do you mean?"

I wish I could tell him. I'm not completely sure myself. But this feels right. For the first time in months—maybe years—I feel aligned. I'm no longer simply surviving. I'm beginning to find my place.

"You'll see." I turn back to the trunk. "We both will."

I straighten my spine and press my hand flat against the symbol of fire. The rune beneath my palm ignites in a soft flare of yellow light. The wheel turns slowly, *click*, *click*, *click*, each quadrant shifting with the same mechanical beat from earlier. The seam along the lid glows, a brilliant thread of fire racing around the edge.

I flinch as the heat kisses my wrist, but I don't pull away.

Click.

The wheel unlocks. The trunk exhales. A warm rush of air spills out, brushing over my face like a memory scented with charred parchment, melted wax, and the faintest trace of cinnamon.

My hand falls away, fingers trembling as the lid creaks open.

Wood strains, copper groans, and then there's light. Soft and smoldering, it slips from the trunk in ribbons of faint gold, candlelight filtered through smoke.

Inside, the trunk is packed with scrolls. They've been clawed through, torn, rewritten, crossed out, reimagined. The ink is blurred in places. Many are singed, smudged with charcoal, their edges blackened and fragile. Wax-sealed fragments are strewn between the stacks like dried blood. Burned scraps litter the pile, twitching as the cool air rushes to greet them.

I lean closer. The tug in my chest pulses. Fortune's quiet *yes* ripples through my mind.

Carefully, I lift one. The parchment is brittle, flaking beneath my fingers. My gaze snags on a phrase slashed through so hard the page buckled:

Speak from the soul

Below it, scrawled in darker ink:

Add fire burst on climactic line.

Another note:

Increase theatricality. Reduce pauses. No weeping!

I stare at the page, throat tight.

Declan crouches beside me, bracing one hand on his knee. He picks up another fragment, brows pinched. "Are these scripts?"

"Spells." I hold up a half-burned page, the ink faded but legible. The parchment is soft in my hands. Ash clings to the edges. "It's written in dual voices."

"Like a duet?"

The tug in my chest sharpens. *Say it.* Fortune's whisper presses in from all sides. *Speak it out loud.*

My lips part, and the moment the first syllable leaves my mouth, something inside me clicks into place.

By fire's command, let falsehood turn to ash;
Speak not for praise, but that thy soul be seen.

Declan shifts closer, his warmth brushing against my side. Without hesitation, he picks up the next stanza.

Let silence break 'neath truths too long concealed,
Let shadowed bonds be burned where lies have been.
No spark for show, nor blaze for fleeting cheer,
But light the dark with that which thou dost fear.

The torch flames stretch taller, orange spines unraveling like ribbons against the ceiling. Shadows convulse across the walls like startled birds. Sweat slicks my forehead, and my breath hitches from the way his dark eyes flick to me between lines, like he's binding himself to me as much as to the spell.

I continue the next verse, though my throat feels dry.

Now let the flame of candor be set free,
And purge the mask that pride would bid thee wear.

Declan's gaze lingers on me as he answers, his lips curving around each word.

Seek not for love, nor fleeting vanity,
But bare thy soul, and speak what lieth there.

The room glows bright, every surface bathed in gold. The parchment in my hands curls, its edges smoking softly but holding. Ash coats my tongue. Magick thrums through the air, through us, and the sound of his voice beside me makes my chest ache.

Together, our voices blend into one.

When fire meets fire, the bond shall be revealed:
Two hearts made bare, in burning truth, are sealed.

The torches roar to life, flames flaring in unison. Light swells, its brilliance holding for a breathless moment before collapsing back into shadowy silence.

Heat stings my fingers, and I drop the parchment. It flutters back into the trunk, edges glowing faintly. My pulse is an uneven gallop in my chest. My breaths come too fast, too shallow. Sweat slides down my temple, and I swipe it away with a shaking hand. My whole body buzzes with heat and magick and the echo of his voice twined together with mine.

Declan cuts gently through the hush. "I wouldn't call that weird."

I look at him. My knees feel weak, the floor unsteady beneath me.

"No?" I breathe. He isn't afraid. He isn't dismissive. He isn't running. He's here, fully present, grounded, watching me like I'm not someone to control or fix, but someone to be in awe of. To follow. To believe in. "Then what would you call it?"

Declan's gaze drags slowly across my face, catching on the shape of my mouth. "Powerful."

My skin tingles with awareness. Heat coils low and hot, sending a pulse between my legs that make my thighs clench.

"I don't know where this is going." I search his eyes.

"What it will lead to." The words are bigger than the spell. I'm not just speaking of magick, and we both know it.

"Amanda…" His fingers brush my temple, sliding through my hair with the softest touch before tucking it behind my ear. "I was ready to follow you into quicksand."

I want to kiss him so badly it hurts. So badly it lives hot beneath my skin like a spark waiting to catch.

His gaze is searing, starving. He looks at me like he could devour me with nothing but his eyes, like if I lean in he'll be on me—hands in my hair, mouth on my throat, burning me from the inside out.

And I'd let him.

Gladly.

Desperately.

I want his hands fisted in my dress, his tongue in my mouth. I want to taste the tension, swallow the groan I know he's holding back. I want to grind against every hard inch of him until there's nothing left between us but heat and skin and breathless want.

I can taste the kiss before it happens. I can feel it ghosting over my lips, making everything inside me clench and ache and beg.

I sway forward.

Just a little.

Just enough—

"I'm only saying"—Tarek's voice comes from somewhere outside the room—"if I had a sword like that, I wouldn't name it *Marshmallow*."

Declan and I jolt apart like we've been struck by lightning.

A second voice responds, deeper and exasperated, unmistakably Dav. "I have not named my sword *Marshmallow*, Tarek. It's *Marrowshard*. It is symbolic."

"Huh, well," Tarek says, footsteps drawing nearer. "It still sounds like something you'd toast over a fire."

Declan drops his head on my shoulder and lets out a strangled groan.

My body feels fluttery, lips tingling, stomach flipping, heart swelling, and I slap a hand over my mouth to muffle the laugh that bubbles out.

In the distance, the drums start to pound, sounding the alarm for the nightly performances.

With a sigh, Declan straightens and drags both hands through his hair. "We need to move."

I turn back to the trunk one last time and close the lid. The copper wheel spins once and locks with a soft, satisfied hiss.

"I still have to coat you in that bronzer the juggler gave us."

His mouth twitches. "Don't pretend like you're not looking forward to it."

I am. Maybe too much.

We wait until Dav and Tarek pass by this final row of tents on the edge of camp before slipping through the silk curtain. Declan props what's left of the shattered door back into its frame and pulls the silks into place until the tent looks like all the others lining the dunes. Together, we step into the shimmer and heat of the Kingdom of Wands—our bodies still humming with magick, our lips still irritatingly, inconveniently unkissed, and another performance looming.

Amanda Ward, Story Witch. Declan Thorne, Brooding

Assistant. Once more returning to the stage for another night of terrible acting, questionable scripts, and the ever-present hope we don't get burned alive.

But something's shifted. And I don't know if it's in the magick…

Or in me.

FIFTEEN

The sun is barely up when the commotion outside the tent pulls me from a dream so sweet I try to fall back into it—something about warmth, safety, a hand tracing lazy circles over my hip.

I blink through the disorienting moment between asleep and awake to realize I'm staring at the back of Declan's head. His dark hair curls slightly at the nape of his neck, mussed from sleep. The sheet is settled across his waist, revealing his naked back. At some point in the night, I must've reached for him, because my arm is draped over him, my hand pinned to his chest beneath his.

He's heavy and warm and solid. My fingers twitch, brushing through the coarse hair on his chest, and I breathe him in—salt, smoke, and spice. I want to nuzzle closer, to stay like this a little longer, to pretend the day hasn't already begun.

"Morning," he murmurs, voice rough with sleep.

"Hi," I manage, which comes out more like a squeak than an actual word.

He rolls over to face me, and suddenly we're eye to eye, the space between us small enough that I can feel the heat of his breath against my lips.

He shifts closer, his voice a lazy murmur. "You talk in your sleep, you know."

My stomach flips. "What did I say?"

"Something about a donkey parade."

I laugh and the sound catches between us. "Fennel's infiltrated my subconscious."

Morning light spills across the sheets from the narrow crack between the door flaps, cutting a bright stripe over the tangled linens. The beam slides across my arm, then over the bare lines of Declan's chest where my hand still rests. His heart beats steadily beneath my palm, grounding and dizzying all at once.

His fingers close gently around mine, and he brings my hand to his mouth. His lips brush my knuckles as he murmurs, "Today might be the day."

The day I stop pretending not to want him. The day I finally tear down the wall between us.

"The day for what?" I ask, voice barely a whisper.

He smiles against my skin. "The day we get home."

The words hit like cold water. I let my thoughts drift somewhere softer, somewhere dangerous and far from the only things that matter: finding Fortune, getting us back before this place or my feelings swallow me whole.

I pull my hand back and push myself up, swinging my legs over the side of the bed.

"Right." I force the words past the lump in my throat. "And we can't do that from bed."

I move to the trunk and pull out another dress similar to all the others, light and silky and long. Declan stays in bed, watching me with that unreadable look that feels like it sees too much.

When we're both dressed and braced to face the day, we push through the tent flaps and step into the sunlit bustle beyond.

The air is thick with the smell of roasting dates and spiced lamb. Fennel presses close to my side, his fur brushing my knees as we weave through the crowd with Declan and his "queen," Cinder resting in his arms.

"What's all this for?" I ask, glancing at the flurry of movement around us. Dancers practice synchronized steps in the sand, acrobats tumble through hoops soon to be set aflame, and young women sit alongside a newly constructed dais stringing together garlands of marigolds.

Cinder hisses and jumps from Declan's hold as he stumbles back, narrowly avoiding two men hauling a massive, gilded throne draped in ribbons.

"Tarek was telling me about this. Damn, what did he call it?" Declan rubs a hand through the scruff on his jaw. "The Festival of the First Flame. Something about celebrating the monarchy." He shrugs. "We were about to go onstage. I wasn't listening all that well."

Something about the pageantry makes my stomach knot. The perfect rows of offerings lining the raised platform. The way groups rehearse chants word for word. The rigid smiles stretched across people's faces. It looks less like joy and more like a rally I once saw in a documentary—flags waving, speeches roaring, everyone pretending to be grateful because the cost of doubt was too high.

It isn't joy. It's control woven through the air like invisible thread.

"It doesn't look very celebratory," I mumble, and my lip curls before I can stop it.

"Careful," a voice murmurs behind me.

I turn to find a boy no older than Nessa carrying a basket of fig tarts. His bright green eyes flick from my face to the dais. "Best not wear such a look," he warns. "Eyes are quick to notice, mouths quicker still to speak."

Heat spikes across my cheeks. "I wasn't—"

"You were." He nods to the basket and lifts it up between us. "Take one. If your mouth is full, no one may claim you forgot your lines."

I take a tart, sugar sticking to my fingers, and the boy slips away into the crowd as quietly as he appeared.

Declan drifts closer. "Making another friend?"

"Making sure I don't get us executed," I mutter, biting into the tart. It tastes like ash under all that sugar.

Tarek barrels up behind us and seizes Declan's shoulders with both hands. "Flaming arrows!" he booms, shaking him. "First to strike the bull's-eye shall be declared victor and supplied with mead for the whole of the four-day festival! What nobler tribute could there be to the Great Families who delivered us from lawlessness?"

Declan's gaze cuts toward the practice area where guards and others taking a break from setting up the festivities dip arrowheads into open flames then loose them at straw targets painted with red and black rings. Fire streaks across the air before thunking into hay, sparks and smoke spiraling upward.

He lifts a brow. "Is there a climbing option? I was never good at archery."

"Come! You will enjoy it." Tarek claps him on the back. "Almost as much as I shall enjoy the endless supply of mead."

Before Declan can protest further, Tarek drags him toward the targets. Cinder bolts in the opposite direction, wisely uninterested in flaming arrows, and Fennel trots after her.

I spot Nessa in the crowd and call out to her. She hurries over, saffron skirts swirling, cheeks flushed, and presses a basket into my arms.

"How pleased I am to see you. You must help with the shrine," she insists, nodding toward the raised dais swathed in garlands. "The queens and the ancestors of the Great Families must be honored before sunset, and we are already behind because *someone*"—her glare slices toward Celine, who yawns and flicks a speck of sand from her dress—"did not harvest the sunflowers. And with no camels left to fetch them from the Everspring we are forced to make do without a symbol of loyalty and devotion."

"Lavender and rosemary," I suggest, peering into the basket of marigold and daisy garlands.

Her blue eyes brighten. "By the gods, yes! You are brilliant."

She links her arm through mine and sweeps me into the shrine's preparations.

The dais brims with offerings: copper basins filled with water where chrysanthemums float beside flickering tea lights, bowls of figs stacked like pyramids, garlands wound around the wooden posts until they gleam gold and white and green. Women sit cross-legged in the sand, weaving crowns of dried flowers from two great mounds spilled onto the ground, stacking them into precarious towers that sway in the breeze.

I kneel beside Nessa as we untangle a stubborn garland from the basket. "How's your fire eating coming?"

"The Player says my flame control is stronger than most apprentices." She grins. "And when I sang at our last rehearsal, she noted how my voice carries even over the drums."

"You're a singer?"

"Since I was small," she admits, tugging the garland free with a triumphant nod. "My first audience were our goats. Now I sing for the queens."

A ripple of unease stirs in my gut. "Won't spitting fire damage your voice?"

Nessa shrugs, careless as only a sixteen-year-old can be. "What is a little discomfort to destiny? Besides, I can't dwell on what hasn't happened. I must do as you do and think positively."

Dav's warning rings in my head—reckless advice, dangerous encouragement. I almost tell her to slow down, to guard herself with more than words and thoughts. But the sparkle in her eyes stops me. This is what she wants. Who am I to strip it away?

"You'll shine brighter than anyone out there," I say instead, stringing the garland around a post.

Her smile widens, drinking in the words like sunlight. But my own chest feels oddly hollow, the affirmation echoing back at me like lines from a script.

"When will you hold another class?" Nessa asks eagerly.

A flash of white fur blurs past.

"Fennel!" I shriek as the donkey barrels straight through the towers of flower crowns, a bundle clamped between his teeth. Petals scatter, trailing behind him as he plows past the dancers.

A woman sprints after him, skirts flying, arms flailing, shrieking curses that only make him tuck his ears back and run faster.

"Fennel!" I call again, and he skids to a halt, nostrils flaring, eyes bright. "Fennel, wait! Stay right there."

With him stopped, the woman makes up ground and shouts, "Damn donkey!"

His ears flick back, his muscles tense.

"Don't you dare," I warn.

He bolts. The crowns dangle from his mouth like he's just been named prom queen.

Cinder streaks after him and leaps onto his back, claws dug in like she's riding into battle. Together, they break through the gathering crowd, sand scattering up from his hooves.

"Shit." I drop the garland and sprint after him. "A little help?" I shout as I bolt past Declan and Tarek.

Declan abandons his flaming arrows with a muttered curse, cutting across the square at full speed.

We fall into a rhythm as we attempt to corral the donkey and cat team. He dodges left, I dart right. He cuts Fennel off near the troupe of acrobats, sending them stumbling out of the way. I reach for the crowns as the little menace swerves.

The crowd claps, cheers, laughs—our donkey/cat rodeo turned into prime-time entertainment.

"Got him!" Declan lunges, catching Fennel's flank.

The donkey bucks hard, nearly unseating Cinder. Declan dodges Fennel's hooves, and I grab his arm to steady him, the momentum spinning us together, chest to chest. We're tangled together, trying to reach around each other to grab a piece of the four-legged trouble-makers. Fennel brays, and Cinder's lemon-yellow eyes go wide as he barrels straight between us. We jump apart as he zooms past, narrowly missing our shins.

We chase the pair in a loop around the festival grounds, dodging onlookers, nearly colliding with a spit of lamb, finally boxing them in against the shrine. Cinder, sensing the end of the chase, abandons ship with a regal leap onto the dais and settles in among the offerings.

Fennel jerks left at the last second, nearly bowling Declan over, but Declan plants his feet and clamps one muscled arm around the donkey's neck. Then, in a move that makes the entire crowd howl, he swings a leg over and ends up straddling the miniature beast.

I dive for the prize, prying the soggy crowns from Fennel's stubborn jaws while Declan hangs on for dear life. Petals fly. Fennel brays. My fingers slide against slobbery teeth, then snag in the woven flowers, and finally the crowns tear free.

The crowd erupts into applause.

Declan straightens, chest heaving, dried flower bits clinging to his dark hair while I wipe sweat and grime from my cheek with the back of my hand. We exchange a glance, shrug, join hands, and take a bow.

Fennel exhales in great gusts, his sides shuddering, nostrils flaring like bellows. He sidles up to me, breath hot against my thigh, and drags his damp nose down my leg.

"Unbelievable," I mutter, petting his soft ears. He snorts, then trots off to a patch of shade and drops like a stone. Within seconds, he's out cold.

The crowd disperses in ripples of laughter, and from

across the grounds Tarek keeps clapping, grinning like a man who's already had too much festival mead. He strides toward us, calling, "Look at you two, stealing the people's hearts before the hour of spectacle! At this rate, they'll be tossing flowers at your feet instead of the queens."

I try to scrub the donkey slobber off the crowns, but the woman who chased Fennel storms up and snatches them from my hands, spitting curses under her breath.

"Sorry!" I call after her, though why I feel responsible for the braying menace is anyone's guess.

Nessa returns to untangling the garland we abandoned, still giggling. "Fennel is rather adorable. Were he not, his theatrics would be only half as entertaining."

Declan brushes sand from his pants, then reaches over to pluck a dried marigold petal from my hair. His knuckles graze my cheek as he tucks the loose strands behind my ear. "Shrine duty or donkey wrangling. Which do you prefer?"

"Neither. Both." I smile and lean into the warmth of his touch. "Depends on if I get hazard pay."

Nessa's laugh dies in her throat. Her fists tighten around the garlands, her whole body stiffening. The crowd straightens as one, lilting murmurs snuffed out like a flaming wick pinched between fingers.

The Player sweeps into view, flanked by robed guards. Dav is among them, his expression hard as stone. Her gown is crimson silk embellished with gold coins, sleeves trailing like banners. She lifts her arms wide, voice carrying like a bell through the hush.

"In honor of the Great Families and the benevolence of the Crown whose hand delivered us from pandemonium, an additional performance shall be given this night. Ready yourselves."

The streak of red paint across her face gleams like fresh blood beneath the sun.

The light seems to fade as she leaves, and the Kingdom of Wands shifts back into a stage. Whether we're ready or not, the show is about to begin again.

SIXTEEN

"Now we know that, as much as Shakespeare should go over well with a crowd like this, they are *not* into *Romeo and Juliet*," Declan says, stuffing his arms into his shirt and pulling it on over his head as he bounds after me backstage.

The air behind the curtain hums with movement. Musicians tune their instruments, dancers adjust their costumes, a man in full body paint sneezes as he applies another layer of glitter. I swipe a squashed fig from my sleeve and flick it on the ground.

"They threw *rotten figs* at me, but they don't like Shakespeare. Make that make sense." I pick another sticky piece of pulp from my skirt. "Maybe I misremembered the balcony monologue. I don't know it word for word, but the vibe was definitely right."

"My monologue was *fire*."

"Aren't you too old to call it *fire*?"

Declan shakes his head, weaving around a contortionist

warming up beside a table covered in masks. "They loved me out there."

I shoot him a look over my shoulder. "You didn't need to take your shirt off."

"Says who?" he asks, brow furrowed. "Do I need to remind you again of how much they loved me?"

"Yes, I know. Your fan club in the front row nearly fainted, and whenever I said any of my lines, I was pelted with fruit."

He grins that slow, infuriating grin that never fails to find its way under my skin. "All good theater involves a little tragedy, a little longing, and a lot of skin."

I snort. "That's not a quote from Shakespeare."

"Should've been."

Nessa's blond hair catches my eye as she slips through the jumble, clutching a polished brass torch and a vial of oil. The torch gleams like a trophy in her grip, and her whole face shines, lit from the inside with giddy nerves.

"This is the moment I was born for!" she whisper-shouts, her voice fizzing like champagne. "Song joined with flame—two arts united. The queens will see me at last. And it's all thanks to you and your teachings, brilliant Story Witch."

"It hasn't been that long." My stomach knots. "Have you had enough time to practice?"

Her smile widens, luminous. "Think happy thoughts, remember? Doubt is poison. Nothing will go wrong if I only manifest love and light."

"Nessa—" I reach for her, but the Player's voice is already rolling out across the stage, commanding silence.

"Behold Nessa Ellesmere, the Songbird of Wands, with a voice like warmed honey and a heart as pure as glass. Listen well to her melodies that speak what mere words cannot. Sing, Nessa, sing so your kingdom may be entertained!"

The crowd roars, and Nessa steps into the light with her chin lifted, torch raised above her head.

Applause shakes the stage, and I try to swallow back the dread creeping up my throat with the same affirmations I spoon-fed Nessa and her friends. She's fine. She's golden. She's aligned.

Nessa joins the tip of her torch with another, and it flares to life. She moves to the center of the stage and sings her first note. The clear thread of her voice weaves through the hush as she glides across the stage, torch in hand. For a few moments, she is everything she's said aloud she would be. She is incandescent, deserving, untouchable. She glides across the stage, mellifluous voice ringing out. She hits a stunning high note, takes a breath, and tips the oil into her mouth. Her cheeks swell with liquid, ready to spit flame when her toe catches the edge of a brazier. A stumble, barely there, but enough to slice the rhythm in two. She inhales a gasp, recovering quickly, but the damage is done.

The sound that rips from her throat is wrong. She doubles over, sputtering and coughing, clawing at her throat, eyes wide and wet. The torch clatters to the stage, sparks spitting across the boards.

Gasps split the audience, and a ripple of horror moves through the court.

Nessa staggers upright, arms outstretched toward the wings. Toward me.

"Nessa!" I crash onto the stage. "I'm here."

She shoves me back with a wild, broken motion.

Her voice is raw, shredded. "Happy thoughts, is that what you've come to tell me?"

Her words bleed fury and grief in equal measure, and my own throat closes around the tears rising fast and hot.

The Player's guards rush from the wings, catching her as she sags between them. She twists against their grip, her gaze finding mine, pinning me to the spot like a spear.

"Tell me, Story Witch," she croaks, every word edged with fury, "what have you gained from your pretty thoughts alone?"

The Player's guards carry Nessa away, her broken sobs echoing behind her.

Queen Solara leans forward in her throne and crosses her arms over her chest.

"A pity," she says, lips curving in something that is not quite a smile. "A spectacle begun in brilliance, ended in ruin."

"And she has always been one of my favorites." Zephara pouts. "Alas, a flame that falters is indeed no flame at all."

A low murmur stirs through the court, and from the corner of the stage, the Player inclines her head, as if the judgment were already written.

Tears burn the backs of my eyes, but I lift my chin and force the words out. "Call it ruin if you like," I spit, "but you'll remember her. You'll remember this. Because it's not devotion you crave—it's spectacle. And she gave her voice for yours."

I rush off the stage after Nessa, world swimming in unshed tears, but Romy and Celine close ranks at the stage's edge.

"You shall not go near her," Celine hisses. "Your *teachings* have cost her enough."

Her words pierce deeper than any blade. For a breath, I can't move. Then the dam breaks. My legs carry me forward, fast and furious, torchlight stretching my shadow long and jagged across the sand. Declan is practically chasing me, his stride eating up the space I'm trying to put between myself and every mistake I've made that led me here.

Dav is planted like a gargoyle outside our tent, arms folded, eyes narrowed.

"I warned you," he mutters. "Had it been up to me, you'd never have left this tent. And no voice would lie in ruins because of you."

"I feel bad enough, Dav," I snap, breath tearing ragged in my chest. "I really don't need this from you."

"You need it most of all," he fires back, stepping closer. "You cannot come into this kingdom with your tricks and infect others with your recklessness. Witch or fraud, it makes no difference if all that is left behind is ruin and regret. Your guilt, *Story Witch*, is too cheap a price."

"Dav, back off," Declan growls, his patience thinning.

But something inside me cracks open, molten and wild. "You think I don't know what I've done?" I scream, every word burning my throat. "You think I don't have regrets?"

Declan grabs my arm, trying to steer me inside.

"Get off me!" I shove against him, heat prickling up my neck.

Dav steps forward, shadow long in the torchlight. "Do you see now? I told you this path led nowhere but ruin."

"Shut up." My hands shake, but I ball them into fists. "I don't need another lecture."

"You need truth," he says, each word precise. "You spilled your empty visions, another paid the price, and now you rage as though you are the injured one."

"I never—" My throat tightens. The image of Nessa's wide, panicked eyes sears me raw. "I never meant for it to go that way."

"Intent won't heal the girl's voice—"

"Enough!" I hold my hand up, palms out. "I already hate myself, all right? I know I ruined everything!"

Declan wedges between us, his hand firm on my arm again. "Let's go inside."

The fight drains out of me in a rush, and I let him pull me into the tent and seal it closed behind us. The moment he does, I wrench my arm free. "Oh, what, now you're my handler too?"

"You don't get to be an asshole to me because you feel like shit," he bites out. "You messed up."

"I know that!"

"And you wish there was something you could do about it. But there isn't."

That knocks the air from my lungs.

I stumble backward, thighs hitting the bed. My purse lies tossed across the covers where I left it earlier, spilling glittery scraps of my so-called magickal life. My pulse pounds in my ears, and my hands shake as I dig into it, the ritual tools spilling out onto the sheets.

If there's nothing I can do for Nessa, then I'll take action for me. I'll do something to prove the wheel is still turning, that I'm not powerless, that all my affirmations and scripting weren't just empty words that broke a girl.

I drag out rose quartz, a crumpled affirmation card, and a candle Romy gave me that she said was imbued with the fire energy of Wands. I place them on the sheet, chasing my own version of control like it might stitch the world back together.

My chest aches with the image of Nessa clawing her throat, her voice splintering like glass. My fault. My words. My empty love-and-light bullshit.

I arrange the candle, the card, and the rose quartz into a triangle on the silk sheets, the crystal gleaming at the top point. I step back to admire the symmetry as if neat angles might disguise the shame tangled around my heart.

"I wish my phone wasn't dead." I tilt my chin. "This would be cute on my feed."

Declan, arms folded across his chest, is a dark shadow in my periphery. "Is that really the priority right now?"

Of course it isn't. Of course I'm being ridiculous. But better ridiculous than shattered. Better cute angles and crystals than the sound of Nessa's voice tearing apart still ringing in my ears. If immaturity is all I've got to keep from unraveling, then fine—I'll take it.

I blink at him, widening my eyes just a little. "What? I'm making a witchy triangle. It's literally cute. My followers would love it."

He watches me for a beat that lasts too long. "You doing this on purpose?"

My smile is soft, practiced. "Doing what?"

"The passive thing," he says. "Pushing. Baiting me. You want me to turn my back on you, walk away so you can say everyone does. So you can have your martyr story, feel justified, be angry with somebody else instead of with yourself."

A hot knot of grief twists in my chest as I force out

a laugh. "That's what you think? You're reading way too much into this. I'm just…trying to make this spell look nice. Magick is real here, so I'm…you know…channeling it."

My pulse hammers in my throat. It's obscene how much I want him to answer by walking away.

He studies me for another long, unbearable second. Then he shakes his head. "I'm not the prop in whatever punishment you've decided you deserve."

"Declan, I really don't know—"

"Stop it, Amanda! Just…stop." He exhales, tired. "Fine. You want me to go, I'll go. I'll give you space to sort this out."

He meets my gaze, steady, and his lips part like he's about to say something that will land with clean, devastating bluntness. I swallow, bracing for the judgment or the lecture I want him to give me. Because he's right. I want to turn my anger away from myself and point it somewhere safe. Point it at him.

Instead, he only shakes his head again. "Try not to light the bed on fire."

And when he finally turns, slipping through the flap of the tent, it feels less like victory and more like confirmation that I've broken something I don't know how to fix.

The silence he leaves behind is unbearable. My chest aches with it, my skin tingling like it can't hold me in. But that's fine. Everything is *fine.* I don't need him. I don't need anyone. I can realign myself, reconnect with my inner power, rebuild my armor.

I narrow my eyes, strike a match with a precise flick of my wrist, and light the candle. The flame wavers, small and steady, mocking in its control. I lift the rose quartz above it, smoke curling up around the edges of the stone.

My chest is tight, my throat raw, but I force the words out anyway, the ones I've recited into mirrors and captions like they were precious. "I am aligned with purpose," I whisper, voice splintering on the edges. "I radiate power."

The flame beneath the crystal flickers.

"I am the fire. I am the flame. I am the light that cannot be dimmed."

The words taste false, but I cling to them anyway, repeat them louder as if volume alone might make them true. I see Nessa's wide eyes, hear the way her voice shredded apart, feel the sting of Declan's absence, and shove it all down under the chant.

"I am the fire. I am the flame. I am the light that cannot be dimmed."

The crystal warms against my palm. Soft at first, like sun on bare shoulders. Then hotter. The petal pink deepens, pulsing faintly.

The crystal flashes yellow. Then orange. Then red. The colors swell inside the quartz like a sunrise. Heat builds, and the crystal vibrates with energy that buzzes up my arm.

The heart of the quartz continues to flare—yellow, orange, red—the colors spiraling inward, collapsing into a single burning point of light.

"It's working," I breathe.

Boom!

The crystal detonates, a fiery shockwave scorching a black ring into the silk bedding. Heat lashes my palm, and I shriek, flinging the stone. It rolls to a stop, glowing like an ember. The candle topples, flame devouring the affirmation card until it curls and crumbles into ash.

Fire races across the sheets. Panic clamps around my throat. My hands flail uselessly, slapping at the blaze.

The tent flap snaps open. Declan barrels in, eyes taking in the scene in one sweep. He seizes the barrel of water we use to wash up and hurls the contents over the bed.

Water slaps the silk, dousing the fire. And me.

I gasp as cold rushes over my skin, thin dress plastered to me, hair dripping, embarrassment and adrenaline making my teeth chatter.

Declan sets the empty bucket down. For a long while, neither of us speaks. The air between us crackles with leftover anger, smoke, and everything I don't know how to say. My throat aches with the things I should apologize for but can't. He doesn't look away, and I hate how much I need that steadiness when I've given him every reason to turn his back.

My palm throbs, skin flushed red and tender. I shift, trying to gather what's left of my dignity and wet spell ingredients, but the saturated silk beneath me squelches.

Declan sits in the dry spot beside me, eyes dark with concern. He leans in, tears a strip from the wet sheet, and gently reaches for my wrist. "Let me see."

His fingers cradle mine. His touch is warm and steady as he turns my hand over, inspecting the burn on my palm.

"Why are you being nice to me?"

His mouth lifts in the faintest curve. "Because you need someone to be."

I slump against him, suddenly exhausted. "I was just trying to… I don't know. Feel like I had control again. Like I wasn't completely at the mercy of this place."

"You're not," he says quietly. "When you patched me up after I clocked Dav, I remember thinking you had it all figured out."

He reaches for a little clay jar the healer gave him and scoops out a small amount of balm with two fingers. Gently, he dabs it onto my burn. My skin stings, but the cool salve soothes almost immediately. His thumb brushes the inside of my wrist as he rubs it in.

He shifts beside me, leg pressing against mine, his warmth curling around me like a blanket. He rests his cheek on the top of my head, breath ghosting over my damp hair. The weight of him, the stability and safety makes the space around my heart unclench.

"I thought maybe…" My throat works as I force the words out. "After everything, I worried you wouldn't look at me the same."

His chuckle shakes my shoulder. "I think I like you even more now that you've become a fire hazard." I feel his mouth curve, the heat in his voice unmistakable. "And I'm not even going to say anything about how wet you are."

"Are you flirting with me?" I ask, smile breaking across my face. "I feel like I need to ask now so I don't automatically assume the worst."

"That's a trade secret. Can't give away all my moves."

"Hmm." I glance down, splashing my toes lightly in the puddle soaking through the tent rug. "Might want to work on those moves."

"I was saving your life."

"You threw water on me."

"Same thing."

Declan's hand stays wrapped gently around my wrist, thumb moving in the barest, most absent-minded stroke against my pulse point.

I catch the faint scent of smoke in his shirt and the earthy trace of salve. I breathe it in. I breathe *him* in.

"I'm sorry," I whisper, the words catching as they leave me. "For earlier. For all of it. I shouldn't have… pushed you like that."

Declan doesn't answer. He just keeps his hand around mine, thumb drawing the same steady arc over my pulse.

That hum in the base of my spine is back. The tug in my chest. The one that feels like something ancient and knowing is threading an arrow through my ribs and drawing back the bow.

I shove myself to my feet so fast the blood rushes in my ears. My gaze snaps to the tent's entrance. The silk flaps shiver in the breeze, but the air inside the tent is heavy. A low sound builds, the crackling of flames, distant at first, then swelling, rushing closer.

Declan's attention turns toward the noise outside, and he goes to stand, but like his limbs suddenly weigh twice as much, his motions slow. His movements take too long. His breathing is so slow, it nearly stops.

The edges of the tent opening ripple as if submerged, silk moving like fabric under water. The air thickens, turning viscous, syrup-slow. Like time itself is falling asleep.

"Declan," I whisper, panic crawling across my skin.

The familiar bite of burning wood and smoldering ash fills my nose.

It's happening again. The world around me is stopping.

Just like the last time Fortune came. Just like the last time she had a message for me.

"Declan," I say again, more urgently now.

It takes full seconds for his dark gaze to drag to mine.

I lunge and grab his hand.

The moment I make contact, heat pulses through me like lava. A pop of static at my fingertips. The air shifts again.

Declan jerks the rest of the way to his feet, sways, catches himself on the edge of the bed. He blinks hard. Shakes his head like he's coming out of a daze. "What the fuck was that?"

"Don't let go." I tighten my grip on his hand. "Please. It's her. It's Fortune."

Around us, the world is suspended in a viscous hush when the smoke thickens.

Fortune glides past the tent, leaving behind a trail of scorched earth, her silhouette flickering like a flame. My body jerks toward the flap before I fully register moving.

"Come on," I hiss, dragging Declan with me.

He pulls back. "Wait."

I spin, breath swollen in my lungs. "She's literally right there, Declan. She has the answers. We need her help. She's the only one who can tell us how to get back."

But he's already moving, dragging me across the tent, dropping to one knee in front of the trunk at the end of our bed. He flings aside a pile of clothes and an unraveled silk sash until he finds what he's looking for.

He lifts a scorched scroll, edges curled and blackened. *The* scroll. The one we read aloud in the only real room in this kingdom. The one that made the torches flare and set something ancient inside me on fire.

"You stole this?" I ask, half shocked, half impressed.

"I rescued it," he says with a shrug. "Figured it might come in handy."

I take it from him, already turning toward the exit. "Fortune led me to that room. This scroll. There's a reason for all of it. She knows what that reason is."

We shove past the curtain into the night. The air is thick and gray with smoke. The torches lining the caravan flicker unnaturally slowly.

Dav stands outside our tent, one finger jammed halfway up his nose.

The ground crunches beneath our feet as we sprint through the camp, following the trail of scorched earth left in Fortune's wake. Its embers glow faintly beneath thc moonlight, charred footprints seared into the sand like a brand.

We weave around frozen fire dancers locked mid-spin and jugglers with their flaming torches suspended in fiery arcs. A woman lurches toward a dropped tray of honeyed figs, the glistening fruit caught in the air like falling stars. Ahead, heat curls into a shimmer where Fortune walks like a dream barely tethered to earth.

I don't stop chasing, and Declan doesn't let go.

But it's not enough.

We reach the edge of camp just as she blurs into the dunes, her figure warping in the rising heat.

And then she's gone again.

I slam to a halt, breath coming hard and uneven. "You've got to be fucking kidding me."

Declan sucks in a breath and scans the horizon, free hand braced on his hip. "Did she just—"

"*Disappear*? Yes." I stalk forward, crumpling the scroll in my fist. "Because apparently two people trapped in a whole other dimension doesn't warrant a proper conversation."

Declan exhales slowly. "This probably doesn't help, but I don't think she's ignoring you on purpose."

"You're right. That's not at all helpful." With a groan, I let my head fall back. "What do I have to do? What am I missing? I've played along. I've said the words. I've lit the candles. I've been patient and polite and open to signs and metaphors. I've tried to be a teacher and a mentor, and all it got me was—"

The thought spikes sharp in my chest. I suck in a breath, shoving it down. I can't go back there. Not to Nessa. Not if I want any hope of moving forward and fixing what I've broken.

"I've done everything I'm supposed to!" My voice rises with every word, until I'm screaming at the endless dunes. "And you still can't manage to have a real fucking conversation?"

The desert stays quiet, frozen.

"Help me!" The plea rips from me like a wound torn open. A cry not just for rescue, but for acknowledgment.

The air shivers and swells with the scents of smoke and ozone. The ground pulses beneath my feet. Heat blooms, heavy and sudden, curling around me like steam.

Fortune steps from the shimmer where she vanished, her silhouette pulsing gold at the edges, her eyes flickering like twin torches.

Declan angles himself in front of me, a shield of quiet

strength. His shoulders are squared, tense, ready to fight if he has to. Ready to protect me, even from something he doesn't understand.

I press my free hand to his chest.

He doesn't move. But he doesn't stop me when I step closer.

"I need help," I tell her. "That's why you keep reappearing, right? That's what you do. You help."

Fortune tilts her head. The copper strands in her hair click together like bones.

"So help me now."

"I did not bring you here." Her voice crackles like wind through embers. "The Tower brought you to this realm. And when you are ready, you will heal it."

"That doesn't make any sense. What does that even mean?" I shake my head, panic rising like smoke. "There's real magick here. I've tried to use it to get us home, to help…" I shake my head. "It keeps blowing up in my face. Literally. I just want to reopen the portal that brought us here. I want to fix what I broke, here and back there. I want to get us home."

"I've worn that look before." Fortune tilts her head and takes one slow step forward. "When you are ready—"

"*I heard you.*" The words slice out of me. "But I'm not ready. Not for what you're talking about. I can't heal this place." My fingers squeeze tighter around Declan's. "I don't even know how to heal myself."

Fortune's gaze shifts to my injured hand, still red and tender from the spell that backfired.

Before I can pull away, she reaches out and gently cradles my hand in both of hers. Her touch is searing. I suck in a sharp breath, shoulders jerking as Declan tenses.

"I was once the balm on the blistered seams of our kingdom. You will be again." Her jeweled thumb glides over the reddened skin, and the pain in my hand vanishes. My skin cools beneath her touch, the angry flush fading as if it had never been there at all.

She looks at me then. *Into* me. Every secret, every splinter, every carefully constructed layer I've ever used to hold myself together.

"The Kingdom of Wands was forged in sacred flame. Its fires once stripped away illusion, burning for truth—for what was real, and only that." Her gaze sharpens, her eyes like twin flares. "Now their flames dance for spectacle. They leap not to cleanse but to please. Monarchs emerged and have bartered authenticity for applause and meaning for the polish of performance.

"Do you not see?" she murmurs, voice low and searing. "Is it so cloaked in prettiness and hidden beneath spell and spectacle that you do not remember? You have chased signs when the answer lives in your blood."

I swallow hard, throat tight. Her words thrum in my chest, pressing against my ribs, against the walls I've built to prop myself up.

Fortune is speaking to every moment I performed instead of listened. Every time I embodied the look of empowerment instead of learning to do the work to achieve it.

My fingers curl around the scroll crumpled in my hand. The paper is soft with age, singed at the edges like it barely survived whatever truth it carries.

"I don't know how to fix any of it," I whisper. Shame grows hot in my chest, presses against the backs of my eyes. "I don't even know where to start."

Her gaze drops to the parchment. "That was written in the days when flame bowed to truth."

I glance down at the smeared ink of the poem, the spell that made the torches leap and the world tilt. The one that didn't feel like performance. That felt like me.

"It was never meant for spectacle," Fortune continues, her voice the dull roar of a bonfire. "It was meant to reveal. To remind. To rend the veil between what is true and what is merely...pleasing."

She looks at me again, and in her eyes, the flames dance wild and ferocious. "You have already done it. You're the echo and the origin, but you cannot burn for that which you are unwilling to be consumed."

Like smoke curling into the sky, she begins to vanish. Her body flickers at the edges, the outline of her softening, rippling like heat rising from pavement.

"No." It escapes me rough and ragged. Then louder: "*No!*"

Declan's fingers slip from mine as I lunge.

"Don't go! Don't leave me with these riddles." I charge into the shimmer. Each step forward feels like moving through oil as her figure continues to blur, melting like wax into the night.

I reach out and catch the edge of her robe—hot silk that unravels in my hand. Ash spills through my fingers, but in that final flash of contact, voices come. They're soft and layered, echoing over each other.

...the wheel turns...

...for the real...

...the willing...

...truth must be chosen...

...and the self...

...unmade...

The heat fades. The shimmer dissolves. The scorched ground beneath my feet returns to sand as the night settles back into its former shape.

SEVENTEEN

The scroll is spread across my lap, the charred edges whispering ash against my thighs as I once again go over the faded script. My back aches from sitting hunched in the sand outside the caravan, and every few minutes I slap at another invisible tickle crawling up my leg.

I've been out here for hours, but I can't stop. Fortune's last words keep replaying in my mind, a needle stuck in a groove:

...you cannot burn for that which you are unwilling to be consumed.

"There has to be something," I mutter to the empty dunes. "Something that opens the portal. That fixes everything and gets us home."

A sting snaps against my arm. I scratch without thinking. Then another. Then five more in quick succession. My legs itch. My arms itch. My freaking eyelids itch.

"I brought you some water."

I start, squinting up at Declan against the gold-drenched

sky. His sun-kissed arms and tousled hair and concerned eyes—he's too good-looking to be tracking my descent into Gollum territory.

He crouches beside me, gaze skating over the scroll and the scattered contents of my ritual pouch. "Everything going okay?"

"Define *okay*." I wave weakly toward the scrap of paper, the sand, the entire kingdom. "I'm hot, itchy, probably dehydrated…" I groan, swatting at another invisible assailant.

He snags my hand and extends my arm. "Have you looked at yourself recently?"

I glance down and register the horror show of angry, red welts dotting my exposed skin.

"Shit." The word doesn't cover it. My fingers hover over the inflamed bumps. "This is bad. They're everywhere. I look like I was swarmed. What do you think Zephara and Solara will say if I go onstage like this?"

"I think they'll say you were bitten by sand fleas." He shrugs. "Got me once on a family holiday in St. Barts. Thought I was going to be scarred forever. Cried in an apothecary shop. My mother still brings it up at Thanksgiving."

"I don't really have the right to freak out about a rash right now." I swallow, and then, softer, "How is she?"

"Celine let me talk to her. You were right about that."

I give a weak smile. "I know a teen girl crush when I see one."

"Yeah." He exhales. "Nessa's with the healer. Said she'll be back to singing by the full moon."

"She's going to be okay?" My voice comes out thin, shaky.

He nods. "She'll be fine."

Relief loosens my shoulders. I breathe out, a short laugh slipping free. It's a small reprieve, and I let it be one—just for a second—before guilt returns, sliding cold into the center of my chest.

"Come on," Declan says, pulling me to my feet. "I want to take you somewhere."

I collect my things and tuck them into my purse as I slide it over my shoulder. Brow raised, I ask warily, "Where exactly are you taking me?"

"That would ruin the surprise."

Sand slips beneath our feet, sun-warmed and soft as we climb over dunes. By the time we crest the last hill, I'm out of breath. The air cools as we make our way down toward the lush, tree-filled hollow hidden from the camp. Palms cluster like guardians, and a spring-fed pool gleams at the center, rimmed in smooth black stone. The water glows blue where streaks of sunlight pierce the canopy overhead, and mist curls from the surface in diaphanous threads.

"The Everspring. How did you know where to find it?"

Declan smirks. "I have my ways."

"Which involve Tarek."

"You know me too well."

I bite my lip. Barely a week ago, Declan Thorne was just a guy in my DMs. A flirt. A fantasy. A series of emojis and late-night sexts that never promised anything real. While I've learned he's much more than that, I don't know him yet. Not as well as I want to.

Declan drags a hand through his hair, raking it off his forehead as he toes off his sandals. He takes his time with his shirt. It clings to his shoulders, sweat-dark and stretched across muscle, and I swear time once again slows. The sun gilds the planes of him—broad chest narrowing to a lean waist, the sharp V of his hips disappearing into his pants.

Cool air brushes my bare stomach, goose bumps rising in a wave as I drop my bag and join him, shrugging out of my silk wrap dress until I'm down to a red linen bra that ties around my neck and back with matching panties secured in knots at my hips.

The pool glows pale blue in the slivers of sunlight. I step in first, shivering as the water wraps around my calves. It's cool and refreshing in a way that makes me gasp, Slowly, I lower myself in. The sandy bottom is soft and warm in places where the sun still lingers.

Declan wades in after me and immediately hisses through his teeth. "It's cold. Why is it cold?"

"Were you hoping for a tepid bathwater lagoon?"

He lunges like he's going to splash me, and I shriek, ducking beneath the surface in a rush of bubbles. When I pop up, his back is turned. I don't hesitate. With a triumphant yell, I leap forward, grab him around the shoulders, and yank him under.

We surface, breathless, and he shakes himself off like a wet dog and grins. "Oh, so that's how we're playing?"

I nod, mockingly solemn, and splash him directly in the face. "You started it."

That's all the invitation he needs.

He scoops me up and spins me in a dizzying circle over his head before throwing me back into the pool. We splash and shriek and wrestle like kids who have forgotten how to be guarded. He springs up out of nowhere and catches me, laughing as his fingers close around my waist. I squirm out of his grip with a giggle and dive under again, swimming toward the edge of the pool like it might save me from the way his hands felt on my skin.

Leaning against the smooth rock ledge, I catch my breath. Declan joins me, his arm brushing mine as he settles in next to me.

"Okay," he says after a beat. "Important question."

I snort. "Shoot."

"Truth or dare?"

I laugh so hard I can't speak for a second. "Umm, truth."

He tilts his head, gaze softening. "All right. Tell me the thing you're most ashamed of. Something you wouldn't tell your best friend."

"We're really getting into it, aren't we?" I force a wobbly smile. The reflex to deflect—tell a cute story, make a joke—bubbles up, but I push it right back down. "Nessa," I say finally, voice low. "I filled her with empty affirmations and let her think that's what it meant to be brave. I wanted validation more than I wanted to make sure she was safe."

He looks at me like he can see the scaffolding I built to hold myself upright, all the props and pretty rituals, and he doesn't flinch.

"Okay, your turn," I say, teasing, even though my voice is shaky at the edges. "Tell me something vulnerable so I don't feel like I'm doing an emotional trust fall by myself."

"There's not much to say." He shrugs.

"That can't be true." I dig my toes into the sand and watch our ripples join on the surface of the water. "Tell me how Declan Thorne became Declan Thorne."

After a quiet, thoughtful moment he says, "My life's been planned out since before I was born. My mom couldn't carry a baby to term. My parents eventually had to use a surrogate, but enough time passed, enough miscarriages happened… I think she felt safer making sure every aspect of my life was mapped out. Like she was ensuring my survival by making me tick these achievement boxes. To me, all it's done is turned life into a task, leached the color from the world, turned everything into shades of gray."

He draws in a breath. Lets it out slowly.

"My dad lives to make my mom happy. I swear he's only in my life to be sure I follow the script, close the deals, hit the metrics, live for her happiness too."

A dragonfly lands on the water, spreads its iridescent wings, then takes off again.

"That's why no more rock climbing."

"You remember that." His smile lifts his stubbled cheeks, and the bright blue water reflects like starbursts in the dark pools of his eyes. "Yeah, my mom found out I was really into climbing. I was good at it too. My dad made sure to put a stop to that." He splashes his face with a handful of water and shakes it off. "Parents, right? No matter how old you get, they always have a hold over you."

"They're not here now. As far as we know, they literally don't exist in this world." I shift, water lapping at my collarbone. "So, right now, what do you want out of life? To find some big rocks or—"

"You, Amanda. I want to be here. With you."

Our eyes meet, and a delicate hush settles over us. One wrong move could shatter it. One right move could change everything.

Slowly, he reaches across the inches between us and threads his fingers through mine. His thumb presses into my knuckles in a small, steady punctuation as he draws me in until our bodies meet.

"Why?" I whisper. "Why do you want to be here with me?"

"You've turned my black-and-white world Technicolor."

His hands slide down my waist. They pause at my hips, fingers curling into the softness. Then he moves lower, brushing over the curve of my ass in a way that makes my pulse skip.

He lifts me, pinning my back to the smooth ledge of the pool. Water trickles down my shoulders as I straddle his waist, the heat of his body flooding into me through every slick point of contact. His hands anchor just above my thighs, thumbs grazing the delicate knots of linen tied at my hips. His eyes search mine, steady and molten and terrifying because of how much they see.

I'm trembling, and it has nothing to do with the cool brush of air on my wet skin.

Declan's lips touch mine, and I fall into the kiss like kindling catching flame. A flare of heat, sudden and wild and hungry, licks up my spine, curls under my ribs, sparks between my legs. His mouth is warm and sure, every pass of his tongue over mine burning through me.

My body arches instinctively, mouth parting on a soft gasp that he swallows like a secret.

I braid my fingers into his wet hair, and his hands tighten at my hips, pulling me impossibly closer.

The hardness of him presses between my legs, hot and insistent. My breath stutters. My pulse punches. It's all heat and promise, straining against the confines of linen, and God, I want it. I want him. All of him.

My hips shift, a slow grind against him, and he groans low in his throat. The sound pours through me like gasoline.

"I've wanted this since that first message." His fingers dig into my ass, his grip possessive. His hips rock, and the friction is enough to drag a moan out of me. It slips between our mouths, and I feel him smile against my lips. "All the things we said we'd do to each other…"

It should melt me. Instead, the line throws me back to the version of myself I used to sell—the filtered, edited woman who hid behind her phone and never had to face consequences.

I go cold.

I'm not that woman. I can't be that woman.

"Wait." The word is small and raw. "This isn't right. I can't."

Confusion flickers across his features. "What happened? Did I—"

"No." I scramble out of his arms, water sloshing over the rocky edge as I clamber up, fingers fumbling for my wrap and my purse. "I'm sorry."

Barefoot, I bolt out of the Everspring. Each footstep kicks up a spray of sand around my calves as I run from the warmth of being wanted, from the way his mouth felt on mine. I run from the persona I sold and from the messy, real woman who's trying to breaking free.

When his guard is down—when he's drunk on heat and sex and whatever spell this place has spun—I can't help but wonder who he really wants. The idea that it might not be me, the *real me*, rushes through me like cold water.

I don't know who I am right now—only that whoever she is, she's too messy, too broken, too real to be anyone's fantasy.

Especially his.

Wind whips my hair into my mouth and flings my wrap behind me like a warning flag. The sunset smears the sky in blood as the faint beat of the drums, the call of the nightly performance, drifts across the dunes from the kingdom's caravan.

"Amanda!" he calls.

I keep running. I need space from Declan's hands, from the fear he stirs in me. He catches up just as I crest the top of a dune, his hand closing gently around my arm.

"Please, talk to me."

I stop. My chest heaves, and I lick my dry lips. Salt stings my tongue from the tears I didn't realize had escaped.

He turns me to face him. His jaw is tight, chest rising and falling just as fast as mine. "You can't keep running, keep pushing me away. We have to talk about whatever's going on. We have to fix it."

Grains of sand scrape my cheeks as I wipe away tears. "I am nothing like the woman I was on the app. I'm messy. I break things." Tears burn as they fall, hot and humiliating. "I don't know how you can see past all the ridiculous shit I've done, because I can't."

"It's okay—"

"No, it's not. This isn't like it was before." I throw up my free hand. "All this—it isn't sexting and flirting. This is real. I don't know how to be real."

"Neither of us do. That's why I'm not walking away."

"Maybe you should." I shake my head. "I'm not doing the passive aggressive thing. I just need to fix myself before I drag another person down with me."

Declan's grip tightens on my arm. "You think we're both supposed to come into this perfectly put together? That's not a relationship, Amanda. We're supposed to be able to lean on each other, be there for each other."

"How would you know? This started as a hookup."

He scoffs and takes a breath, ready to say more, but I don't let him.

"Don't pretend otherwise. We were practically fucking each other in DMs. If we hadn't ended up here, we probably would've had sex, I'd have left before morning, and we would've never seen each other again. I haven't been honest—about why I perform, about what I'm afraid of. And you—" I swallow. "You were raised on a to-do list. We're both...*frauds*. I can't be your soft place to land, and you could never be mine."

His expression falls then twists like I reached into his chest and crushed something vital. Like I confirmed whatever worst thing he already believes about himself.

"Declan, I'm sorry. That was—" My voice catches on the knot swelling in my throat, which is a good thing since I have no idea what to say. Maybe I'm being a coward. Maybe I'm finally telling the truth.

His jaw sets, and he shakes his head.

Silence folds in around us.

I step back, this time needing distance from myself. From the sharp, cruel things I continue to let out just to keep from feeling vulnerable.

My heel clips something hard, half-buried in the sand. I stumble and look down.

Stone, blackened and weatherworn, juts from the dune. Faded sigils, carved deep, catch the last light like wet teeth.

I kneel, brushing the sand away with my fingers. More stone is revealed as a hum slides under my skin in a low electric pulse. My fingertips tingle, and that feeling swells, fierce and alive, beating beneath my ribs like a second heartbeat. I press my palm to the stone, and it answers.

The sand around the spire trembles with a long, low groan. Cracks spider out from under my knees, thin as lace at first, then widening until the ground at our feet sighs and the dune cascades in a great, roaring slide.

"Hold on!" Declan shouts.

I seize his hand. Maybe he grabs mine. It hardly matters. The world tilts. The dunes fall away in columns, pouring like waterfalls of sand.

We tumble down, down, down, the air full of grit.

Stone slams into my back, knocking the breath from my lungs. My palms scrape the ground as I push myself upright, coughing until my lungs burn. I blink through the dust. Declan's a few feet away, rubbing the back of his head as he stares up. I follow his gaze, my head tilted all the way back.

We stand in a chamber carved deep into the desert's belly. It's vast and open to the sky now. Evenly spaced columns thick as sequoias shoot up from the stone floor. Flame-shaped spires crown each, their tops black and sharp against the sky. We're within a ring of ancient stones, the desert exhaling around us. Above, the first stars prick the dusk.

We've fallen into a memory long forgotten, a secret swallowed by the earth itself.

Declan groans, brushing sand from his clothes. "Fuck being dropped into things."

I smell smoke and ash, fire and ozone. The air thrums with heat and something that feels ancient. Something that vibrates against my bones and whispers beneath my skin.

Magick is on fire behind my heart as Fortune's words echo through my thoughts:

...the Tower chose you... The Tower brought you to this realm. And when you are ready, you will heal it.

I blink up at the circle of dusk, wide and gleaming like a god's eye. At the columns and their stone flames. At the sand that is held at bay around us by some other-worldly force.

"I think..." I swallow, throat raw. "We found the Tower."

Or maybe it found us.

EIGHTEEN

I should feel empty after what I said. That Declan's basically a to-do list. That we're frauds. That he could never be my haven. After the way Declan looked at me like I'd ripped the earth out from under him and offered him nothing to hold on to, I should feel hollow.

But then the sand opened up.

And now I'm not empty.

I'm *brimming.*

Something timeworn and hot is coiling in my chest, pressurizing with every breath. Like the Tower planted its magick inside me the moment it cracked open. Magick that's growing, expanding, aching to burst free.

At the center of the Tower sits a forgotten shrine. It rises from the stone floor like the spine of an ancient beast. The pedestal is carved from obsidian, edges chipped and softened by time. Ash clings to the base like a shadow while traces of red pigment bleed into the sunken lines and faded symbols etched into its surface. A clay offering bowl rests on the podium. It's cracked down the middle and blackened by fire, its rim warped and melted.

Around the shrine, stone steps lead to a sunken circle—an ancient gathering space carved into the Tower. The floor is smooth beneath the drifting sand. Obsidian inlays glint faintly beneath the dust in jagged, interwoven flame-like patterns.

A deep bench curves along the circular wall, polished to a dark, oil-slick sheen. Nestled on the stone are cushions draped in rust-colored velvet and gold brocade, their fabric worn thin in places. Golden tassels glint beneath fine layers of dust, and thick fur pelts spill over the seats.

I follow the steps down, drawn to the altar, the magick in me recognizing the magick in it.

I trail my fingers over the faint veins of red etched into the smooth black base. There's a rhythm beneath the ash, a pattern I recognize. Brushing gently, I hold my breath and coax the soot away. And there it is. Revealed in fragments, but whole enough to understand: *Naught but truth shall feed the sacred flame, and in so doing, preserve the realm it guards.*

The words hum beneath my fingertips. The stone warms, almost pulsing as my hand moves over the weathered letters. The pressure in my chest intensifies—sharp, restless, hungry. It coils behind my ribs, alive with heat and wanting, burning its way to the surface, burning to be seen.

Fortune's voice comes back to me all at once, crackling through my memory.

The Kingdom of Wands was forged in sacred flame. Its fires once stripped away illusion, burning for truth—for what was real, and only that.

Stripped away illusion.

Burned for truth.

"It wasn't a metaphor," I say aloud, my voice barely more than a whisper. "She meant what she said."

Declan furrows his brow. "What who said?"

"Fortune… She knew." I press my palm flat against my chest, trying to contain the blaze climbing beneath my skin. "The Tower—*this Tower*—it brought us to this place, to Towerfall. She said I had to heal the realm. That the wheel would keep turning. That true transformation asks a price, and I have to be ready to be changed—even consumed—by it."

The words tumble out, spilling faster than I can catch them. The air around me thins. The pressure behind my ribs spikes. Flames lick the inside of my chest. I gasp. Gulp in breath after breath but can't get enough air. My body vibrates, pulses, runs away with me.

Declan's hands close around mine. His palms are rough and steady, and the solid strength of him grounds me to the stone beneath our feet. To this place. To this moment. To him.

"Slow down," he says gently, thumbs brushing my knuckles. "Breathe."

I do. One slow inhale. A long exhale. Then another. My lungs stretch, and the blaze within me cools into an ember I can hold in the hollow of my ribs.

That he keeps staying, even after everything I've broken, shows me who he really is. And who I've been too frightened to become.

"Declan, I know I've said it before. I've apologized and then made the same selfish, hurtful choices. I don't expect you to forgive me right now, but I am sorry, and I want the chance to prove it."

He meets my eyes. “Then show me,” he says plainly. “I’m not going anywhere.”

My next exhale leaves me in a rush as another wave of magick funnels up through the floor like heat through a grate, and everything in me tilts. There’s pressure between my temples, a hot tightness behind my sternum, a rush of images and scents and voices that shove at the edges of my mind.

I crumple, and Declan catches me.

“Breathe,” he says again.

In the thin quiet between inhales, a parade of images flips behind my eyes, snapshots that are wrong and right at the same time. A ruby-encrusted hand closes around a child’s small fingers. That same gem-studded hand presses sigils into wet clay. The hand pours oil from a pitcher into a bowl and sets it in front of an altar. They aren’t memories, exactly, but they feel like echoes of something I once was or might one day become.

Fortune’s voice rides under each image. Fragments of words at first, like someone yelling in a windstorm. Then they stack on top of one another until they’re a chorus, loud and urgent in my head.

“Slow down! I can’t understand you. I can’t—” I bury my face in Declan’s chest, cover my ears, and pinch my eyes shut against the noise.

The Tower thrums beneath my bare feet, a low metronome that steadies the noise in my skull until I can make out the shape of the words forming.

The flame eats not the prettified offering. It consumes the true thing given without costume. Present truth, and be fed.

Fortune’s voice arrives, and I can breathe again. My head is clear, and the images recede.

"I get it now," I murmur against the hard planes of Declan's chest. "The Tower doesn't want perfection. It doesn't want handpicked rituals or performative strength or some carefully crafted illusion of healing." My throat is tight, heart thudding. "It wants what's real."

Declan lifts my chin, runs his thumb along my jaw. "And what's real, Amanda?"

The moment I open my mouth to answer, the Tower groans. A sound like the earth exhaling. Wind rips through the chamber like a beast unchained, whipping sand into a spiraling column of smoke and dust.

Declan folds his arms around me, using his body as a shield. I curl into him. Sand lashes my exposed skin, and even with him holding me close, grit stings my eyes. I bury my face deeper into his chest and try to breathe, but the air is a furnace, every inhale a scrape.

He holds me tighter and presses his face in my hair. "Are you doing this?" he shouts, straining to cut through the roar.

"No!" I yell back, my words nearly swallowed by the wind. "I have no idea what's happening!"

On the altar, the offering bowl trembles. Its broken edges draw toward each other, seams knitting themselves together until the cracked vessel re-forms into a massive, seamless vessel.

A jet of fire lashes up from the center of the bowl in a sudden explosive column of flame.

The blast rips us apart and flings us in opposite directions. I fly backward, skidding across sand-covered stone. I slam into the ground with a breath-stealing crack that sends pain streaking up my spine. Heat washes over me in a scalding wave. For a disorienting second the world inside the Tower is a smear of light and smoke.

Across the altar Declan hits hard, the sound of him striking the stone muffled by the roar of wind and flame.

Plumes of dust and smoke rise in choking clouds around us. I cough until my eyes water and my throat feels raw. I shout for him, but the cyclone and the crackle of fire answer instead, swallowing my voice whole.

Flames continue surging from the mouth of the bowl, snaking up into the spinning vortex of sand and smoke. The fire grows, stretches, a serpent of orange and red that twists higher and higher. It coils inward like a clenched fist, and with a thunderous crack that ricochets off the columns and vibrates through the stone beneath my feet, it slams down into the offering bowl.

A wave of heat tears outward, thick and shimmering, warping the air. The burn licks my cheeks, races down my arms, slips beneath my wrap, and scalds my skin. I brace for more, for flames to engulf us, for the Tower to crumble, but nothing comes.

The cyclone unravels. The wind dies. The flames settle. The roar dwindles to a hush.

When the dust clears, the fire has changed.

Flames peel out of the bowl above the altar and stretch into moving pictures of firelight. Movies drawn in fire.

First, a row of tents forms in the flames. Then, the images of people appear. The fire figures pin sheets across lines, flames of laundry fluttering against the backdrop of the night sky. A man kneels to lace a child's sandal while another child blazes past, barefoot and shrieking with laughter, a comet trailing sparks.

Tables appear in silhouette, heat-rippled heaps of bread and roasted meat rendered in shimmering orange. The whole caravan blooms in ember and smoke.

The vision inhales and exhales, growing and contracting like a living thing as branches of light arc from the bowl. Trunks of fire knit into trees, their leaves tiny tongues of flame. The canopy lifts and arches until the tents are crowned in fire-forged shade. Flames lay themselves out like rivers, long braids of fire that thread through the camp. Glowing bridges arch over channels formed of heat ripples. Orchards bloom in sparks, fruit rendered in orange fire—a garden of light that once held the whole kingdom.

From the other side of the altar, Declan's breath ripples through the fiery image. "It's the kingdom."

"But from the past," I add. "Like Tarek said. When the Everspring covered the whole desert."

Through the flicker, I see Declan lean closer, pulled toward the flame. "How does something like this turn to sand?"

As if in answer, heat flushes over my skin, threads through my blood, and everything narrows to a single pull. To the flame. My fingers tingle, then glow with a light that isn't mine. A thread of smoke reaches from my palm to the flames. Without thinking I move, following the smoke to the vision of what once was. I reach for the nearest slender flame—an instinct to touch what feels like truth—and heat bites my fingertips. The pain is fierce and instant. I snatch my hand back. My touch ripples through the flames and, impossibly, opens the picture wider.

The flames carry us forward, winding through the

caravan of the past. Children dart between the tents, waving palm fronds drawn in whiplike curls of flame. The murmur of voices ripples through the air. Two women sit together, passing a steaming platter between them. A woman holds a cup to a child's lips. A group of men roar with laughter, and one of them lifts a cloth to wipe his grinning face. There are no rehearsals, no performances, no roaming guards. Just life, simple and sacred, shaped from heat and memory.

The flames press onward, guiding us toward the center of camp, where the stage stands now. But here—in this memory of the past—there's only the Tower.

A fire burns in the center of the altar, and gathered around it is a ring of flickering figures. They sit close, shoulder to shoulder, knees tucked beneath them. Smoke rises in glowing coils, curling through the space. The scents of cedar and cinnamon wind through the air.

Although I'm not a part of this vision, the flames pull me so close it feels like I am.

A woman leans forward in the firelight, her outline wavering. Her voice comes with the crackle of coals. "My husband left with the last full moon," she says, thin and frayed. "He spoke no farewell. Walked beyond the reach of the kingdom and…never returned."

She draws a steadying breath without looking away from the vision's sacred flame. "Still, I set two places at my table."

Her words fall into the altar fire like an offering. The flames before her jump. Sparks lift and spin. She holds out her hands, and one by one they drift down and settle on her outstretched palms. Her lips part on a sound that is half gasp, half laugh, and when she smiles it's small and stunned and somehow whole.

Beside her a man's outline bends forward, his figure rendered in a long, loping ribbon of orange light.

"When my brother took ill," he says without looking up, "I bade him speak to the sun. Told him faith would mend what flesh could not. Belief alone would carry him through." He pauses, and his eyes burn like lit coals. "When he died, I told the others the wheel had turned as it must. I told myself to keep away from the Tower, that I did not belong. But the truth is, I fear it. I fear I do not deserve its mercy."

He drags a fiery hand across his face. The motion doesn't erase the tears of flame that fall in the heat.

The circle leans in, holding him with their silence, their presence and peace.

"I gave my brother hope. Sent him to the grave with promises I knew I could not keep. If I stay in the hurt, perhaps I can pay for the harm I caused him."

The offering bowl before him stirs. A burst of sparks surge from the flames within. A burst of bright golden motes that lift like fireflies. One arcs toward him, and he lifts his hand as if catching a snowflake. The spark settles into his palm. Grief shakes his shoulders as he presses it to his chest.

He inhales, and his spine straightens, eyes wide with a look caught between joy and wonder. A long, shaking exhale leaks out of him, and the sound carries the words like an offering: "Thank you."

The man looks unmade and rebuilt at once. Whatever had been broken stitched back together by the Tower's light.

One after another, the stories continue. People bare their truths. Some speak softly, their voices thin as thread. Others shout, raw and shaking. And each time, the Tower responds. Its flames consume their confessions and return light in exchange. A quiet kind of healing.

A deep ache breaks open and spreads through my chest as I watch them. This Tower, this circle, this truth is what healing is meant to be. Real and messy and unpolished. Spoken aloud with cracked voices and red-rimmed eyes. People shaped by grief and guilt and the desperate hope that they are deserving of grace after the truth is known.

I've spoken so many words about healing, but I've never done this: Been soul searingly honest. Let myself burn. Trusted I'd still be whole on the other side.

I wrap my arms around myself, fingertips digging into my sides, trying to hold the ache in place.

I'm glad Declan's gaze is fixed on the memory playing out in flames. Glad there's a wall of heat and smoke between us. If he looked at me right now, I don't know if I could hold myself together.

Flaming grains of sand overtake the image—piece by piece at first, then in great, flaming gusts. They devour the oasis, stripping away the trees, the orchards, filling the rivers and canals. The ring of honest confessions fades like smoke on the wind, swallowed by the rising hiss of dust and heat.

What remains is a husk of what came before. A barren encampment bleached by sun and silence.

This burnt-out echo is the present. The kingdom we fell into.

Guards march through the camp in rigid lines, their

armor sculpted from flame. Villagers drift between tents—flickering shapes caught in the firelight—but something is off. Their joy is too bright. Their smiles too wide. They move like dancers performing steps they don't dare stop. Costumes shimmer into place. Silk spills down their limbs in ripples of flames. Flaming jewels burn along their cheeks like frozen tears.

The vision shifts again.

The stage takes its place as Wands' new heart, rising from the sand like a crown. On it, performers bow and twirl, movements perfect, rehearsed to each breath. They dance instead of speak. They spit fire instead of share truth.

Pain becomes performance. Confession becomes monologue. Applause replaces connection. And behind every perfect bow and beaming grin—they are silently breaking.

It's in the tightness of their shoulders. In the tremble of their hands before they clap. In the flicker of panic in their eyes as they scan the shadows, hoping no one saw the moment their mask slipped.

In a kingdom built on performance, silence is safer than truth.

The flames flicker and morph as next vision rises, conjured in coils of orange and gold.

My heart lurches in my chest, and I suck in a breath. "It's me."

The fire draws me in arcs of light—shifting, flickering, uncomfortably precise. She lifts her arms and lights candles, arranges crystals and herbs with meticulous care. Each movement is smooth and practiced.

Her head tilts.

She smiles. A carefully measured upturn of her lips, perfectly angled toward the glowing outline of her phone.

"I invite you to breathe. To trust the process. To be gentle with yourself." Her voice, *my* voice, flows out in streams of fire and smoke, slow and honeyed. Overly rehearsed. "And, of course, you must remember that healing is a journey, not a destination. Be kind to yourself as you go down this path."

But I know the truth.

She hasn't been kind to herself in years. This woman doesn't know the meaning of *healing*.

She posts. The caption glows. It's soft and lyrical and clean. I want to think this version of me mirrored in flame believes what she's writing, but I know better.

The fire shifts, and the performance sloughs off like melting wax.

I watch her fold in on herself. The fire turns to smoke around her, and the only glow is the one from the screen in her hands.

She scrolls. Scrolls. Scrolls.

Searching for validation. Proof from others that she matters.

I know that she believes if she just keeps looking, the ache won't catch up.

The image moves again. And there she is. There *I* am. She is a figure of motionless grief at a kitchen table made for two but with a single chair. She's bent over a glowing screen, face caught in the silent scream of editing.

And then she breaks.

Flames erupt as she slams her fists against the table.

The fire surges with her, violent and white-hot, reacting to her pain like it's its own.

Her voice erupts from the flames, raw and ragged and undeniably mine. "Not good enough. Not good enough. You are *not enough*."

The words tear through me. Hot tears sting my eyes as I press both hands to my heart like I can guard myself from them. Like they haven't already carved themselves into the softest parts of me. The ache in my chest rises until I'm choking on it, until I want to turn away. But I can't. I won't.

This is me. This is what I've hidden from everyone. Even myself.

The flames ease, and in the center of the fire, she starts again.

She rebuilds the smile. Reapplies the mask. Smooths her clothes. Lifts her chin. Again and again.

Each time it takes longer.

Each time it costs more.

The burning light behind her eyes fades with every reset. And still, she keeps going. Because she believes—because *I* believe—that if I let go even for a moment, if I breathe too deeply, if I let the pain rise, let the truth spill that the personality I've created, the version of myself I've pretended is real might collapse.

And who will I be without it?

So she keeps performing the part. *I* keep performing the part, hoping that eventually I'll become it.

But I haven't.

And witnessing her try—witnessing *me* try—is the most painful thing I've ever seen.

The Tower knows, and its fire draws that collapse too.

My mirror image flickers. Her silhouette splinters. Ash blooms from her skin. It spreads like ink dropped in water. Soft at first. Then unstoppable.

She turns to dust. Scatters. Rains down in silent spirals over me, over Declan, over the altar fire that spoke her truth. That burned her down.

The flames churn. The fire splits. And the vision twists again.

Declan sits behind a sleek desk carved from flame, phone pressed to his ear. Behind him, a man materializes from the heat. He's older than Declan, his expression severe, face wrinkled, but the cut of their jaw, the smoky, coal-black eyes are the same. Declan's father. Numbers flicker in the flames around them—profits, projections, check marks stacked like logs waiting to be tossed onto his pyre of success.

A young woman stands in the doorway, etched in firelight, a small suitcase clutched at her side. She waits for Declan to see her, to choose her. Finally, he notices. His flaming face brightens, and he reaches to set the phone down and rise. The older man's hand clamps onto his shoulder. The smile slides from Declan's face. He stays seated, takes another call, seals another deal, ticks another box. She exhales the last breath she'll give him and walks out. The door clicks shut.

Declan's fiery image shudders, then splits. It fractures him into two separate beings. The other Declan—drawn in red, flickering heat, palms ashy white with climber's chalk—rushes to the doorway.

The chalk-handed Declan grabs for the woman, but it's too late. He's too late.

The fire moves, and the vision shifts.

Suit-clad Declan stands before a polished boardroom table of flame, ringed by specters of smoke. They nod and twitch like hungry things while Declan's father lurks in the shadows. His father moves in the smoky black, and a thin whip of fire flicks out from his hand. The flaming leash snaps through the air and coils around his son's throat. Declan paws at his neck, but the flames only race down his arms, through his body, consuming him. From the shadows, the burning coals that are his father smile.

Across the room, the chalk-handed version watches, rages, burns. Anger clings to him in searing red flame as he paces. His fists clench. His shoulders shake.

"This deal will destroy everything it touches," he roars. "We'll win on paper and lose everything that matters."

The leash tightens, and the suited Declan crosses the burning floor in three precise steps. His eyes are empty, and his mouth wears his father's smile as he seizes the screaming, pleading version of himself by the throat.

"You were made for a purpose," he hisses, each word a hot snap. "You will see it through."

Red flame lashes across the struggling Declan. Disbelief warps his features as his form stutters in and out of focus. His hands claw at the grip burning into his throat, his mouth forming words that vaporize before he collapses into a writhing coil of smoke.

Again, the image warps and changes.

Declan kneels before a towering pyre. Each log is carved from flame and branded with a checked box. One by one, he picks them up and throws them on the fire. As the flames grow higher and hotter with each glowing chunk of timber, a piece of him sloughs away.

Embers hiss as his fingers break off into ash. His arms are next, then chest, stomach. The pyre grows. A structure made of sacrifice and fed by what he's lost, what he's chosen to leave behind.

Finally, when there's nothing left to give, the last of the fire holding him together snuffs out. What's left of him collapses. Ash scatters through the Tower in a quiet gust, and Declan is nothing but smoke, a man who carved out every tender thing inside him just to check a box.

The flames crash down into the altar bowl, pulsing like a dying star before they flicker out completely. Only the soft glow of embers remains, cradled in the offering bowl between us. Their dim light casts a faint halo across the stone, illuminating the silence swelling between us.

We stand on opposite sides of the altar, smoke clinging to our skin, ash dusting our hair. Every mask that once protected us has burned away. The personas we wore like armor, the crafted versions of ourselves we used to feel valued—they've been stripped clean by truth and flame, leaving nothing behind but the raw, exposed heart of who we really are. Now, neither of us can hide behind who we've pretended to be.

I meet Declan's gaze, and something inside me swells under the weight of it. He sees me. All of me.

My throat tightens around the words I've never said aloud. "I don't know how to believe in myself," I whisper. "I only know I'm tired of pretending."

The wind stirs, slow and mournful, lifting the last threads of smoke from the air. It sweeps our ashes from the stones and scatters them into the sky like constellations.

Declan rounds the altar, the fire's dying light catching in his dark eyes. "If it's too much to believe in yourself, you can start by believing in me." He holds out his hand in quiet invitation.

I stare at it, then at him. The fully and painfully real Declan Thorne. A man who's made mistakes, who's suffered losses, who has scars no one can see. A man just as broken and uncertain and lost as I am.

Maybe that's what makes him exactly who I need.

For the first time in a long, long while, I don't wait for a sign.

I make my own.

And I take his hand.

NINETEEN

Declan's fingers wrap around mine. The truth lingers in the air, humming between our bodies, breathing on its own. When he tugs me forward, I go easily, willingly. I fall into him because I want to. Because everything the Tower burned away made room for things I never thought I'd be brave enough to hold—stillness, desire without performance, want without fear. And him.

His exhale is long and uneven, a sound more like a release than a breath. His hands find my waist. Mine curl into his shirt, fingertips pressing into the fabric like I need to feel how solid he is. We stand like that, our foreheads touching, suspended in something quiet and tender and unfinished.

We've both been burned down to our bones. And here, in the ashes, we choose to start again.

Maybe this is what beginning feels like.

"I didn't realize how bad it'd gotten," I murmur. "Bit by bit, I edited myself down. Smoothed the edges.

Cleaned up the rough spots. Kept rebranding until there wasn't much left that was actually me."

His thumb strokes the small of my back, grounding me with that quiet, steady pressure.

"It's not surprising she never loved herself," I whisper. "How could she?"

"I could." Declan's breath is warm against my cheeks. "If she let me, I could love her enough for both of us."

I look up, searching his face. Searching for the catch. The hesitation. The lie.

I want to trust him. I want to let myself trust him. But habits don't die in a night. The woman I built—polished, made palatable—still lives under my skin, cataloging every way I fall short.

"I taught myself that love is just another thing to manifest, to earn. Do everything right, be smaller, quieter, prettier, and one day someone picks you."

Declan doesn't rush to fill the silence, to fix what I'm learning is broken. I'm grateful for that because something in me is spilling open, pouring light into the places I've tried to keep sealed.

Declan brushes my hair back, his palm warm as he cradles my face. "Would it be weird to say that I think I might have manifested you, like this, just as you are?"

"In the messy middle of healing?" Tears press against my eyes. "I've spent so long building the appearance of being okay, I'd forgotten what it feels like to actually become it."

The Tower gave me permission to move forward, burn myself down, and rise from the ashes like a phoenix. Declan did too. But more importantly, *I* have finally given myself permission to stop performing. To stop contorting into something worthy. To stop chasing validation like it's a prize to be won with perfection.

This experience, this kingdom's magick, has awakened a part of me, brittle and buried, and I know if I let it rise into the light, I'll never be able to shove it back down into the dark.

But maybe that's the point.

"Do you know what that looks like for you?" I ask. "Moving forward. Living the life you want. Healing."

He blinks like the idea hasn't fully landed.

I lay my hand on top of his. "Your softness can't only be for me. You have to turn it inward too."

He looks down, lashes casting shadows over the sharp lines of his stubbled cheeks. "It's easier when I'm..." He searches for the word, jaw flexing. "Checking the boxes."

"Is it?" I lift my hand and trace the sandpaper edge of his jaw. "Because what I just saw didn't look easy."

His eyelids shutter for half a second. "I don't know how to bring that other version of myself back. The one who knew how to live life for himself."

"You don't have to bring him back. He never left." I press my palm flat to his chest, over the steady beat of his heart. "He's right here. He just got buried. But while we've been here, I've seen him. He's fun," I continue, an almost cheesy grin pulling at my lips. "A kind, knight-in-shining-armor type. And in spite of the fact that I've seen him shove five figs in his mouth at once, he's ridiculously sexy."

His brows lifts, mouth quirking. "You think he's sexy?"

I shrug one shoulder. "Occasionally. Under very specific lighting."

"Specific lighting?" he echoes, his hands sliding into

place around my waist like he already knows the blueprint of my body.

"Moonlight with a dimming fire. Maybe a little ash smudged across his jaw." I brush my thumb over the stubble at his chin. "You know...*hypothetically*."

He exhales a sound somewhere between a laugh and a growl, then pulls me flush to him, one hand sweeping up my spine with aching slowness. His chest presses to mine, solid and warm. Then he lowers his head and buries his face in the curve of my neck, breath hot against my skin.

"Are you flirting with me, Amanda?"

My fingers slide into his hair, damp with sweat from the Tower's heat and flame. Pulse skipping, I turn my face toward his, a slow, wicked smile curving my lips. "I hope to do a lot more than flirt."

Declan's lips are soft when they brush mine once, twice, testing the shape of us. His hand slides to my jaw, and he tilts my face enough to open me to him. A promise written in the way his lips part mine.

When he deepens the kiss, I meet him halfway, melting into him inch by inch.

His tongue strokes mine with unhurried intensity, learning me, tasting me. Like every slow glide is a question, and every sigh I give in return is the answer. His thick fingers splay against the small of my back, and the contact sends a pulse of heat up my spine.

I sigh into his mouth, opening wider, burning hotter. His teeth catch my bottom lip, and I gasp, the sound echoing off the Tower columns. He groans low in his throat, the vibration sinking straight into my bones.

The more he kisses me, touches me, the more of myself I want to give. The whole, broken, burning truth.

"Declan—"

His name slips out before I know what I mean to say. There's so much rising at once—want, ache, uncertainty, the edge of something that feels like surrender.

He pulls me closer, one arm tightening around my waist, the other sliding higher up my back, palm pressing flat between my shoulder blades.

"I'm not going anywhere," he murmurs. His voice is gravel and honey, rough and sweet.

My knees buckle, and I collapse into him fully, letting him take my weight. Letting him hold it. Letting him hold me.

His hands move slowly up my arms like he's afraid that one wrong touch might fracture whatever fragile, sacred thing has opened between us. His fingers trail beneath the loose edges of my wrap and find the tie at my waist. He pulls the string and pushes it away, knuckles brushing my ribs, leaving trails of fire behind.

He pushes the silk, and the wrap slips from my shoulders. Before it's even reached the sandy stones, I reach for him, needing him closer, his skin against mine. My hands slide under his shirt, palms skimming the ridges of muscle carved along his stomach.

I lift the fabric up his chest. He takes it from me, ripping it off and letting it fall, his mouth catching mine in a kiss that's harder now, hungrier, like something inside him has also been bared.

His callused hands scrape my shoulders to the ties at the back of my neck. His lips never leave mine as he tugs them loose, and the moment the fabric slips away, cool night air licks across my skin. My nipples tighten instantly—sharp, needy points that ache for his touch.

He kisses a line down my throat, stubbled jaw burning a track in my skin. He trails lower, breath coming in hot plumes against the swell of my breast. My toes curl against the stone. I rise onto them, lifting into him, offering. Begging.

He groans, low and broken, then closes his lips around one aching peak and sucks.

A moan punches from my lungs like it's been tucked inside my chest waiting there, waiting for him.

My spine bows. My fingers dig into his shoulders, nails scoring flesh. His free hand finds my other breast, thumb brushing the tight bud in slow circles, over and over, until my legs tremble.

Pleasure pools low and deep, heat slick between my thighs. Every pull of his mouth draws more from me. Every breath makes me needier, more desperate.

He releases my breast with a soft, wet pop that makes my knees shake. His tongue flicks once more over the peak then he drags his mouth back up to mine. His hands slide lower, fingers scorching a path along my ribs, tracing the dip of my waist and the curve of my hips with unbearable patience.

Rough fingers find the knots of my panties on either side of my hips. One tug, then another, and the ties unravel in his hands, whispering against my skin as they fall open. The fabric slips down my thighs in slow surrender, catching briefly at my knees before pooling at my feet.

When he sinks to the ground, rough palms sliding down my ass, the breath leaves my lungs in one violent rush.

"Spread your legs for me," he rasps, his hands anchoring at my thighs.

My body listens before I can think, hips tilting, feet parting in silent invitation.

He pulls me closer, presses his mouth to the inside of one thigh. The sandpaper scratch of his cheek against my soft flesh shoots hot sparks beneath my skin. The heat of it coils deep in my belly, spreading lower, dripping between my legs.

I reach for the altar to steady myself, fingers curling against the warm stone.

He looks up at me from under his dark lashes, hair wild and damp, delicious mouth curved in a sly smile that makes my stomach clench. "I've been dreaming of this every goddamn night. What you smell like." With a sharp inhale, he drags his nose through my wet heat. "What you taste like."

I don't get the chance to respond. His mouth is already on me.

He licks a long, flat stripe through my slickness. He groans into me, and the vibration rocks straight through my core, stealing the breath from my lungs. I clutch at his hair, fingers twisting in the damp strands, tugging without meaning to.

He sinks his fingers into the meat of my thighs, holding me open, holding me steady. His mouth is relentless, tongue flicking and rolling and dragging until I'm shaking, panting, grinding against his face.

"Oh—fuck—Declan—"

He seals his mouth around my clit and sucks.

Lightning bolts through me. My back arches, and a strangled moan tears from my throat as my orgasm hits, wave after wave crashing through me. I pant his name, begging without knowing what I'm asking for as I shatter on his tongue. His strong hands hold me there—mouth latched, fingers gripping, feeding off every twitch and cry that rips out of me.

When the stars fade from my vision, and I can finally remember how to inhale, he rises.

His face is flushed, his mouth wet, his eyes so dark there's no light left.

"If I had to die between those thighs," he growls, licking his bottom lip, still tasting me, "it'd be the best fucking ending I could ask for."

My body clenches around nothing, desperate and wet, already aching for more. That line shouldn't do what it does, but I am ruined.

I lunge for him and crash my mouth to his. I taste myself on his tongue, and I suck, dragging a guttural sound from his throat. My teeth scrape his bottom lip, and I bite down until he groans into my mouth, hands flying to my hips.

I want to devour him. Or be devoured.

The ties of his pants resist for half a second before they give way beneath my fingers. I dip my hand inside, skin already fever hot, and curl my fingers around the base of his cock. He's so thick, velvet stretched tight over steel.

I drag my hand up the full length, then use my thumb to circle the swollen tip, which is already leaking for me.

He snarls against my mouth, hips jerking, and starts to back me toward the bench.

I shake my head and press my hand to his chest.

"Sit."

His eyes flare, and he kicks his pants the rest of the way off before sinking back onto the stone bench.

Declan spreads his legs wide. His cock juts up between us—thick and hard and absolutely fucking perfect.

I climb into his lap, and his hands lock onto my hips, fingers bruising, desperate. I reach between us and wrap my fingers around him, slower this time, savoring the way he twitches in my grip.

"Fuck," he hisses between clenched teeth.

I drag the head of his cock back and forth through the mess between my thighs, teasing us both. The swollen tip bumps my clit, and I jolt, a gasp tearing from my lips.

"Goddamn, Amanda," he growls, jerking up into my fist, barely holding himself back.

I rock forward, slow and merciless, taking the tip. Enough to tease, to burn.

His head snaps back, teeth clenched like he's fighting for his last shred of control. "You're gonna kill me."

I lean in, brushing my lips against the shell of his ear, letting my teeth graze the curve of it. "For the man who always does what he's told, who's always in control, you sound a little wrecked."

He grabs my jaw, and his thumb slides along my lower lip, dragging down until my mouth parts for him.

"You think I'm wrecked now?" His voice is molten, blazing, scorching. "Sit all the way down, baby. *Break me.*"

So I do.

I tilt my hips and sink down on his cock.

Every thick, perfect inch stretches me open, heat flooding between my thighs, flames racing up my spine in a wild, uncontainable blaze. My mouth falls open, breath caught somewhere between a gasp and a plea as I take him fully. My head drops back, a moan finally tearing loose from my throat. The stretch is obscene. Perfect. Too much and still not enough.

"Fuck—*Amanda*—" His voice breaks around my name as his fingers bite into my hips.

I rock in slow, grinding circles, rolling my hips, watching him unravel one thrust, one unhurried grind at a time. His eyes flutter shut, his jaw tight.

But I want him here. With me.

I reach up, both hands cradling his face. "Look at me."

His eyes open, and his gaze is bare, defenseless, all storm and surrender, firelight flickering in those coal-dark pools.

His hand lifts, brushing the hair from my cheek with a tenderness that slices something open in my chest. I whimper as his thumb drags slow across my skin like he's memorizing the shape of this moment.

"I've never wanted anything like I want you," he says, voice splintering. He pulls me down until our foreheads press together, breath mingling. "You make everything beautiful, colorful. You make me want to live."

His words shatter the cocoon around my heart—the part of me that believed I had to earn love. Perform for it. Be perfect for it. My body trembles, clenches around him, tears blurring my vision even as I ride the edge of something I've never let myself feel before—being wanted without performance. Being chosen for exactly who I am.

My mouth finds his again, and I kiss him like it's the only proof that any of this is real.

His hips roll up, slow and deep, filling me with that perfect, devastating stretch. I gasp, nails digging into his shoulders as the pressure builds. His next thrust is harder—deeper. The moan I let out is ragged, shaking.

Another thrust that slams my ass into his thighs, and my back bows.

My toes curl as he grips my hips and uses them for leverage, dragging me down to meet every merciless stroke.

I can't think. Can't breathe. The world narrows to the stretch, the slick drag of him inside me, the filthy sound of skin on skin echoing off the stone as he fucks up into me.

He grunts out a curse, sweat beading along his brow as I brace my hands on his chest and start to move like I mean it—like right here, on his cock, is how I break myself apart and rebuild into someone new. My thighs burn, my rhythm turns frantic. Every time I slam down, his dick hits a spot that makes my vision blur.

"You feel me right here?" He presses a hand to my stomach, just below my navel.

I nod, desperate, frantic. My nails score his chest. My thighs quiver around him.

He slides his hand between us. "You're so wet," he grinds out, thumb circling my clit in tight, ruthless spirals. "You gonna come for me again?"

"Yes," I pant. "Yes. I want to come on your cock."

His head snaps back like I yanked a leash. "*Fuuuck.*"

The sound he makes is primal, feral. His hands clamp down on my hips, and then he's thrusting up into me again, brutal, relentless.

My moans turn into cries, each one louder, more desperate than the last.

It hits like an inferno, violent and all-consuming. I shatter around him with a scream, my thighs clenching, body spasming.

"That's it, baby," Declan groans. "Come for me. Drench my fucking cock."

My vision whites out as pleasure blazes through me. I ride it out, writhing, gasping his name like it's the only word I remember.

He lifts me enough to pull out and comes with a broken curse, his release spilling hot across my thigh.

We collapse into each other, sweat-slicked and breathless, and his arms wrap tight around me. We're both shaking, both breathing like we've crawled from the smoke and finally found clean air.

His chest rises and falls against mine in uneven waves. My hand settles at the nape of his neck, fingers threading through damp strands of hair as I press closer, needing the feel of his skin against mine to keep from floating away.

"I think you broke me," he murmurs, voice rough and raw at the edges.

A slow, shaky laugh bubbles up from deep in my chest. "You asked for it."

He pulls back enough to look at me. His eyes are heavy-lidded, pupils still blown wide, but behind the wreckage is something gentler. Something new.

"Amanda..." He says my name quietly, and it lands differently. Like a hope. Like a wish.

"What is it?" My fingertips run along the rough scratch of his cheek as my thumb sweeps beneath his eye. Vulnerability flickers in his gaze, and it makes my heart squeeze. "You can tell me anything, Declan."

The nod he gives is thin and unconvincing. He grabs the nearest fur throws and wipes up the mess on my thigh before draping the second around my shoulders.

His arms slide around me, his hold tightening at my waist until I'm pressed flat against him as if he's afraid the moment he lets go I might run away.

"I don't want to be the man I was. Not after this. Not after you."

"I don't want to be the woman I was either," I whisper. "I want—" My throat tightens, the words snagging on old patterns, old fears.

But I won't let them win. I deserve to say what I feel. And Declan deserves to hear it. All of it. The truth in its full, messy, unfiltered form, and nothing but the truth.

I sit up. Declan needs to see me when I say this, to know that it's the truth.

"I want this. *Us.* Whatever we become, I want it to be real."

His brow furrows slightly. His lips part like there's something else he needs to say, but the words catch on a rough inhale.

I press a kiss to his cheek. The slope of his nose. The space between his brows. "We don't have to go back to who we were."

"No," he says softly. "We don't."

Hope is a dangerous kind of fire. It burns just like fear. I've spent my whole life flinching from joy the same way I do from pain, well aware that either one can turn me to ash if I'm not ready.

I draw the fur throw tighter around my shoulders, trying to hold the moment in place. Like our softness might be enough to make me safe. Like if I stay still enough, quiet enough, maybe the universe won't notice I finally have something to lose.

"Hey," Declan murmurs, his hand finding my waist

beneath the blanket and squeezing. "You're here. I'm here. That's real."

My mouth finds his again. The kiss is deep and aching, more need than heat. His hands cradle my face like he knows exactly how fragile I am. My fingers knot in his hair, trying to memorize the way he feels when he's not holding anything back. I want to stay here forever.

Unfortunately, forever lasts less than a minute.

Voices echo through the Tower. Fast footsteps across sand. The crackle of torches.

"Keep searching! Their footprints led this direction." A voice I know all too well barks orders.

Declan's body goes rigid beneath me, every muscle wound tight as a spring.

"If they're not dead now," Dav snaps, "they will be soon."

I tilt my head back, gaze searching the dark ring of sand that surrounds the top of the Tower like the rim of an ancient hourglass. The blanket falls to the floor as I move, and Declan slides out from under me. He snatches up his pants. Then my wrap. Then my bra and panties.

"It's the guards," he says, handing me my bundle of clothes. "We missed our performance."

TWENTY

I'm halfway into my wrap, one arm through the sleeve, hair sweaty and sticking to the nape of my neck when a shout rips the air above us—a muffled command that plainly says Dav and the others are close.

Prickles of energy start to snap against my skin. This is more than the adrenaline of throwing on clothes and knowing we'll have to pay the price for not performing for the queens and their court. Magick coils in my chest. A low, patient pressure that settles behind my breastbone and won't be ignored. The Tower hums through the stones under my soles. Its magick is talking, speaking directly to me, warning me, and I've learned enough about the Tower and this kingdom not to ignore it.

"I don't know how," I say, breath shallow, fingers fumbling with the ties of my wrap. "But we need to get away from here before the guards find this place."

Declan finishes pulling on his sandals, his brow

drawn tight as he studies the ring of packed sand. "We could try to climb it."

We cross to one of the walls that hems the Tower in, a smooth curve of compacted sand rising above us. I press my hand to the wall. The surface gives, melting beneath my palm, grains slipping between my fingers like flour.

"*Can* we climb it?"

As if on cue, the sand along the wall shifts. A few grains sift over my toes, then a soft, hissing cascade slides down the face with a low *shh-shh-shh* like someone tipped the hourglass. The sand bulges and settles. Holds take shape—ridges, shelf-steps, and fist-sized nubs push out where there were none. Sparks drift along the new features in two parallel columns, markers lighting side-by-side paths up the face of the wall.

Declan tests the first handhold, then grins. "We can now."

He gives the sand an approving tap and nods for me to try. I edge closer, skeptical, and slip my foot into the lowest pocket. I press my weight into it, and it doesn't budge.

With a wobbly smile, I say, "Seems solid enough."

He rubs his hands together then shakes them out and rolls his neck. The motions are small, muscle memory, but there's an eager looseness about him I haven't seen before. "Don't think of it as pulling yourself up with your arms. Push with your legs," he instructs. "Let those bigger muscle groups do the work."

"The only thing I've ever climbed is a ladder, and that wasn't even recently." My throat tightens as I track the lit paths up the sand. "What if I fall?"

"You won't." He presses a soft kiss to the top of my head. "I'll be right next to you the whole time."

He points to a shallow ledge. "Plant the toes of your right foot there. Keep your arms extended and grip the holds for balance, then drive up. *Push*—don't pull."

I do as he says—press my toes into the pocket, feel the wall take my weight, and reach for the first set of ridges.

When his hand steadies my hip it's a coach's touch, firm and correcting. "Watch your feet and use your toes. Push, Amanda. Good. Now reach."

My lungs work. My stomach churns, but motion settles the panic, and Declan's voice is a rhythm I can lean on.

"Keep breathing," he murmurs, a buoy I can cling to. "I'm right here."

Sparks gather like moths, signaling where I should place my hands and feet next, then moving up as soon as I pass. A breadcrumb trail built of flames and magick.

Declan climbs beside me, damp hair sticking to his forehead, grin wide and boyish and beautiful. He moves naturally, the muscles in his back and arms tightening and relaxing in easy motions. Every so often he throws me a glance, and his smile is not just about the climb—there's adoration in it, like he's watching something precious learn to move.

Halfway up he glances over at me, eyes bright with the reflection of the sparks guiding our path. "So this is magick."

I breathe, then laugh, and the sound is thin in the open air. "Incredible, isn't it?"

He tilts his head, watching me, and his voice softens. "The most incredible thing I've ever seen."

A few more feet up, and I realize it's been a minute since I last heard the guards' shouts. The quiet makes my stomach tighten. I can't shake the feeling that we'll breach the lip of the dune and be met with shackles and swords. If they look down into the Tower—if it's exposed… I don't know why, but the thought terrifies me.

I peer up into the silver glow of moonlight spilling across the upper edge. No silhouettes. No movement. But the stillness only winds the tension tighter.

My mouth is dry, my swallows thick as I glance over my shoulder at how far we've ascended. At this height, the embers smoldering in the altar offering bowl are a small blur of orange light. My legs start to shake, my hands instantly clammy. The drop would be over in seconds. Then my body would meet stone, and that would be it.

"I can't—" I start, my throat closing up as I stare down at the ground.

"You can. I'm right here. Don't think about what's below. Think about the next hold."

"But what if I miss it?" My heartbeat echoes in my ears. "What if I slip? What if—"

"Satan wouldn't let his worshipper smash into the ground."

I whip my head toward him, almost losing my balance in the process. "Excuse me? Did you just call me a Satanist?"

He shrugs as well as he can with his arms stretched over his head. "That's the old conspiracy theory, isn't it? Witches dancing naked in a circle, sacrificing goats to the Dark Lord." He grins, daring me to argue. "So technically you're safer than I am."

His fingers find the next hold. He tests it, then moves, pushing himself higher.

"Two things: one, I wouldn't call myself a witch." The words rip out in a mix of fury and disbelief as I scramble up the wall after him, anger firing hotter than fear. "And two: even if I did, that is centuries of misogynistic propaganda wrapped up in one asinine sentence. *Satanist*?! I have read hundreds of books on witchcraft, and that is not how any of it works!"

He only climbs higher, shoulders shaking with silent laughter.

"Oh, I see what you did there. You say something heinous so I forget about dying and focus on how much I want to murder you. Real clever, Declan. *Real* clever."

He looks down with a wicked grin. "It worked, didn't it? You're arguing and moving up instead of panicking and looking down."

It did. The ridiculous, infuriating moment is a handhold I hadn't expected—something to steady my mind when my muscles were about to betray me. I move, following his path, my body remembering the rhythm he's been giving me: breathe, push, reach.

My muscles burn as we ascend. Every step drags fire through my thighs. My lungs and heart keep trying to convince me I can't continue—that I've used up all my oxygen, all the energy I have left—but I do.

I have to.

"You've got the strength, Amanda," Declan says as if he can sense the exhaustion creeping in. "Keep going."

I can't tell if the holds are narrowing the higher we go, shrinking from ridges into little more than crumbling nubs or if the muscles in my hands are so tired the wall might as well be smooth. My palms are slick, my fingers and toes aching, and every breath I drag in is laced with sand. My arms ache, my calves twitch with warning spasms, but I don't dare look down. I won't make that mistake again.

Declan climbs a half step higher, his body angled against the wall like it was carved to fit there. He moves with skilled ease, fingers and feet precise, confident. I mimic him, slower, trembling, my nails scraping into the next handhold.

"Breathe," he says, steady and calm, the sound of his voice like a rope between us.

"I am breathing," I grind out.

"Not enough. In through your nose, out through your mouth. Keep the rhythm."

I try. I try. My chest heaves like I've been sprinting uphill. Sweat rolls down my forehead and stings my eyes.

We're nearly to the top of the wall when the foothold beneath my left toes crumbles away in a spray of sand.

My weight shifts. My stomach plunges. The wall seems to sway, and I'm hanging by my arms, feet scrabbling against nothing.

A throat-shredding scream rips out of me.

"Amanda!" Declan's shout cracks like thunder.

My grip falters, entire body hanging on by the tips of my fingers. "Declan," I whisper as if speaking to loudly will dislodge my hand. "I can't—I can't hold on."

"Yes, you can." His voice cuts through the panic, hard as steel as he climbs down to me, muscles taut. "Look at me. Only me."

I force my eyes up, away from the dark hollow yawning below, and fix my attention on him. He's close enough that I can see the moonlight tracing the paths sweat has carved through the dust on his skin.

"Do you trust me?" he demands, taking a wide stance and digging his feet into shallow pockets in the wall.

"I—" My fingers burn. My nails rip against the wall. "Declan, I'm slipping—"

"Do you trust me?!"

"Yes!" The word explodes out of me, broken and terrified and true.

"Then let go."

The world lurches. My vision tunnels. "What?"

"*Let go*," he grunts as he anchors his hips and chest to the wall. "I'll catch you."

The command slams into me. Impossible. Unhinged. Every instinct screams against it. But the truth blazes like fire in my bones. I do trust him. More than I realized. More than I've ever trusted anyone.

I suck in a strangled breath and let go.

Weightlessness claws at my stomach as gravity reclaims me and drags me back to earth. My purse slips from my shoulder, falling into the dark until it hits the stone below with a hollow thud that echoes up the void. I'm falling, shrieking—

Declan's hand seizes my wrist, iron-strong, jerking me out of the void. My shoulder wrenches, sending spots of pain bursting across my vision, but his grip is unbreakable.

"You're safe. I promise," he forces out. "Now eyes on me. Breathe. I've got you." His voice is ragged, every sinew in his body straining as he braces himself against the wall. His arm knots with corded muscle as he pins his body against the stone and hauls me up.

"Here." His voice is rough, urgent. "See the footholds between mine?" He jerks his chin down, sweat dripping from his temple. "When I move, put your feet there."

He shifts, bracing with one arm and a single foothold, his body straining as he frees the other leg. As soon as he moves, I scramble to dig my toes into the sand where he showed me. Knees shaking, teeth rattling, I wedge myself between him and the wall, willing it to take most of my weight to give him even a moment of relief.

With a grunt, Declan regains his hold. We're pressed so close I feel the heat radiating off him, burning through every layer of fabric between us. His breath comes in harsh bursts against my hair, and the solid pound of his heart rattles through my back.

"Good," he breathes. "Press in. Hips to the wall. Use your legs. Where my hands are—grab the holds."

My hands, slick with sweat and sand, tremble as I reach up and lock my fingers around the same ridge. His knuckles are white, fingers straining where they hold on next to mine.

"Now push," he orders, shifting his weight just enough to give me a boost.

I shove off, muscles screaming, hooking my foot on a jagged tooth of sandy stone. Declan guides me higher, talking through each move, grab by grab, so close behind me that the heat of him rises with me. My trust in him, more than myself, is what keeps me climbing, what holds me together.

Finally, with one last desperate heave, the wall gives way to open air. I spill over the edge in a tangle of limbs, rolling onto a hill of soft sand. With a groan, I drag up the last scraps of strength in my body to twist and look down the dune. The guards' torches wink against the dark like a scatter of fireflies—fragile, distant, far smaller than their shouts had made them seem. Their voices sounded so close. They must have veered off, driven in another direction before they ever reached the rim of the Tower.

Declan hauls himself up and over the edge and rolls onto his back beside me. "The guards?"

"Ten minutes," I breathe. "At least."

We take a second to lie there. The cool night air sears my lungs, each gasp cutting deep, but I'm alive. We're alive. Thanks to him. Something hot and wild floods my chest, more than adrenaline, bigger than terror. It's him. It's always been him.

Declan props himself on one elbow, his chest rising and falling in rough, ragged pulls. His hair sticks to his forehead, a streak of blood smears down his forearm. He looks wrecked—and devastatingly handsome.

The dam inside me breaks. The fear, the trust, the passion—it all floods out. Tears blur the stars above us, and I laugh through them, shaky and wild.

"I love you." The words tumble out, uncontrolled, unstoppable. "Holy shit, Declan Thorne, *I fucking love you*."

Not just because he literally saved my life, but because he's seen every awkward, shameful, messy part of me and stayed. Because he wants us to grow into something better *together*. I finally found him. The one person who won't shatter my heart, who won't turn away once he sees me completely. The one I can trust more than I even trust myself. For the first time, it feels like I did something right.

He closes his hand over mine and cups my face with the other, thumb swiping a tear off my cheek.

"I fucking love you too."

We crash together in a kiss that's all heat and teeth and panic. His mouth is hot against mine, the taste of smoke curling over my tongue, the faint tang of ash clinging to his lips. I fist my free hand in his shirt like I can hold us in this moment. If I just squeeze tight enough, the guards, the queens, the whole magickal kingdom, won't be able to touch us. Our lips break, our breath mingling, smoke sweet and ragged.

"Let's get out of here," I whisper, the words falling over themselves in their rush to escape. "We can figure out where to go after—once we've escaped. How about the Kingdom of Cups? They think we're from there anyway. We'll just…keep running until we figure out how to get home." I pull back enough to meet his eyes, my grip on him aching, my pulse pounding so hard it hurts. "Whatever we decide, we'll be together. And that's what matters. That's all that matters."

For a heartbeat, he's with me in that fragile, impossible hope. Then, the air shifts, and his hand slips from my cheek. He sits up, creating space that wasn't there a breath ago, and brushes the sand from his hair.

"I want to be with you, Amanda, I do. But…" His throat works. "I need to be honest. About everything. Even if it risks this."

I blink up at him, teary, blotchy, smiling like a buffoon. "You're not about to tell me you secretly hate cats and cuddle Cinder to rub in how much she despises me, are you? Because that would really kill the vibe."

A strained laugh breaks out of him, quick and fleeting. Then his expression sobers. He brushes his knuckles along his jaw.

My heart gives a single, hard kick, like it's trying to break free of my chest. It knows before my brain fully has time to register that this is a deathbed confession. A final declaration before our story ends. And the way he's looking at me… I already know it's going to hurt.

"No. Nothing like that." He swallows, gaze flicking away, then back to mine. "But I have been keeping something from you."

"*Okay…*" The word comes out thinner than I mean it to.

An icy prickle rushes under my skin. I shiver and sit up. I'm suddenly too aware of how little I'm wearing in this desert realm, how bare I've become with him. As if on instinct, my arms fold over my middle, protecting myself.

"Fuck, I hope this isn't a mistake."

"What is it? What aren't you telling me?" My voice is brittle. My nerve endings frayed, muscles braced for the blow.

"When we matched on Flutter…" He pauses, shaking his head. "It wasn't supposed to be real. We weren't supposed to end up like this."

"You didn't want to be magickally dropped into another world?" I try to laugh, a weak spark in the gloom.

"You were market research. I was considering funding a dating app company. Wanted to get an idea exactly how it worked. Us matching…" He pauses, dragging his hand down his cheek as each word sticks like a hot coal against my skin. "I wanted to see firsthand how effective the algorithm was. I didn't want to be with anyone, but I did need to know if it would pair me with someone I connected with beyond the physical. Would my money be going toward a product that could create real relationships?"

The breath leaves me in a pained exhale, sharp enough to feel like a blade slipping between my ribs. My body still aches from the Tower, from the fall, from what I let happen between us. What I asked for. What I surrendered to. The places where he touched me still hum with the ghost of his hands, and for the first time, that memory feels like contamination.

I clamber to my feet, anger blistering to the surface. Heat floods my limbs, my face as my mind claws back through every moment, dragging red ink across every touch, every yes, every truth I thought we'd whispered into being. One by one, the ink bleeds through until the memories are illegible, until I can't tell if any of it was real.

"I'm a case study."

Declan scrambles up beside me. "Not anymore."

"But I was."

Every beat of my heart chars its edges, turns it to ash inside my chest.

"Amanda—"

He reaches for me, and I back away, pressing my hands to my chest, like I can hold my heartbreak together while everything else falls apart. "Don't touch me. You don't get to touch me. Not after—" My teeth sink into the inside of my cheek hard enough to taste copper. "Not after telling me I was an assignment. A line item in your fucking market research."

"I didn't expect any of this," he says, voice rough, like he's trying to hand me a piece of himself. But I don't have the ability to hold anything from him. Not when my own insides are scraped raw. So I turn to deflection, barbed and ugly, the armor I wear when the truth cuts too close and thinking positively, using affirmations and crystals, won't dull the pain.

"Should I be grateful you caught feelings instead of just meeting up to fuck me for the sake of your spreadsheet?" My laugh is flat and humorless. "Is that what your mommy and daddy wanted for you? Because it sure looks like you *can* make your own choices. You just hide the inconvenient ones."

He looks at me like I've just torn the last piece of him out of his chest.

"I should have known better. Even though this is the worst possible setting, you were—" I falter, because if I try to name what this man means to me, it will consume me whole. "This was all too good to be true. I should've known it wouldn't stick."

"You're wrong, Amanda," he says, the edges of his words rough. "I am so sorry I hurt you. But what we had—what we *have*—is not too good to be true. It's real. *I love you*. That's real. That will never change."

"*You lied to me*," I cry. "About what you wanted. What you were even doing on the app. That you were using me. Everything between us is built on that lie. And of course you made the best of a shitty situation. You didn't have much of a choice. Kind of hard to gather data about how well the algorithm picked a partner for you and then ghost me when you got your answers when we're trapped in the same nightmare."

"Amanda, I—" he starts again, another apology already forming.

"Don't," I cut him off, the single word a door slamming.

If I let him keep going, I might break, and I've already done enough of that in front of him. His *sorry* doesn't unmake his choices. It doesn't pull out the knife after it's already sunk deep.

"You've spent your whole life chasing the version of you your parents decided was worth keeping. Always selling. Always winning. Always putting on the perfect show." I let my gaze drag over him, slow and cold. "Grow up, Declan. Stop worrying about how Daddy sees you and whether your mommy is happy. Maybe then you'll figure out love isn't something you can close like a deal. And if it were, you just lost mine."

There's a heat in my chest that has nothing to do with the Tower or this kingdom's magick, a sharp sting that settles in places I don't dare touch. It feels hauntingly familiar. Pieces of my life playing out the same way over and over again. But everything I think is real is always just another performance.

I shove the ache down deep, sealing it inside the container I know best. The one I can always reach for. The one that's never failed me. The one labeled *I'm fine.*

I turn my back to Declan, brush sand from my skirt, flick grit from my lashes, and sweep sticky strands of hair from my temples. Behind me, the Tower's rim gapes. The columns glow slate gray, casting strange shadows across the curved sand walls. Below, dunes roll away like a black ocean under the half moon. The kingdom's torches stitch a line of fire across the horizon. Farther down the ridge, the guards' torches bob like angry stars.

Figures I'd end the night on the verge of being arrested. The cherry on top of this shitstorm of a sundae.

"Ahead!" Dav's voice booms up the ridge as the

guards break into a run, boots kicking up arcs of silver-dusted sand.

The feeling in my chest hits harder. This time I know it's otherworldly, the magickal thread that's attached to my heart, and right now it's knotting around my lungs, squeezing them tight. "I can't let the guards find the Tower."

Declan clears his throat, the cool, disconnected edge from our first meet up back in his voice. "Why can't they see it? Wouldn't the kingdom finding out it's here—knowing it's real—help you do what Fortune said you were brought here to do? To heal it?"

For a second I'm furious in a way that feels embarrassingly small. Declan should know better than to question me right now. The Tower is mine, the kingdom revealed its magick to me, and I don't want anyone else messing with it or taking it from me. I want something I can keep. Something I can believe in.

I drop my hand to my sternum, fingers flat against the hot, steady thrum there. I breathe into it, let the rhythm steady my breath. The sharp, broken edge softens. When I actually listen—not to the frantic voice in my head that keeps me stuck but to the Tower's magick under my ribs—the meaning shifts. This isn't a warning to hide. The wheel is turning. Change is coming.

Declan's expression hardens. "What will they do to us if they drag us back? That's the more dangerous question." He glances down the slope, then back at me, shoulders squaring. The set of his jaw says he's about to do something reckless and chivalrous, and I don't need or want any grand gestures that prove how he feels.

"You're not seriously thinking of fighting them."

He doesn't answer, which is its own answer.

Dav's voice thunders up the dune. "By command of the Kingdom of Wands, halt and yield your weapons!"

I lift my hands. "Dav, we don't have any weapons."

"Then yield your designs!" he calls, stopping a few feet below us and drawing his sword with a flourish. "Confess you were sent to spy upon our great kingdom for Cups. Skulking off before your report is due, are you not?"

"This again?" Exasperated, I shake my head and toss a glance back at Declan. His arms are crossed, jaw set, teeth grinding like he's chewing rocks. Heat flares in my cheeks. He doesn't get to be angry. He's the one who lied.

Tarek jogs the rest of the way up the ridge to meet Dav, panting, his hair plastered to his sweaty forehead. Three more guards are at his heels, palms resting on the hilts of their swords. He wipes his brow with the back of his hand and grins. "Accusing them of espionage again, are you?" he pants, bent over and breathless. "Like I said, I gave Thorne directions to the Everspring. They deserve a bit of a respite as much as the rest of us."

Dav's blade glitters in the moonlight. "They are not at the Everspring, Tarek. They are here—in the dunes—attempting to flee."

"Well, perhaps," Tarek says breezily. "But I've shared many words with Thorne. They will not escape to Cups. They have no route and scarce provisions. They've merely..." He shrugs. "I don't know...gotten lost. One wrong turn is all it takes. Out here, the dunes look the same until the caravan fires show the way."

Dav narrows his eyes. "Do you listen to yourself?"

"I do, actually." Tarek replies, chin lifted. "I find myself charming. My mother often says—"

"Your mother is a cur," Dav snaps.

Tarek straightens to his full height, which is admittedly not that impressive, but he pulls it off with the indignant stance of someone six inches taller. "Take that back."

Dav lifts his chin. "Make me."

The guards behind them shift, trade knowing glances, then collectively take a half step down the slope.

"Can you two just shut up?" I press my fingers to my temples. "It's been a really long night, and I would love to get whatever this is over with. Tarek's right. We weren't skulking off to Cups or committing treason. We were—"

"Scheming," Dav interjects. "Plotting. Sabotaging."

"*Taking a break*," I bite out. "As Tarek said."

"In the dunes, under cover of night?" Dav's lip curls in a slow sneer.

"*Ohhhh*," Tarek breathes. His eyebrows shoot up, and he elbows Dav with a ridiculous grin. "They were *taking a break*."

The words punch the air out of me, sadness pressing down until it's hard to breathe. The moment we shared in the Tower felt like everything, and it all shattered so quickly.

Push it down. I'm fine. I'm fine.

Behind me, Declan clears his throat in a way that promises trouble.

Dav's gaze lifts over my shoulder. "What's the matter? Can't find your tongue without your handler's permission?"

Declan steps forward, fists clenched. "You don't want to fuck with me right now."

With a smirk, Dav tightens his grip on the hilt of his sword and starts to close the distance up the slope like he's been itching for an excuse. "It's in this very moment I should most delight in crossing you."

The guards flanking Tarek draw their swords with a sharp hiss of steel as Declan takes another step forward, sand shifting under his feet. The air crackles with the tension between Dav and Declan. One spark and the whole dune will ignite.

Declan's mouth curls into a cold smile. "If you want a fight, Dav, you'll get one."

"Oh, for fuck's sake. You two want to whip out your dicks and measure them? Better yet, maim each other. Prove which one's the biggest through violence. I'll wait." I throw my hands up and step back, giving them plenty of space to square off.

The tension holds, the guards' torches snapping light across steel, every man waiting for the first strike.

"Most convenient," Dav drawls, circling Declan, "that you slipped away just before your performance."

Declan squares his shoulders, eyes fixed on Dav. "We didn't run. We don't need to."

"We were going to come back!" I shout, my voice carrying down the slope. "But then we got held up. Not by some espionage mission. By *that*." I stab a finger toward the Tower looming just beyond the lip of the dune. From a distance it could be mistaken for the slope of a collapsed ridge, the shadow of a cloud pressed into the sand. It's easy to mistake unless someone knows what they're looking for. "Your kingdom is rotten with secrets, and you're too stubborn to see them."

"A convenient tale," Dav sneers. "Or a trick."

Tarek bounds the few paces up the ridge to the edge where the Tower plunges into the earth.

"Tarek!" Dav's smirk breaks as he points his sword up the dune. "Get away from there. This reeks of ambush."

Eyes wide, Tarek drops to his knees, leaning over the rim, torchlight painting his face burnished gold. He's silent save for the breath whooshing from his lungs, and then he presses one hand to his heart like he feels the same magick that's been beating in mine.

"It's not a trap," he says, voice soft enough that the wind almost swallows it. "'Tis a legend risen. The Tower of Fire, called back from the sand. The very thing the old songs sing of."

The guards murmur, shifting uneasily, their blades wavering in the firelight. One even lowers his torch, craning to glimpse what Tarek sees.

"Enough," Dav snarls. In two strides he's beside me, his hand lashing out. He seizes my arm and yanks it behind my back, pulling until pain sparks up my shoulder.

"Ow!" I twist against his grip, teeth gritted. "What the hell are you—"

"By decree of the Queens of Wands, you are under arrest for defiance of the Festival of the First Flame." A cold cuff snaps shut around my wrist, the metal biting into my skin.

"Get your hands off her!" Declan roars, his voice ripping through the night.

"Cuff him," Dav barks. "Before he injures himself on my sword."

I wrench around in time to see Declan meet one of the guards with a brutal right hook that cracks loud enough to echo across the sand. The man crumples, and another lunges. Declan catches him by the throat, slamming him backward into the slope.

He looks unstoppable—rage and muscle and sheer will. But there are too many.

The first guard staggers back to his feet and drives a fist into Declan's gut. He doubles over with a sharp gasp, knees buckling, and they seize the opening. Three guards pile on, forcing his arms behind his back. Another pair of cuffs clanks shut.

Declan grits his teeth, chest heaving, sand clinging to his sweaty skin. His gaze never wavers from Dav. "Touch her again," he growls, voice low and ragged, "and that sword won't be enough to stop me."

My heart squeezes so hard it hurts, but instead of letting it show I go sharp, biting. "Very knight-in-shining-armor of you. Too bad we're both handcuffed like criminals."

Dav smirks and tightens his grip on his blade like he's hoping for round two.

"Well!" Tarek claps his hands once, the sound loud and absurd in the tension. "What say we all take a breath and not end one another before we reach camp?" He flashes a grin. "Besides, the queens will want their tongues before their blood. A legend risen from the sand? That's worth more than bodies left to the dunes."

He steps in and gently relieves the guard of me, looping his arm through mine like we're heading to a ball, ridiculous as it feels with my hands chained behind my back.

Dav's groan is deep and long-suffering. "For the love of the sun, Tarek. They defied the Festival of the First Flame. They vanished during their ordained hour. The queens and their court will decide their punishment."

Tarek winces then gives me a sidelong glance. "The queens will be merciful," he says like he's trying to convince us both. "Probably. Maybe."

The guards shift formation, flanking us with swords drawn but lowered. Declan is kept a few steps ahead, shoulders taut, fury rolling off him in waves under the silver wash of moonlight. Together, cuffed and bound, we're marched back across the dunes toward the heart of the Kingdom of Wands.

Back to face the queens. Back to face judgment.

TWENTY-ONE

We're marched through the sand in a silence so loud it feels like its own indictment. Declan and I are a living cautionary tale paraded through the kingdom, and the caravan watches our punishment more closely than it watches a show.

Performers pause. Silks fall slack from fingers. Dancers extinguish their flaming hoops. A drummer's stick clatters. The music dies, replaced by the sound of our footsteps and the rustle of people retreating.

"Are they—" an apprentice whispers under her breath.

"*Shh*," a nearby performer snaps.

One by one tents close like eyelids. People flatten into shadow as if proximity alone could make them complicit.

I turn toward Tarek for answers, but he won't meet my eyes. He shakes his head once, almost imperceptibly, and stares down at his feet.

My heart pounds hard enough that I feel it in my throat. The guards keep moving forward, their grip firm, their pace unchanged as they drag us toward the stage.

It looms in the torchlight. The same one we've stood on night after night, smiling through smoke, playing our parts. I expect to be taken there again, have the kingdom called to bear witness. Bend the knee to the queens and put on a public show of repentance that feeds the court's appetite for spectacle and lets the kingdom forget its truth.

At least, I hope that's the worst of it.

"Please, Tarek, what will they make us do?" I ask.

He continues to avoid my gaze as he answers, "The queens and their court, they shall—"

"Hold your tongue, Tarek, lest a blade teach you how swiftly silence comes." Dav's hand drifts to the sword at his hip, the message clear.

At the center of the crescent-shaped dais with its dark stone polished to a mirror sheen, its edges etched with gleaming flames, the queens sit like statues against a backdrop of firelight. Solara in white and gold and Zephara in burnt orange with flames painted on her forehead and across the bridge of her nose to frame her eyes. Their court fans out around them, the elders of the Great Families that took control of the kingdom and extinguished its flame long, long ago. Each is draped in robes the color of fire and ash—scarlet, marigold, coal black—every hem lined in jewels, every collar sculpted high and sharp like rising tongues of flame. Their faces are painted or powdered or masked, and they sit bloated with authority, content to watch, to judge.

I see it now. This place is a mockery of the Tower. All the familiar shapes are here—the columns, the ring of flame overhead that mimics the sunlight, a stage at the center where the altar should be—but there's no heart. Whoever built this knew exactly what they were doing. They took the Tower's bones and dressed them up as spectacle, swapping living ritual for a neat display case. The Tower breathed. It burned. It healed. It held space for truth without demanding performance.

Here, truth is edited and repackaged and placed on display by those who profit from deciding which stories count. History is rewritten into tiny, digestible versions of events taught to children so subjugation feels natural and questions feel like trouble. Outrage is entertainment, dissent a plot point to be managed. These queens and their "Great Families" can keep the pageantry and the platform, they can vet the versions of reality that suit their power—but the truth has heat, and sooner or later it will burn through the hypocrisy.

"Kneel," Dav orders as the guards shove us forward.

Spectators funnel in, taking their seats to see how our story will end.

Declan and I go to our knees on the stage. I brace myself and try not to flinch as one of the nameless guards steps forward and releases the metal cuffs around my wrists and then does the same for Declan.

Queen Solara sits with her chin balanced on her ringed fingers. Her posture is perfect—still, straight, sovereign. Her gaze is fixed and unreadable and as dark as the stone around us. Her braids are twisted into a crown that rises from her head like a ring of flames.

Beside her, Queen Zephara lounges in her throne with the bored grace of a lioness. One elbow hooks over the chair's edge, her fingers drumming a lazy rhythm against the carved stone. Her mouth is a taut line as her gaze flicks over us, and the streaks of flame framing her eyes in fiery red makes every look she gives feel like a slow, deliberate burn.

The guards fan out in a tight semicircle behind us, hands resting on hilts as the court's narrowed eyes look down at us.

Dav steps forward, all sharp angles and smug obedience. He bows low at the waist, his sword jutting from his hip. "The accused stand ready."

Solara lifts her chin and nods to the stage. The guards around us part, and the Player steps out of the shadows. She's draped in black silk shot through with gold, and a layered necklace of orange, red, and yellow glass beads that loops down to her navel and glitters like embers.

"Good people of the Kingdom of Wands," she begins, "lend me your ears and steady your hearts. Tonight we are offered a rare thing—a story unspooled before our very eyes, hot with disobedience and the stench of betrayal. Watch closely, for what is shown will teach us what we may keep and what we must burn away."

She paces the lip of the stage in a careful arc, letting the beads washing down her chest clink like wind chimes. "Here kneel two whose acts have rent our script: the Story Witch and Mr. Thorne, the shadow who accompanies her. They are accused of defying your queens and this court, of abandoning their ordained performance."

Jeers and boos rise from the crowd, and she lifts both hands to silence them.

"This, however, is not merely condemnation. This is theater made moral. We are not met here to pry at private motives. We are met to reckon the shape of our kingdom. Shall such transgression be corrected by penance? By exile? By a far greater act of sacrifice?"

She sweeps her arms out, and the crowd answers in shouts of encouragement that make my stomach twist.

"Tonight, you will judge the form of the lesson to be taught. The center of our great kingdom is our stage, and you, the people of Wands, our actors' greatest critics." She finishes with a flourish, never once looking our way, folding us into the set as if we're props. "Watch and learn the shape of mercy or, perhaps, the cost of deception."

Torchlight picks out eager smiles and wide eyes. Children are hoisted onto shoulders as people crane their necks for a better view. The more excitement lights their faces, the colder my dread grows.

Solara rises from the dais, and her movement instantly hushes the buzz of the crowd. "What say you, sister? Are these traitors, or simply wayward performers who have mistaken our generosity for weakness?"

Zephara leans forward and purses her lips. A slow, wicked smile unfurls across her face until she seems to glow with pleasure from the thought. "Guilty," she purrs, not so much a judgment as an appetite for spectacle.

"Hmm." Solara taps her chin. "Tell me—why guilty and not simply naive?"

"They disrespected us, dear sister. On the night of the Festival of the First Flame, no less. Such insolence ought to be answered with consequence. And what a marvelous spectacle! I have been desperate for the pyre—a show to break up the boredom. Does not the notion delight thee, Solara?"

The pyre?!

The air in my lungs turns to ash. A chill slips down

my back, pouring icy water into my legs. This is a performance we're not meant to survive.

"They're going to burn us alive." Declan stiffens, and I feel the shift roll through him like a fault line quaking beneath the surface. His shoulders go rigid, arms tense at his sides. His jaw clenches, and a vein pulses at his temple.

His wide-eyed gaze finds mine, edged with disbelief and something else. His confession is still between us like shards of broken glass, and he looks away as if his shame hurts more than whatever the queens decide.

Solara settles back into her seat and tilts her head, her mouth twisting in something like indecision. "I have not decided if death is fitting. There is cruelty in ending a life for spectacle's sake," she says slowly. "It has been many seasons since an act has made my heart quicken. This Story Witch, her performances seem like true magick."

Zephara lets out a sigh and stomps her feet against the stone. "But, sister, I am *bored*." A faint smile creeps up the corner of her mouth. "I wish to be entertained."

Solara meets her sister's petulance with an unreadable gaze. "We shall not be rash. Let the court speak its judgment."

"Very well." Zephara pouts. "Let the court decide. But I shall look forward to the drama."

Solara turns toward the elders seated around the ornate thrones. "Court, speak." Her voice lays the matter open like a book.

A murmur rises, a thousand small wagers voiced in the hush.

Something hot and bold releases in me. I've had enough of being a prop in other people's stories.

"Is that how you'll decide what happens to us?" My voice cuts across the sand. Heads whip in my direction as I rise to my feet. "You're going to let a handful of people decide what happens to us without ever speaking to us directly?" My hands are fists at my sides. "Is this all a big performance to you?"

Zephara throws back her head and claps, delighted. "Oh, how wonderful!" she cries. "Very bold of you, Story Witch."

A sharp, cruel laugh peals from the court. It ripples outward until the crowd takes it up, hundreds of throats returning the sound as if on cue. The echo lands on me like cold hands. Heat floods my face, and my mouth goes dry as the amphitheater narrows to that mocking sound.

It shrinks me until everything inside gets tight. The same tangled knot of anxiety I feel after launching a new class that flops, or a polished post on socials that gets three likes and one spam comment. All the rehearsing, the risk, the parts of me I lay bare reduced to someone else's amusement.

Declan grabs for my arm in a quick, possessive tug. "Kneel." His whisper is urgent. "Don't give them anything."

I draw in a breath and steady myself before turning and leveling my gaze on him.

"They're going to decide our fate, and if we don't speak up, we'll never get the chance," I say low enough for only him to hear beneath the laughter. "At the very least, I want to be able to tell the truth before…" I shake my head. I can't bring myself to say it. "The people deserve to know what's out there. They deserve to know what's happening to their kingdom. It's the only chance they have to save the Everspring and themselves."

Declan's hand hovers, caught between the impulse to pull me down and the urge to stand with me. Then he rises. Warmth floods my chest. I am so full, I can't hide my grin. He meets my smile with a light in his eyes that feels dangerously close to hope.

It's almost enough. Almost. Then his admission, the fact that I am market research, slices back into me. The grin curdles, and I let it fall away.

He reaches for me, sensing my retreat, but I don't take his hand. Instead, I fold mine into fists and clear my throat.

"We saw something in the dunes." I try to speak over the laughter, but my voice is just another sound amid the chorus of jeers.

There's movement behind me, then the boom of two men's voices colliding.

Laughter dies. The crowd goes silent as every pair of eyes angles toward the two guards. Tarek jerks away from Dav, who drops his hand to his hip. Dav's scabbard sings a long, metallic note as steel slides free.

Tarek plants both feet, wood creaking beneath his boots, and squares his shoulders. "I will speak on their behalf. Cut me down if you must, but I will not stand silent while the truth is snuffed out."

Dav levels the blade so the tip catches the torchlight, a thin, lethal star. "You do not know what you are doing, Tarek," he spits. "Soft-bellied, soft-minded... enchanted by the witch's tricks."

Tarek's hand moves to his sword, fingers closing on the hilt, but he does not draw. "Better to be soft and true to the oath I swore—to protect the people—than to be hard and bought by coin and theater. My duty is to Wands, not to gilded pockets."

He pivots and lifts his chin toward the audience, toward his queens and their court. "The Story Witch speaks the truth. They did not abandon the festival. They were drawn—*pulled*—by an idea long thought dead but now resurrected out in the dunes."

Zephara's body snaps forward like a whip, painted flames along her temples shimmering under the firelight. "And we are to believe you, *guard*?" she hisses, and her fingers flex against the carved arm of her throne. "Your compatriot is willing to slit throats for a good show. What makes your tale more exciting than his?"

Tarek's eyes harden. "Does truth need a richer voice to make it credible? Or do we listen to whoever suits the court's appetite?" His stare flicks to Dav and then out over the rows of faces. "If we will not protect what's real because it hurts the story, then we are not guardians. We are actors in a lie."

Solara raises her hand, and Zephara settles back in her throne. "Story Witch," she calls, "what did you find?"

The Tower's magick thrums beneath my ribs, and my voice rides that current, lifting my words until they land like thunder. "We found the Tower."

A slow exchange of looks threads through the dais. At first, I think they're astonished. Then I follow the way their gazes slide to one another, and the nuance of those looks, the pinched mouths and clenched fists, has me tumbling toward another conclusion.

Solara's smile is small and careful. "Story Witch, you are mistaken. The Tower is legend."

"The sand caved in, and columns rose from the dunes. We were inside the Tower. We saw the altar. The Tower showed us visions—the way things were before your families rose to power."

The Player steps in like a director, waving her arms. "Blasphemy!" she cries. "She speaks of flames that have not burned in the memory of this court."

"Go out past the Everspring," I snap back. "You'll find columns bigger than these rising from the sand. This stage, this whole amphitheater is a cruel imitation of the real place. A place that wasn't built to worship performance."

A tremor runs through the court as the crowd begins to murmur, soft and uncertain.

Declan squares his shoulders and calls out, "The Everspring is dying. One day, it will be gone for good. This land used to be a part of it. Has anyone asked why it's failing or who profits from the inaction of letting it fade away?"

That line loosens something within the court. Expressions go tight. A man in an embroidered collar leans close to his neighbor. A woman with rouge-covered cheeks lifts an eyebrow and shows a smile that's all teeth. Like dry brush catching flame, the accusations begin.

"They wish to see the return of the old ways."

Another voice from the court cuts through the murmuring crowd, breathless and high-pitched. "An age without rulers? Anarchy!"

"This is Cups' doing," someone hisses. "A plot to see Wands drowned."

The rhetoric swells fast, fear breeding fury, a fever spreading from mouth to mouth.

The sisters fall suddenly silent. Their faces drain to

the pale of old bone, lips thinning. The stillness feels practiced, and my skin tightens with understanding: They know. Every person on that dais knows the truth.

My anger burns hot and bright. They are choosing power over the very lives of future generations.

Solara looks to the Player, who claps her hands. "Let us not lose the plot," she says, quieting the murmur. "This is not a scholarly inquiry into legend. This is a question of betrayal brought before our queens. Our great, wise monarchs and their court will not fall victim to a tale told by the Story Witch. Is this not what she does?"

The murmurs settle into relieved exhales as the crowd buys what's being sold. The Player's job is to shape the audience, cue emotion, time the reveal, and hand the crowd exactly what will push them to the queens' desired outcome. It's clear how she's kept her place beside the monarchs.

"Do you, people of Wands, believe we should take the word of this traveling conjurer?"

The answer comes in a roar of jeers and boos crashing like waves. The noise hits me so hard I gasp and clamp my hand around Declan's.

Taking her cue from the audience, Queen Solara rises once more. "We have our verdict. Bring forth the pyre."

TWENTY-TWO

They wheel out the pyre like a parade float, its weight groaning on iron wheels that squeal against the wooden planks. A team of guards strains at the ropes. "Heave! Pull!" they shout, shoulders bowed, boots skidding as they drag the monstrosity onto the stage.

The pyre rises in a pyramid of thick wooden beams stacked and bound tight, the gaps stuffed with bundles of herbs meant to catch fast and burn sweet. The scents roll over me even before the fire touches it—rosemary, cinnamon bark, something bitter and leaf green underneath that coats the back of my throat like bile.

This was always the ending they wanted—our ashes carried off on desert winds.

Zephara leaps to her feet, clapping and jumping up and down like a schoolgirl, her painted flames shimmering in the torchlight. "A pyre at last!"

Solara approaches the edge of the dais, chin lifted

high. "These flames shall entertain the kingdom, and in their rising smoke, order shall be restored."

Declan squeezes my hand, and my gaze finds his. His eyes are midnight-black, pulling me in with an intensity that feels like the only real thing in this nightmare of fire and spectacle. This kingdom, the crowd, the scent of herbs, the groan of the wheels, all of it is staged and hollow, but his gaze holds me steady, an anchor in the storm.

His mouth forms the shape of words, but the sound never reaches me. The lumbering thud of my pulse drowns him out, matched beat for beat by the creak and protest of the pyre's old iron wheels.

The Player, arms wide, drinks in the crowd's roar and smiles. She plucks a torch from its holder, and the firelight catches the red slash of paint across her face. Her beaded necklace sways as she moves—a metronome ticking down the last minutes of my life.

"Take them to the pyre!" she shouts above another wave of cheers and applause.

Tarek jerks forward with a shout. "You must not see this through!"

The reaction is immediate. His fellow guards are on him, their hands clamping around his shoulders. Tarek thrashes like a man possessed.

"They do not deserve this! They have not lied! Go out into the dunes. See for yourself!" His words ride above the roar of the crowd.

Tarek slams his heels down as he moves forward, dragging the men who hold him and nearly breaking free. More guards swarm him, locking his arms, forcing him down.

"*Traitor*," Dav snarls, stepping in close, blade flashing as he presses it to Tarek's throat. "Do not make me add you to the fire. There would be no pleasure in watching you burn."

Guards descend upon Declan and me, grabbing each of us and forcing us to the pyramid of wood. Declan's grip tightens in a final, desperate squeeze before they pry our clasped fingers apart and wrench him away.

This is it.

We're going to die.

It's embarrassingly ordinary, the way my chest folds in on itself—an old, familiar collapse I've rehearsed so many times it feels like muscle memory. I've lived here before, in this suffocating corner where hope shrivels and self-pity takes root. Every failure, every betrayal, every door slammed in my face always seems to end with me curled around the ache, whispering that this is what I deserve. I am too much, not enough, too loud, too quiet. Always the problem, always the punchline. I can summon a thousand reasons why the universe delights in watching me break, and I cradle them like proof that my suffering is earned.

The universe has never been on my side. That isn't news. What stings now is that I let myself forget it. The burning brilliance of my own naivete blocked out the shadows and let me believe that maybe I was finally on the cusp of change. That maybe *this once* the wheel would turn in my favor. When we first landed here, I should've just gone limp, rolled over, played dead, let the Kingdom of Wands take what it wanted. Every act of resistance since has been nothing more than stalling, a doomed performance delaying the inevitable.

The pyre's shadow stretches like a beast across the stage, long-limbed and ravenous. Hands clamp down on my arms, bruising in their certainty, and I'm shoved forward so hard my knees slam against the beams. Splinters catch in my palms as they force me to climb onto the wood.

Every staggered step feels less like moving and more like surrender. Just as the last shred of fight drains from my body, the world itself starts to slow.

The air changes. Everything around me gives way to that placid, syrupy hush—the telltale sign Fortune is near. Sound lengthens into vibrating ribbons, motion smears like wet paint. The guards' rough pushes move forward in frames rather than smooth assaults. The Player's laugh hangs in the air, broken into bubbles of sound.

Fortune's magick sparks in my chest. This is her. It has to be. She's bending time, freezing it, swooping in to save us at the last possible second.

I spin around to Declan. He's frozen in time, his arms outstretched toward me, a promise that might as well be a map to a country I no longer belong in. His eyes are wet, shining in the firelight, and his mouth forms words that stretch soft and thick as taffy. The words stick before they can spill across his lips, but I hear them in my head as clearly as if he's speaking.

I'm sorry. I'm sorry. I'm sorry.

"No!" My voice rips out of me, clanging through the frozen silence. I twist hard, wrenching against the guard's petrified grip. My gaze sweeps the crowd, the tents, the shadows. "Fortune! You came to save us! Tell me what to do."

She doesn't answer. No ribbon of smoke, no scorched earth marking her arrival, no shadow slipping between the cracks of time. Just silence and the acrid bite of herbs waiting to burn.

I scream again, my throat tearing with it. "Where are you?!"

Silence.

Fortune isn't coming.

The realization knocks the wind from my chest. Despair swells so fast it drowns me, filling every hollow place inside until I'm choking on it. I was obtuse enough to believe Fortune had stepped out of the dark to hand me a miracle. But the truth is cruel and simple—there is no miracle. Not for me. No matter where I am, the universe will always let me down.

If I wasn't so broken, a single tarot card wouldn't have been enough to end our lives. If I wasn't so hopeless, so fucking chaotic, I would've already figured out how to get us home. I have real magick here. But even that doesn't matter with how broken I am.

The world is syrup and glass as I inch around the pyre until I'm face-to-face with Declan.

My fingers tremble when they close on his. I squeeze like I mean it—hard enough to make the skin at his palm blanch—because if I let go I'll lose the only thing I have left that matters. And he does matter. *We* matter. There's still a wedge between us—his confession like a cold pebble pressed into my heart—but even with that, I can feel what we've shared, what we still share. It doesn't erase what he did, and it won't be fixed with a single apology, but maybe, if we ever get the luxury of time, we could untangle it, stitch the edges back together.

His hand is warm in mine, and for a breath I think maybe we'll get out of this. Maybe this is why Fortune came but isn't revealing herself—to give us time, a seam in the world to slip through. The hope tastes like smoke and copper, fragile as spun sugar. It arrives and flees in the same heartbeat, but in that small, precious moment it's everything.

But Declan is still frozen, reaching for me. There's a limit to what I can pull free. Towerfall's magick hums in my chest, coursing through me in fiery currents, but it flinches away when I try to tug him out of the spell.

"Why can't you just do it?" I roar at myself in a voice that sounds like someone else's. "What are you waiting for, Amanda? You have the power. Use it. Save him!"

I'm furious at myself for letting his admission fester and rot within me. My pride, my doubt, my need to be right. How selfish I am. Petty. A coward. I pummel myself with the thoughts, with names that sting because they're true. I hate that I'm thinking about being hurt when he's the one who might burn. I hate that my righteous pain is a chain around both our throats. I hate that this magick bows to feeling and that my feelings are messy and loud and useless.

Of all the ironies, the cruelest is that I have the power to save him, to save us, but the thing that's actually blocking me is not the kingdom or the queens or the pyre. It's this bright, ratty heap of emotion tangled around my heart. Pain and fury knotted around the mechanism this realm's magick needs to work.

I suck in a breath, set my jaw, and stop hoping for miracles and feeling sorry for myself. This isn't the end. Time's frozen. Great. I'll use the pause to find a way out.

My fingers slip away from Declan's—my own unformed apology.

I'm sorry. I'm sorry. I'm sorry.

I climb down off the pyre and jump off the stage. My lungs squeeze, and tears threaten to form, but I keep my spine straight and push through the statues of the crowd and away from the stage before I can memorize the shape of him reaching for me.

I don't look back. I know myself well enough to know that if I do, I'll stay. I'll stand here, watching him while I replay everything I could have done differently, until the memory of his hands is the only thing keeping me alive. I'll rewrite my story as the woman who froze instead of fought. I will become a martyr of my own indecision. And when Fortune releases her hold and time undoubtedly starts again, I won't let my grief be this kingdom's show.

TWENTY-THREE

Sand whips at my calves as I sprint away from the stage, the pyre, the court—away from the only person I almost let myself believe would stay. I don't stop at the camp's edge. I push into the moonlit dark, lungs burning, feet sinking into loose sand.

I run for the dunes because that's where the Tower woke, because if anything in this place can help, it's there. I run because I'm desperate and afraid, and desperation is a tool if it's used the right way.

I crest the final dune, lungs raw, and the Tower rises out of the pit in the sand like broken matchsticks, its columns blackened, splintered, reaching for the sky. My hands go cold and clammy, and I have to close them into fists so they won't shake.

"Shit. How am I supposed to get down?" My throat tightens at the thought.

I can't climb down the way Declan and I came up. Not alone. The only reason I didn't end up splattered on the stone before is because he was there to catch me. He kept me from falling. He kept me from breaking.

Tears burn at the corners of my eyes, but I won't cry.

"I'm fine," I tell the dark as I shrug away the memories. I don't have time to untangle them properly. Right now I have to find a way down, trust the magick on fire inside me that's screaming that the Tower can help, or watch everything that matters go up in smoke.

"Whatever magick is here, Fortune or whatever energy brought the Tower back to life, I need your help. I was brought here for a reason. I can't fix it from up here. Give me a way down. Please."

The sand shifts under my feet. It melts, soaking into itself like water through cloth. The ground exhales a low groan. A staircase pushes out of the wall. Each steep step is rimmed in gold and orange sparks that hang in the air like tiny, impatient fireflies.

I lean down and press my palm to the first step. It's warm and solid and buzzes with the same current that lives in my chest. The vibration rolls through me, familiar and fierce. An invitation.

The sandy steps are soft but steady beneath my feet. My lungs burn as I race down the stairs. The air cools as I descend. By the time I reach the bottom and drop to my knees on the shadowed stone, my breath comes in jagged bursts.

My purse is where it fell, dusted over with sand. I snatch it up, unzip it, and dump it out. It gives up what's left of the life I used to have: a half-crumpled pack of gum, a receipt for groceries I'll never eat, an empty tube of lipstick, along with the last of my witchy tools—a bundle of rosemary, a box of matches, a vial of salt, and the expensive green fluorite crystal cluster Alder gave me.

The fluorite is a gleaming piece of home. The proof that I exist somewhere other than this sand. That I have friends, a life.

The idea that I might never get home, that I might never see Gemma again, never sit on her couch with too much wine in my glass, retelling this wild adventure while she makes me laugh through my tears and helps me make sense of what Declan means to me—the grief at it is sharp enough to buckle me. Tears press in, hot and relentless.

"I'm fine." My voice snags on a cry as I brush my fingers over the glittering green cubes pushing out of their bed of ice. "I'm *fine*. I have to be fine. Falling apart now will get Declan killed."

The Wheel of Fortune card slips free and flutters onto the stone. I scoop it up. The edges are soft, the wheel stamped in glinting gold, a ring of symbols orbiting like little planets.

"Nice of you to show up." I wipe the tears from my cheeks and grab the card, feel the weight of that mocking promise—change, destiny, divine timing.

A laugh claws out of me, jagged and accusing. "Speaking of the Wheel of Fortune—where is she, anyway? What good is an omen, a goddess, if she doesn't bother to show up when she's actually needed?"

Remember...

Fortune's voice coils through my mind, echoing between my ears.

"Remember what?" My voice cracks between a shout and a sob, bouncing off the Tower's columns. "How do I remember something I've already forgotten?"

The Tower hums around me, low and steady, and the silence it and Fortune offer is worse than any answer.

The word keeps drifting through my thoughts—*remember, remember, remember*—like it should unlock something if I hold on to it long enough. I scan the scattered contents of my purse as if they're the pieces of a puzzle. Nothing screams salvation. Nothing whispers instructions.

I dig the heels of my hand into my eyes, furious at the wetness there.

"Remember what? My past? A ritual or a spell I've read? Some hidden meaning in the tarot?"

The fist-sized cluster of fluorite catches the moonlight, a green wink flashing through the dark.

Remember...

The word reverberates inside me, and this time it lands. I know how to find what I've forgotten. I've always known. The answer was in my purse all along. I've just been too tangled in my emotions, too distracted to see it.

Fluorite cuts through fog. It steadies the spin, clears the static, makes the truth bright enough to see. It's a stone that will break open the third eye and connect straight to intuition, to deeper meaning, to whatever's real beneath the noise.

"Of course." I blow out a shaky breath and blink away the press of tears. My magick has been flailing, pulled in a dozen directions by every messy, jagged feeling inside me. "I don't need more power. I need focus."

I curl my fingers around the crystal, pressing it into my palm until the edges bite.

"Oh, Alder. You billionaire angel. If I get out of this, I swear I'll forgive you for being such a douche."

My hands move on their own, the choreography etched into muscle and bone. I strike a match and touch the flame to the rosemary. Smoke rises in fragrant curls, bitter and sweet.

"Cleanse me," I whisper. "Make me mine again."

I waft the smoke over my arms, my chest, my face, the way I've done a hundred times before. I drag the scent deep into my lungs, begging it to scour out the ache. To still my pulse. To free me from the throb of heartache and make me strong enough to hold what's coming.

The fluorite waits in my other hand. I know I can't use it, can't focus, until I strip away the mess inside me. I cling to the ritual's rhythm. Inhale, sweep. Exhale, sweep.

"Calm me. Cleanse me. Give me strength."

Tears sting, and grief digs in like it has no intention of ever leaving. But if I fall apart now, I'll never put myself back together.

"I'm fine. I'm fine. I'm *fine*—"

The last one catches, snagging in my throat. My lips keep moving—*I'm fine, everything is fine*. I grit my teeth and force the words back into the air, as if sheer volume can hammer them into reality.

"I'm fine!" The shout ricochets off stone. "I'm fine, I'm fine, I am fine!"

The syllables rip from my mouth in sparks—bright, angry comets that hiss into existence and burn hot against the night. They streak through the dark, spitting embers as they go, until they slam into the altar. Ash stirs and lifts at the impact, and the whole bowl catches, fire leaping higher as if the Tower itself is feeding on the sound of my lie.

Fortune's voice swirls around me.

Remember…

"Shut up!"

I sink to my knees and sob, shoulders heaving, lungs wheezing, the noise filling the hollow until it sounds like the whole place is breaking with me. The sobs are proof. I am anything but fine.

Fear begins to take hold. It combs through my insides, twirls my veins around cold fingers, and whispers that this is all I'll ever get. This is what I'm worth. That I have broken something in myself that won't stitch back together.

Remember…

"I can't! I don't know how!"

Remember…

Fortune's haunting me now, mocking me with something she knows I can't reach. I am falling apart, and I cannot stand it. So I stop being small, stop trying to decode the magick, stop letting this realm run over me, and I let the anger move in.

Rage burns through me, scorching the edges of my despair until it becomes something sharp. I welcome it as it sears a path through me. Anger for letting Declan into the parts of me I shouldn't have given. Rage for the universe for dangling hope like it was ever mine to keep. Contempt for myself for ever believing the tease.

My voice tears raw as I curse it all—every affirmation, every magickal card, every single thing that's ever put me on my knees like this.

"You ruin everything!" I shout at the fire, at the Tower, at the universe, myself. "I am done! I am fucking done! Do you hear me? Done with all of it!"

Movement flickers in the corner of my eye. The

Wheel of Fortune card lies where I left it. The wheel in its center turns slowly, mocking me.

"Oh, fuck you." I snatch it up, strike a match, and feed the card to the flame.

The paper hisses and curls. Gold flakes blister and fall away in sparks.

The stone vibrates beneath me as the altar fire expands, and the flames swell and stretch into a single column of heat that claws the sky.

Shapes emerge within the inferno. Faces swim into focus before collapsing into ash. From the flames their voices take shape. They hum at a pitch just shy of pain, the sound crawling over my skin like static, pressing against my teeth, making the hairs at the nape of my neck rise.

Control…burns. Worthiness…rage… Love…unlovable… Died with lies in our mouths.

The figures begin to circle, every movement scattering a shower of embers that whip between them like snapping chains.

My gaze jerks from one spectral face to another, never certain if I'm looking at the same figure twice or if they're shifting between forms to keep me unsteady.

Remember… Fortune's voice fills me, pressing in until my heartbeat rattles my ribs like a cage.

Part of it clicks. I've heard these specters before—when I touched Fortune. The cryptic riddles, the sense of being chosen. It felt like I was being handed a key I didn't yet know how to use. Now it feels like they're furious I never figured out what it unlocked.

Remember!

And Fortune is too.

...waited for the right moment...called it fate. ...stayed small...called it safe.

The spiral of apparitions tightens. Their heat pulls at the hairs on my arms, and I taste ash on my tongue.

...nothing changes if nothing changes...

The ghosts lean in, their forms stretching taller, their faces flickering in and out of focus. The heat surges, a blistering wave that forces me to take a step back.

"You don't get to cast stones, tell me this is my fault. I have done everything I can. I *always* do! Some people are just unlucky." My voice is ragged, but I don't stop. "Some people are disappointments. Some people get stuck."

...nothing changes if nothing changes...

Their judgment circles back, insistent, like I missed the words the first time. They land heavy, searing against my skin like hot iron, branding me with shame I already carry.

"I didn't make the world this way," I snap, my voice cracking. "I just live in it."

One breaks from the circle, its form flickering violently as it glides closer. The face it wears is almost human before the flames take it again. Its voice is layered with all the others, the words resonating through my very being.

Fear...lies...feed the flames.

The fire writhes higher, twisting with the smoke until the two are indistinguishable, a serpent of gold and black coiling skyward.

I open my mouth to shout back, to swear I'm not afraid, not a liar, but the words wither before they leave my tongue, singed to nothing by the heat pressing in from all sides.

Lies!

The specter spits the word. Its body splinters into a shower of sparks that rain across my shoulders, stinging as they land.

The others fly toward the middle of the Tower in a single, furious rush, their forms unraveling into ribbons of flame that fold into the altar's heart. The column of fire surges, roaring with the sound of a thousand breaths exhaled at once. Then it fractures, bursting apart in a storm of embers that spit from the altar and streak outward, arcing toward the sand walls that encircle the Tower. They wriggle through the air like something newly hatched, and when they land, they burrow into the grit with a hiss, disappearing beneath the surface.

The ground bucks beneath me, the low tremor swelling into a deep, rolling quake that rattles my teeth and thrums up into my bones. The crystal in my hand shatters. The rosemary crumbles into blackened ash. The sand walls shiver. Each grain glows as the buried embers take root. Heat pulses out, lashing my skin with waves of smoke. The breeze turns feral, kicking up grit and fire. The walls ripple like muscle, then lift from the ground. In a rush of wind and fire, the sand surges out into the open desert in a blazing storm.

My heart hammers in my throat as I stumble forward, bare feet skidding on loose sand. I sprint up the low slope the tempest left behind, lungs filling with smoke until every breath scrapes my lungs raw. Grit lashes my cheeks. The air tastes of ash, hot enough to scald my tongue.

Ahead, a monstrous, towering wall of fire-streaked

sand devours the horizon as the storm barrels straight for the heart of the Kingdom of Wands.

This magick isn't Towerfall's. It's mine. It's been mine all along. My emotions gave it teeth. My lies gave it form. And I've just set it loose.

TWENTY-FOUR

"I didn't mean to..." The wind rips the words away before they're fully formed, scattering them into the howl.

It doesn't matter. It's too late.

The storm is a beast, stitched from fire and sand and every scream I ever tried to bury. Its body writhes across the horizon, a twisting wall of flame-veined dust, alive and ravenous.

I run to catch it. To throw myself between its teeth before it rips through the heart of the kingdom. My chest heaves, each sand-laced breath scrapes the back of my throat as heat lashes my bare arms and legs. The ground bucks beneath me, dunes slithering like snakes, a tide of sand writhing forward, dragging everything toward the kingdom.

I run harder, faster, legs pumping, muscles burning. I've almost caught up with the storm when the first curling lash of fiery sand slams into the outer tents. Silk rips like paper. Wooden poles snap like kindling, cartwheeling end over end before vanishing into the maelstrom. Torches tear free, each wink extinguished as the wind devours them.

Figures stumble and scatter, silhouettes blinking in and out of view as the storm whirls them into its throat. I throw myself into it, and the world convulses. Sound goes wrong first. The roar stretches, pulled thin and taut as wire until it sings, sharp and brittle. Even the slap of my footsteps sounds distant, as if someone else is running.

Behind me the corridor seals, a wall of heat and dust closing tight, hemming me into the path I've carved. Shapes waver inside the haze, outlines that don't quite belong to the storm.

An ex, one in a long line of relationships doomed from the start, steps forward from the grit, grinning, lips smeared with the wrong shade of lipstick, the stain bright across his teeth.

His form swirls and twists, collapsing in on itself before another takes its place.

My mother. Just her back, always her back, moving through a doorway away from me. The door closes behind her. The lock catches. She kept herself hidden from me, and I grew up learning love as a hallway of closed doors.

The storm is splicing betrayals into a mural. Every ounce of pain I've ever tucked away flares back to life in unbearable detail, the storm pressing the memories close.

Friends blur into view at the edge of the corridor, then begin to fade. The ache of being left alone spreads like a bruise under my skin. It's always been this way. People orbit close for a season, then slip out of reach.

Making friends has never been easy. With the exception of Gemma, keeping them has felt impossible.

Tears carve tracks down my cheeks, and I force myself to look away, to keep moving. If I stare too long, the wounds gape wider. If I linger, I'll drown in them. But I can't shut them out. The storm knows me—it *is* me—and it's offering me back to myself in jagged pieces. It wants me to bleed with every wound I've ever carried.

I almost do. The taste of iron fills my mouth, my ribs ache with the pressure, and I want to let the storm swallow me whole. But I don't. I take the pain and use it. Every memory it throws at me fuels another step. I refuse to stop long enough to let the storm, let myself, tear me apart.

The camp bleeds into view through curtains of sand and fire. I stumble forward, breaking through the last wall of the storm into what's left of the kingdom. The wind drops, sudden and brutal in its silence, and the only sound is the ragged chorus of moans and crying that leaks through the smoke.

Shredded tents flap like torn flesh. Pieces of wood lay broken, snapped, scattered. Small fires lick at tattered fabrics and light up the eye of the storm in a tangerine glow. Ash drifts like snow, brushing my arms and sticking in my lashes.

Guards and other members of the kingdom haul people clear of the rubble. Solara stands on the lip of the dais, jaw slack. Her arms are wrapped around her sister as they survey the wreckage. Zephara presses a hand to her mouth to cover her sobs. The court clusters in tight knots, twittering like frightened birds, eyes darting between the queens and the debris. From the stage, the Player hurls herself forward, red paint smeared across her cheek, her shirt ripped. She limps toward the shocked queens, flailing her arms, saying something I don't catch because my attention is focused back on the stage.

Tarek and Dav lift planks of wood from the collapsed pyre off a body. When the last beam comes free, Declan's shape comes into view. His chest lifts in shallow, fragile hitches.

"*No*. No, no, no." I don't feel the splinters of wood that bite into my bare feet as I scramble forward. Smoke claws at my throat, and ash streaks my skin as I climb onto the stage, clambering over the wreckage like none of it matters.

Because it doesn't. Only he does. Only Declan.

I drop to my knees beside him. Blood seeps through his shirt in a dark stain that spreads like ink across the fabric. His face is pale beneath streaks of sweat and dirt. His hair is plastered to his forehead, his lip split, his mouth trembling around the edges of another breath.

Tarek and Dav keep pulling wood off him, fingers gray with ash, palms scraped and bloody. Declan blinks at me, the corners of his mouth trying for a crooked smile. "Thought Dav would be happy finding me like this," he says, voice paper thin.

Dav grunts as he and Tarek lift another piece of wood and throw it off the stage. "I do not delight in bloodletting if it's not by my own hand." His mouth is tight as he bends down and squeezes Declan's shoulder.

Hot blood slicks my palms as I press against the wound. "Tarek, Dav, please. You have to help him. We have to—"

They share a look that wrenches the air from my lungs.

Dav's jaw sets. "There's nothing we can do for him."

"Perhaps the healer..." Tarek's words fade as he looks down at Declan then back up to Dav.

"We can try." Dav gives Declan's shoulder another squeeze before the two men jump off the stage and rush into the mess of injured bodies and wreckage.

"I am so sorry," I sputter when Declan and I are alone.

The last conversation we had—the confession that left me gutted—feels so far away now. I thought I needed distance, thought I needed time to make sense of it, of us. But all that feels small and foolish in the face of him, broken and bleeding.

Declan's dark irises find me, and even like this, even when he's wounded and on the brink of death, they burn through me. He drags his hand across the sand-covered stage with a slow, stubborn effort until his fingers find mine.

"You're here now." His swallow is thick, and he winces on his next inhale. "That's what matters."

"Don't talk. Save your strength—" I choke on the rest as tears prick my eyes, stream down my cheeks.

He tries to push himself up, and the movement seems to take every ounce of strength he has left. "I have to tell you—"

"Shh." I shake my head frantically. "Declan, please." I wrap my hands around his and squeeze like it's the last time I'll ever get to.

"Amanda, you need to hear this." He sucks in a breath and bares his teeth against another wave of pain. "You've been acting your whole life. You think other people, the universe broke you." His breath shudders out. "But they didn't."

I shake my head so hard it rattles my teeth. "Stop. Don't—we don't need to talk about that now."

He squeezes my fingers and wets his cracked lips. "You broke yourself. You…walled off. Never let anyone get close enough to stay."

A sob tears through me. I bend over him and press my forehead to his. "Please, Declan. Please, don't leave me."

"I wish you would have let me love you."

The words land and split me open. Tears come hot and sudden. They run down my cheeks and drip onto his skin until they streak his face. I want him to be wrong, but the truth is, I wish I would have let him love me when I had the chance. I wish I would have loved myself.

"You still can. I want to let you." I lean down and kiss him, my lips damp with copper and salt. "Stay with me, please."

My hands are slick with his blood. They tremble so hard my fingers ache. I press down where the wound is. My breath is a ragged, convulsing thing. Sobs break free and rattle up my throat. They sound like the storm, wild and animal.

"I'll fix this," I promise. "I'll—" I choke on the rest.

He squeezes my hand once more, thumb tracing the back of my knuckles. "I love you, Amanda," he breathes, voice tearing out of him like paper.

"I love you too." I press my lips to his again, clinging, willing. "I love you."

His fingers loosen. The squeeze unravels like a thread. A final breath trembles in his chest, small and brief, then the empty, sinking whoosh of it slipping away.

My brain offers me soft denials: it'll be okay, this is temporary, you're fine. But I'm not fine. I haven't been for a long, long time.

The realization seeps in slowly, and I feel it like winter in my bones—cold, patient, impossible to shake. I broke myself. Not betrayal. Not abandonment. Not the universe turning its back.

Me.

I am the only one responsible for how my life has turned out.

Every betrayal left me wounded, but it wasn't those cuts that left me bleeding. It was the armor I built after. The bitterness I spit before anyone could hurt me again. The walls so high no one could climb them.

It's all here. It became this very storm. My fear transmuted into ruin.

The fear that I am powerless—so I clung to control in the form of affirmations and positivity until they burned everything in reach.

The fear that I am unlovable—so I created a smiling, love and light persona, and when that didn't work, I lashed out, raged before rejection could land.

The fear that I will always be left behind and alone—so I forced others away thinking that if I could control how they left, it would hurt less, keep me safe.

The storm is every one of those fears made flesh. Alive now, tearing across the edges of the world with my voice in its throat, my fire in its veins.

"*Remember*!" The word lashes the sky, stitched into the throat of the storm.

"Nothing changes if nothing changes," I whisper, and the words aren't an empty affirmation. They're a vow.

I broke this—myself, this kingdom, Declan—and I am the only one who can put it back together.

The storm claws at the stage and the rest of the camp, a living wound roiling up from the sand. Fire threads through the funnel of dust like veins lit from within, and the sound of it makes my teeth ache.

"*Remember*!"

Fortune wasn't asking me to remember one moment, one lesson, one fixed truth. She wanted me to remember all of it—every scar, every joy, every sharp edge and soft place. A lifetime. My history. The collection of broken and burning pieces that made me into who I am.

And that's what this kingdom needs too. Not a script or a performance. Not a single, polished story. It needs to remember itself—the whole of it. The fire and the ruin. The beauty and the grief. The truth it buried long ago.

Declan's hand slides from mine as I push myself to my feet. The storm shoves me back, but I stay upright. My hair whips across my face, and sand bites at my skin like shards of glass. I know what to do.

I turn toward the storm and hurl my voice in a command that blazes a trail through the sky. "Hear me! I remember!"

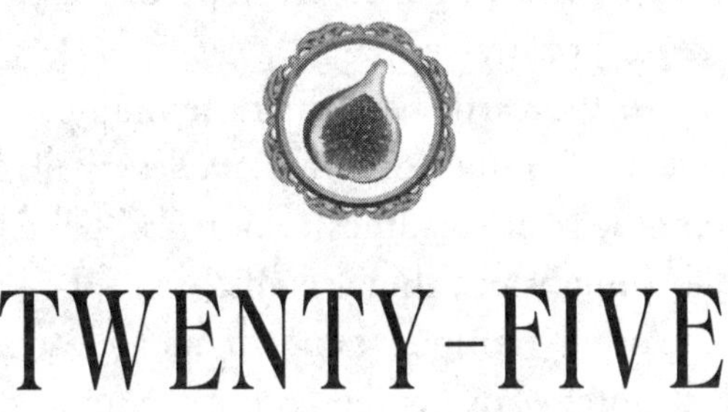

TWENTY-FIVE

"I know what you want from me! I know what to do now."

The queens and their court watch from the safety of their platform, waiting for a miracle or a spectacle. I'm still not completely sure which they would prefer. Either way, they're going to get the truth.

I climb down from the stage, and the moment my soles kiss sand, the ground answers. A shiver ripples out from my bare feet, concentric rings thrumming under the skin of the desert.

The Kingdom of Wands has been waiting. So have I. Every moment of my life has been preparing me for this one.

I reach up, visualizing my hand stretching through the clear, glassy eye of the storm to the heavens beyond.

"I call to the sky above, to the burning stars and endless dark. Lend me your light, your vastness, your fire. Lend me your magick so I might put things right."

Heat licks down my arm, curious at first, then

insistent, a swarm of small, wild creatures climbing down from the sky, burrowing into my fingertips, claws scoring along the path of my veins.

"I call to the earth below, to the molten rivers that churn beneath, to the stone that cradles us all. Lend me your strength, your steadiness, your fire. Lend me your magick so I might put things right."

The ground trembles beneath me. Heat swells up through the arches of my feet as if the core of the world has opened to me. It surges through my legs, into my belly, burning as it rises.

The two currents braid. Earth climbs. Sky descends. Terrestrial heat threads up my legs as starlight pours down my arm, stretched high overhead. They meet in the beating hearth inside my chest, and everything that has felt ragged, messy, broken snaps into place.

Old wounds stitch closed with a warmth that is made both of comfort and recognition. A silent healing that says I knew what to do all along. I had the tools, I only had to learn how to use them.

"Thank you." My voice wavers as tears prick my eyes.

Beings shimmer in the fire threaded through the storm. This time, I am not afraid. I finally know what they need from me, and I am more than happy to oblige.

Thank you, the ghosts whisper in return, voices soft as ash.

I am a conduit between sky and sand, between above and below, the past and the present. I am rise and ruin, mercy and consequence, the turning point that rewrites every small undoing into a new beginning.

My hands go to my chest, fingers splayed over the hot, steady beat behind my sternum. Power gathers there, and I walk toward the storm with that drum in my mouth.

A shape moves in the flame. Fortune steps out of the cyclone. Her cloak billows around her feet. Everywhere it touches turns blackened, charred. The sight of her is not a surprise so much as realization, as if a thought I never finished has finally finished itself.

She reaches for me with that hand covered in gem work and glowing like rubies trapped in flame. I reach back. My palm meets hers. The jewels are hot as lit coals, but I don't pull away.

"You remember." The shadowed line of her chin dips as her fire-bright eyes meet mine.

"I remember," I answer. "And now they need to." I motion toward the people of Wands who have gathered their injured and are cowering from the storm. "Show them what they were before the script. Show them how they hurt, and how they healed. They are ready to remember."

My magick answers. Heat blooms across my right hand, a blossom of fire under the skin. Blisters rise along my fingertips like small moons. I taste ozone and ash, smoke and char.

As she receives my magick, Fortune sucks in a breath and closes her eyes, her whole face going dark beneath the shadow of her cowl.

"We will help them to remember." Fortune's body jerks, pulled by some will of the storm. She's sucked into the whirlwind, a living shard of light dragged back into the sand and fire.

A crack races through the storm like lightning, splintering the cyclone's body. The current rips along my palm, scouring nerves raw and leaving a trail of pain that blazes up my arm. Like with Fortune, I don't let go. I've run from hurt my whole life, but sometimes pain is the price of moving forward.

I dig my fingers into the storm. The wind howls with a sound that is part thunder, part chorus. The blisters along my fingertips bead, swell, then burst. Stars of pain flash at the edges of my vision, but I keep my palm pressed to the storm.

"Show the kingdom!" I command. "Make them remember!"

The cyclone reels, then bends, arcing toward my outstretched hand. Sand around my feet vitrifies into a sheet of glass that sings under the pressure, then shatters back into grit with a brittle groan.

From within the storm, the specters wail, echoing Fortune, echoing me, their mouths shaping a single word until it's everywhere.

Remember! Remember! Remember!

TWENTY-SIX

The storm shudders.

The kingdom holds its breath.

The spell ignites.

Sand rains down in a furious sheet as specters of fire burst from its heart. They shoot out by the dozens, then in hundreds, like flint meeting steel. Every eye in the kingdom tilts toward the horizon as the howling fire ghosts streak straight for the Tower.

The storm reshaped the land. The tower now stands tall and proud, obsidian columns thrusting from the sand like black spears piercing the pale throat of dawn.

The specters converge on the Tower in a spiral of light. Flames burst to life like fireworks on top of the Tower's columns, detonating the skyline and throwing a brilliant, beautiful light across the sand that travels like an aftershock. It rips through the desert and washes the kingdom in true memories of the past.

Where the Tower's light touches, flames paint moving

pictures. Sand becomes lush greenery. A river of embers glitters, molten light tracing the outline of a stream. Palm trunks rise as columns of coiling flame, fronds unfurling in tongues of heat. Vines are thin snakes of fire that wrap the bones of broken tents, forming pavilions of shade. The flames cleanse the air, and the sweetness of wet stone and tilled earth rises from the images made of light and heat.

The vision drapes itself over the kingdom so perfectly that, for a breath, we are living in it. Fire as change. Fire as promise. Fire as healing that reaches beyond applause and into the slow work of becoming whole.

The crowd ripples as everyone scrambles to the edges of the light, eyes wide. An adviser from the queens' circle drops to her knees and presses her forehead to the sand. Children peer out from behind their awestruck parents. Dav and Tarek stand ankle deep in the vision of rushing, white-capped flames, dipping their hands into the river of fire. People stand still, wide-eyed and amazed, singed clothing hanging off their shoulders. Others laugh and cry in the same breath. Everywhere, hands reach toward the Tower's light, fingers brushing at fiery visions, and the whole kingdom hums with the small, fierce note of wonder.

Again, Fortune says. Though maybe she doesn't speak at all. Maybe the word comes to life inside my head, sounding exactly like her.

The Tower pulses in the distance, its glow surging upward like a beacon.

I pull air into my lungs and open my burned hand. I let the pain anchor me as proof of my purpose. This is why I was dragged through worlds, and I will not flinch now.

"Return," I tell the Tower. "Remember."

Sparks lift from my palm like they did from the altar, bright and buzzing as I pour myself into the kingdom, a living channel between the magick of the tower and the Kingdom of Wands.

The shredded tents quiver. Threads begin to glow at their ripped edges, tiny veins of light that seek one another out. They lift and pull, and stitch by stitch the rips close until the fabric is once again whole. Splintered poles groan and tilt toward each other, halves of snapped wood finding the right angle to fit back together. The jagged ends bind. Sap bubbles warm and clear where the breaks meet, then hardens with a soft hiss.

Cries break across the camp as wounds knit closed. A boy's split lip smooths under his mother's shaky fingers. A dancer who had been clutching a twisted ankle lets out a sharp little sound as the joint rights itself with a pop. A man who'd been cradling his arm and panting beside a shredded tent exhales as bone slides back with a wet, settling click.

I feel it all flow through me: the loosening of muscle, the settling of bone, the pain extinguishing. Around me, the kingdom exhales a ragged mix of sobs and laughter and astonished gasps as what was broken stitches itself back into being.

A cool breeze blows in from the Tower and gusts across the dunes, carrying the scent of wet clay. Ribbons of water burble up through the sand like veins drawn onto the earth. They widen into channels that rush between ridges and pool in low bowls, catching light like quicksilver. Tiny shoots unfurl with shocks of green so bright they're almost glowing. Moss gathers along the shoreline of the rivers and grows over scorched patches in the sand until they're fuzzy and bristly. In minutes blades thicken into grass, grasses gather into tufts, and what was a dry and barren plain becomes a verdant crush.

The Everspring has been remembered, has returned, and with it the Kingdom of Wands rises again, an oasis reborn.

TWENTY-SEVEN

There is a fierceness in my chest that wasn't there before, a proof left on my skin and in the way the kingdom breathes that I've done something enormous. I did this. I pulled the Tower and the kingdom back from the ash, and in doing so, I pulled myself a little straighter too. I have unlearned a hundred small lessons and learned, with a terrifying, thrilling clarity, that I have the power inside me to heal more than myself.

Still…Declan is gone.

The finality of it sits like cold iron in the pit of my stomach.

His body is a shadow at the edge of my sightline. It anchors me in the worst and truest way. I learned, painfully and proudly, how to make the kingdom remember. Now I must learn what to do with memories I cannot possibly forget.

Around me Wands mends, the Everspring sings, and people reach for one another, mouths shaping grateful, unbelieving laughter. I want, with a fierceness that squeezes my heart, to pull that same healing around him, to have enough magick to unmake his ending. But it seems that some healing is only for the living.

It doesn't stop me from hoping, from casting a whispered plea to the universe, "Please let me save him. Let me bring him back." Tears press hot against my eyes as I hold those impossible wishes in my chest.

I force my fingers open, a small gasp shredding out of me as pain flashes up my arm.

I sway on my feet. My legs are rubber, my hand throbs, every nerve in my body collapsing into wet noodles. The world tilts, and warm callused hands close around my shoulders and catch me before I fall.

My heart vaults with the impossible hope as I whirl around to face—

Tarek.

"Are you feeling all right?" he asks softly.

"Yes, I—" I try to answer, but it's hard to form words around the despair sinking my heart. "I'm tired. And Declan—" My eyes sting, and I squeeze them closed.

Tarek pats my shoulder, then quiet and practical, he asks, "What would you have us do with him?"

I don't know how to be anything but small and broken and messy in that moment. And that's okay. So I give myself permission to be imperfect.

Air wheezes out of me in one long, wet sob that feels like it might never stop. My body trembles, chest convulsing as I cry. Tarek wraps me in a hug, and I let my tears soak into his shirt, leaving hot, dark tracks.

I wish the arms around me were Declan's. I can

almost feel the memory of his hands on me, the comfort of his touch.

I press my cheek harder against Tarek's shoulder and let the grief be as big and as ugly as it wants to be.

Finally, this bout of grief drains away. Taking a deep breath and wiping my face with my good hand, I say, "I want to say goodbye."

The watery light of the rising sun pools around me, haloing the stage with something tender as I kneel beside Declan. Hiccuping back sobs, I place my head on his chest because that's all I can do when there's nothing else left.

His skin is cool under my hands, the blood dark and dry at the edges where it soaked through his shirt. A crimson smear of dried blood crosses his lip, and I brush my fingers over it as tears leak from my eyes.

The wheel is turning, and everything is changing, but even with Fortune, with magick and the Tower, I can't bring him back.

"I'm sorry." I sniffle, my tears dotting his shirt. "I'm sorry I pushed you away. I'm sorry for not letting you in sooner."

The list is clumsy and useless and also the only offering I have. The only thing I can give him before they take him away, and he's gone forever. When I'll have to live with his absence, build a life around the hollowness he left behind.

"I'm sorry, Declan. Forgive me."

My hand throbs where I press it to his chest, and I splay my burned, blood-smeared fingers over the place where his heart should beat. Heat answers the wound in my palm, and a sharp pain flares up my arm.

Dawn washes over us, and a hush falls across the kingdom so complete I can hear the sound of the wheel.

Click.

Click.

Click.

Ash coats my tongue, and smoke curls into my nose. When I look up, Fortune is there, a heat shimmer between the trunks of two great palms, burning a path between the trees.

"I remember," I tell him, her, the universe. "I remember how bad you are at flirting. I remember how your skin feels against mine. I remember the way you smell—clove and spice and home. I remember how you listened to me talk and never once thought I wasn't enough. I remember the way you laughed and would carry that damn cat and how you were just like me, pretending to be the person you thought others wanted. I remember the taste of your mouth and how you made me feel like the world had room for me. I remember that I love you, Declan Thorne, that I will *always* love you."

The sunlight around the stage swells, and the air thickens until its crackling around us, filled with smoke and heat. The *click* of the wheel quickens into a cadence I can feel in my teeth, and I clench my jaw. Sparks spill from my fingertips and arc into the pooled light. I press harder, emptying myself into the magick taking hold.

Declan's chest twitches under my palm. Then, impossibly, he inhales. His small, ragged gasp is the most beautiful sound I've ever heard. Cold, stiff fingers curl around my wrist, his touch light as ash, then warmer, firmer. Color washes back into his face like a tide discovering the shore.

Under my hand, the wound on his chest draws together. Blood dulls to dust and flakes away as the gash draws closed from the inside out. Skin smooths around the puckered edges until it's whole again.

The magick in my palm folds back on itself with a soft, sibilant note. Threads of smoke draw back into my fingers, into the living drum under my ribs, until the fire is gone and my hand is only heat and damage. A fresh pain flares along my fingertips and the curve of my palm, a bright, piercing ache. But I can barely feel the hurt beneath the tide of joy that has just come in.

Tears spill hot down my cheeks as I release all the grief I was still holding.

With a groan, Declan sits up. His dark eyes find mine, and the world contracts to the shape of them. I cup his face with both hands, my thumb tracing the thin line where blood became ash on his lips.

"So," I say, voice breaking more than I'd like, "you do exist."

The corners of his mouth curl into a smile I know and love. "Don't sound so disappointed."

He pulls me to him and wraps his arms around me. He holds me as I sink into him. His palm slides up my back to my neck, fingers threading through my hair as he presses his lips to mine. I part my mouth and his tongue sweeps in, warm and tasting of smoke and salt.

"I love you, Amanda."

And this time, I let him. I let him love me, the woman who once carried laminated affirmation cards in her purse because saying the words felt safer than living them; the woman who treated manifestation like control; the woman who built walls and believed they were shelter.

I let him love me, the woman who is messy and imperfect and learning and healing and powerful in ways I am only just beginning to understand.

He drops his forehead to mine and blinks down at my hand. "Are you okay? That looks terrible. What happened?"

I grin, wincing a little as he turns my hand over in his. "It's kind of a long story."

Fennel finds us first. His bray cuts through the quiet like a trumpet as he barrels toward me with all the subtlety of a stampede. He pushes his shaggy head into my chest, rough fur scraping my cheek.

"I'm glad you're okay too," I whisper, looping my arms around his neck. He smells like dust and sunlight, grounding in a way that steadies my pulse. I press my face into him and blink hard when my throat tightens. "Thank you for forcing me to be your friend."

Cinder pads up behind him, tail flicking. She circles Declan once before springing into his lap and curling up like she belongs there.

"My queen." He kisses the top of her head as his fingers drag slowly through her sleek coat.

I lean into Fennel's shoulder and watch them together, emotion swelling in my chest.

This unbelievable, magickal place has been hot and horrifying and terrible, but it's also given us so much—truth, healing, and family in the most unlikely creatures.

Fennel flicks his ears, distracted by the rattle of a grain bucket somewhere within the tall grasses. I kiss his soft nose and inhale his earthy scent one last time before he lumbers off toward the promise of food. Cinder lifts her head, blinks her lemon-yellow eyes up at Declan, then leaps onto Fennel's back. Together they disappear into the gilded shimmer of dawn that bathes the camp.

Across the expanse of leafy green, I spot Nessa with Romy and Celine. The three of them are huddled together near the edge of a mended tent, skirts streaked with ash, faces smudged, hair coming loose.

"I need to go talk to them."

Declan follows my gaze and squeezes my hand. "I'll be right here."

I approach, and when Nessa sees me, her mouth tightens. Romy hooks her arm around Nessa's, and Celine shifts, stepping as if to shield her, but I raise my hands.

"I'm here to apologize." I swallow, my mouth dry. "I failed you. All of you. I told you to manifest and handed you empty affirmations when what you needed was someone to see you. To listen."

Nessa's chin trembles, and for a tense minute she doesn't answer, just stares at me like she's weighing whether this is another performance. Finally, she exhales.

"I was angry. And scared. But you…you did see us, Amanda. And you listened to what we most desired. You pushed me to reach, even though I did not succeed. While thinking only good thoughts is a bit naive—"

"Yeah"—I shake my head—"that was terrible advice."

Celine snorts, her ash-streaked arms crossing over her chest. "Useless, more like."

Romy elbows her. "She's apologizing."

Celine softens a fraction, tilting her head.

"You did show me," Nessa continues, "show *us* we could have belief in ourselves and aspire to more than what we are given."

"Can I—" I open my arms, hesitant, asking without demanding.

Nessa's smile breaks through the ash and exhaustion, and she barrels into my chest. Romy follows, wrapping her arms around us. Even Celine grudgingly steps forward, muttering under her breath as she burrows into the embrace.

A lump swells in my throat. I pull them all closer. "I'm sorry I hurt you," I whisper. "I care deeply about each of you. I hope you know that."

Sniffling fills the space between us. Three heads nod against my shoulders.

"You can do great things. I believe in you."

Nessa tilts her face up, eyes shining with unshed tears. "And now, we believe in ourselves."

The embrace lingers, then one by one the girls peel away. Romy tugs Nessa toward the healer's tent, and Celine mutters something about needing to scrub the ash from her skin. I watch them go, my chest tight but lighter, as if some snarled knot has finally come loose.

My gaze drifts over the lush landscape and rippling waters. The Player is on her knees, tears cutting fresh rivers through the makeup. Around us the caravan hums with a dozen new conversations, but the dais is empty, thrones abandoned in the wake of this remembered world.

Hand in hand, Solara and Zephara pick their way toward me through the lush grasses swaying around their knees.

Solara stops and looks across the verdant landscape at the Tower—at what it was and what it has become—and then her eyes find mine.

"You brought it back." Her voice is loose with astonishment, wonder, respect. She is no longer a monarch but a woman who has watched the rebirth of a kingdom and now must decide where to go from here.

"No," I answer, throat thick. "You chose to remember."

Zephara squeezes Solara's hand and turns to me, admiration softening her sharp features. "We are not naive. We were taught the old stories—that the Tower took and kept, that its light must be guarded against. We were taught the Great Families rose to power to keep the peace and provide for our kingdom as the Tower bled it."

"We were taught wrong," Solara adds. "We were taught fear and hate and were raised to prize pageantry and to fold emotion into performance. Spectacle made it tidy and kept it contained."

Zephara nods, the painted flames at her temples lined with ash and sweat. "In doing so we let show become the substitute for the truth." She takes a deep breath and the corner of her mouth slides into a small smile. "We see that now."

I bite my lower lip and sweep my gaze across the camp. "If you mean it, then do the work. Let your actions prove you understand the truth."

"We shall." Solara's brow furrows, and her eyes narrow, the gears of a plan clicking into place. "No one party will own the story of our kingdom. We will honor the past, and we will change what failed us."

"We will do it together." Zephara claps her hands. "As a kingdom united."

The sisters walk away, and I watch them tend to their people. Unburdened by the old lies and no longer chained to spectacle and secrecy, they will be the kind of rulers this place needs, the kind of rulers this kingdom deserves.

Tall grasses graze my legs as I climb back onto the stage.

"What's next?' Declan asks, smiling up at me.

"Dying and being brought back wasn't enough?"

A cool breeze encircles us, and the Wheel of Fortune card flutters down from the dawn-lit sky. Like it did all those days ago in Declan's club, it lands between us.

I can't help but laugh as I help him to his feet and we stare down at the tarot card.

The image begins to move. The wheel turns, the designs around it shifting as if they can't quite decide what they want to be. The card's edges curl and smolder, sending up the scent of cinnamon and dust.

A hairline split races out from the wheel and cuts across the stage. Red, orange, and yellow light wells up beneath the boards in a surge of molten color that brightens and pulses until the planks bow with the heat. The fissure yawns open, revealing a rift in the center of the stage.

I know immediately: It is a way home, a new beginning.

Declan closes his hand around my uninjured one. His shirt is crusted with dried blood, his scruffy cheeks are streaked with ash, his hair clings to his forehead in dark, sweaty ropes. He looks like hell. He looks alive.

And I can't look away from this man who infuriates me, who told me the truth even when it gutted me, who died and came back because of my choices, who I love with my whole heart.

He leans close. "I think that's for us," he says, nodding toward the wheel burning at center stage.

I lift my face to him and smile. "Are you ready?" I ask. "When we go through, everything changes."

"I'm not afraid of change anymore. I'm not afraid of living." He brushes my hair back and kisses my forehead. "Not if it's with you."

I squeeze his hand until my knuckles ache. Together, we step into the glowing rift between worlds.

The last thing I see before the fire closes in around us is the Everspring unfurling, green and endless, across the Kingdom of Wands.

Beneath that new life, beneath *all* life, the Wheel of Fortune continues to turn.

EPILOGUE

New York hums outside the window. A taxi honks, a siren keens somewhere in the distance, the faint bass of an outdoor speaker beats against the windows.

Declan's kitchen looks like it was ripped from an architectural magazine—glossy white marble counters that waterfall into wood floors, black cabinets that close without a sound, knives that cost more than my rent.

I sit at the island that's as big as a car, laptop open, deleting piece after piece of the persona I built. Canva mockups of curated affirmations. Prescheduled Reels with sparkly captions about "five-step manifestation hacks." Witchy lip syncs that have stopped trending in the week I was gone.

Delete. Delete. Delete.

The bandage mummifying my hand makes it hard to move the cursor, my fingers clumsy on the track-pad. Luckily, the ER doc didn't press too hard when we stumbled in streaked with blood, sand, and ash. I chalk it up to Manhattan being Manhattan. This city has seen worse stagger in off the subway at three a.m.

A soft thump lands on the stool beside me. A tiny gray kitten mews, tail flicking, golden eyes round and warm.

"Hello, Ash." The kitten presses his head into my palm, purring like a motorboat, jellybean paws kneading my thigh. Then he turns to Declan, hisses, arches his back, and leaps from the stool to tear off into the living room.

I laugh. "He likes me better."

"Of course he does," Declan mutters and refills his wineglass with a rich Silver Oak cab.

"But I do miss Fennel. I keep thinking I feel him right behind me. Like a phantom limb."

Declan pours me a glass and slides it across the counter. "I'm sure he and Cinder are somewhere in Wands living it up."

I exit out of all the tabs cluttering my screen, take a deep breath, and close the computer. "It feels so good to let all that go."

"I bet." The pan Declan's holding sizzles, and he flicks his wrist. The pancake soars up, flips over, and lands back in the skillet. "*Now…*"

"Now I'm going to finish my outline and start writing."

Since I've been back—and after a long talk with Gemma and Alder, er, *Alderic*—I've officially found myself and my true calling. I'm putting my editorial and storytelling skills to use and am writing a book. A memoir. Sort of. But dressed up as a cheeky fantasy romance, because no one wants to read the raw confessions of a not-famous woman. Honestly, not many people want to read the confessions of a famous one.

"Good girl." He winks and takes a sip from the wineglass in his other hand. Standing barefoot in jeans and a long-sleeve black shirt, pan in one hand, glass of wine in the other, he looks like the ad for a cooking show no one asked for but everyone would watch.

"I really hate that Gemma taught you all those book tropes." My cheeks heat despite myself. "And I don't know if I would have decided to move in if I knew how much you like breakfast for dinner."

His phone buzzes against the counter. He glances at the screen, grimaces, then answers. "Dad, what can I do for you?"

Even from the other side of the island, I can hear his father's anger boil over with words like *irresponsible*, *disgrace*, *reckless*.

Declan rolls his shoulders, sets the pan down, and leans back against the counter. "When you want to have a real conversation, you can call me back."

He ends the call with one efficient tap.

"I'm sorry." I slide off the barstool and wrap my arms around him. "That was…"

"A long time coming," he says. His jaw is tight, but his eyes soften when they find mine. "He'll live. So will I."

"I'm proud of you. Of us." I reach for my glass of wine to make a toast to our growth, separately and collectively, lift it too quickly, and slosh crimson across my bandaged hand. "Shit."

I slip out of Declan's arm and head for the sink. The wine has soaked through, ruining the gauze. I tug at the tape with my teeth and peel the wrappings back. Declan joins me, sleeves shoved to his elbows as he washes his hands, ready to assist.

My stomach twists. I don't want to see my raw, red healing skin. It's bad enough when Declan helps me clean my wounds and apply medicated ointment throughout the day. Although, I am lucky I don't have to have skin grafts.

The gauze tears away in strips, and with it, bits of me. I suck in a breath, ready for the sight of ruined flesh. Except the skin beneath isn't torn. It isn't even healing. It gleams.

Rubies stud the curve of my palm and fingers, catching the kitchen light and splintering it into shards of red across the ceiling.

Declan goes very still. "Whoa. That looks like—"

"Fortune."

Water hisses out of the faucet, forgotten gauze clumping in the drain as I stare at my hand like it belongs to someone else. I flex my fingers, and the stones shift with me. We're fused. They're a part of me now.

Smoke tinges the air, and I whirl around wide-eyed, my heartbeat roaring in my ears. Then the smoke alarm shrieks.

Declan swears, rushes for the stove, and kills the burner. The pancake is scorched, blackened at the edges.

"Shit, Declan—" I swat at him as he darts past me to open a window.

"Sorry, sorry."

I clutch my jeweled hand against my chest, heart hammering. "I thought it was starting again. I thought we were about to get dropped back into Towerfall."

Declan glances over his shoulder, one brow arched.

"Would you want to go back? I mean, if we had a choice and didn't get dropped from a portal in the sky."

"I don't know." I shrug. "It must be so different over there now. But it would be good to see Fennel."

"And Tarek."

"And check on Nessa and the girls."

A memory dances through my thoughts, and a laugh bursts out of me. "Do you remember—"

The word catches. Sticks in my throat.

Remember…

The kitchen falls away, New York dissolving into smoke and shadow. A rush of images slams into me—fire-lit stages, storm-torn skies, the wheel spinning through centuries. A hundred lives burst into flame across my mind, stacked like cards in a deck, each one burning bright before giving way to the next. Queens and deserts, altars and ashes. A thousand names, all of them mine.

Not just this one life. All of them.

I *am* Fortune. I have always been. This body, this love I share with Declan, this moment in Manhattan is only a single spark in the wildfire of my story.

I suck in a breath, and the kitchen reappears around me.

"Oh, shit."

Declan stops waving away the haze and looks at me, the smoke curling around him like a ghost. "What?"

"I remember."

Acknowledgments

Thank you to the people who kept me going while I wrote this book. You're the reason I made it to the finish line with my anxiety (mostly) in check.

Some days were saved by simple texts. Falyn, Alisha, and Melissa, thank you for being my friends.

Krysta, your outlook and your help to turn 2026 into my best year yet were priceless. I'm so glad our paths crossed.

As much as I'd like it to, life doesn't pause while I write. Debbie, thank you for always being there for my boys. And Douglas Bean, you will forever be my soft place to land.

The end of this book nearly broke me, and Phyllis and Emily found solutions beneath all the muck. You rescued me when I thought my creative well had run dry, and I am grateful for each of you.

I'm a better writer and I will continue to improve thanks to my brilliant editor, Christa Desir. I cannot wait for what's next.

Kate, Brooke, Cindi, and Gina, whenever the urge to give up started to creep in, you were always there with sprints, advice, encouragement, and inappropriate humor. Let's write another book!

Keeping my life from unraveling behind the scenes fell to Sedona, my assistant extraordinaire. You organized, steadied, nudged, and somehow made every task (even creating Reels) feel doable. I owe you so much coffee.

Steven, you deserve a trophy for being the best agent alive! I didn't cry once this time. I'm basically a professional now.

This book found its way into the world because of the powerhouse women at Bloom Books—Letty, Alex, Brittany, Holly, Jolene, and Stephanie. Working with you still feels like hitting the jackpot.

And finally, to you. Thank you for choosing this story, for taking Amanda and Declan home with you, and for reading every last page.

About the Author

Kristin Cast is a #1 *New York Times* and #1 *USA Today* bestselling author with over 30 million books in print.

She is proudly neurodivergent (ASD + OCD) and deeply consumed by character-driven chaos, emotionally vulnerable heroes, and smart, sexy heroines who always get the last word *and* the hot guy. When she's not writing, you'll find her devouring thriller, horror, and romance novels, practicing witchcraft, and being the exact kind of unhinged that makes group chats worth opening.

Connect with Kristin on Instagram and TikTok @kcastauthor.